NEVER AGAIN

FRANCIS KING was born in Switzerland in 1923 and spent his early years in India before being sent back to England to a boarding school. A bright student, he earned a Classics scholarship to Balliol College, Oxford, but later changed to English literature, and published his first novel, *To the Dark Tower* (1946) while still an undergraduate. This novel, and his next two, *Never Again* (1947) (an autobiographical novel based on his childhood) and *An Air That Kills* (1948), were published by Home and Van Thal, which then went bankrupt, but not before King had established himself as a promising young novelist.

Beginning in 1949, King worked for the British Council and travelled extensively, including to Italy, Greece, and Japan, all of which would provide settings for his novels. His next book, *The Dividing Stream* (1951), set in Florence, won the Somerset Maugham Award and cemented King's status as one of the bright young literary stars of his generation. During the 1950s and 60s, King published a string of excellent works, including *The Dark Glasses* (1954), *The Man on the Rock* (1957), *The Widow* (1957), *The Custom House* (1961), and *The Waves Behind the Boat* (1965).

In 1966, King resigned from the British Council to devote himself to writing full time and supplemented his income by writing book and theatre reviews and working as a literary adviser to the publishing house of Weidenfeld & Nicolson. He continued to write prolifically, and notable highlights include the gay-themed novel *A Domestic Animal* (1970), which drew a threat of a libel suit, *The Action* (1978), which narrowly missed the Booker shortlist, and *Act of Darkness* (1983), which, unlike many of King's books—which were usually well-received critically—was relatively successful commercially.

King went on writing until his death in 2011, making the Booker longlist with *The Nick of Time* (2003) and publishing a revised 60th anniversary edition of *An Air That Kills* with Valancourt Books in 2008; his final novel, *Cold Snap*, appeared in 2010.

ROBERT KHAN earned his Ph.D. in Classical Japanese at the University of British Columbia in Vancouver and has taught at universities in the United States, Japan, and England. He presently teaches at SOAS (School of Oriental and African Studies), University of London.

By Francis King

* Available from Valancourt Books

NEVER AGAIN

A Novel

BY

FRANCIS KING

With a new introduction by
ROBERT KHAN

VALANCOURT BOOKS

Never Again by Francis King
First published London: Home and Van Thal, 1947
First Valancourt Books edition 2013

Published by Valancourt Books, Richmond, Virginia
http://www.valancourtbooks.com

Library of Congress Cataloging-in-Publication Data

King, Francis, 1923-2011.
  Never again : a novel / by Francis King ; with a new introduction
by Robert Khan. – First Valancourt Books edition.
    pages ; cm. – (20th century series)
 ISBN 978-1-939140-32-6 (acid free paper)
 I. Title.
 PR6061.I45N44 2013
 823'.914–dc23

                              2013008115

All Valancourt Books publications are printed on acid free paper
that meets all ANSI standards for archival quality paper.

Cover by M.S. Corley
Set in Dante MT 11/13.5

INTRODUCTION

FRANCIS was making his way slowly, painfully, and with shortness of breath, from his hospital bed to the end of the ward. It was 2011, and he was eighty-eight, but despite his infirmity he was upright and walked with a determination, gaze fixed ahead, that belied the fact that within days he would be dead. His calm demeanour and his air of assuredness seemed to me to derive largely from the support, both physical and psychological, of his partner Karim, who walked patiently beside him, holding him with a firm, steadying arm. A couple of days later, Francis was sleeping restlessly when I arrived at his hospital bedside. He was muttering and tossing and turning, then he awoke with a start and fixed me with unexpectedly calm blue eyes. "I suppose this is the end," he said, and indeed, that was the last time that I saw Francis King.

These two scenes came powerfully back to mind as I read Francis's 1947 novel *Never Again*, although "Hugh", the young protagonist of the novel, is based in so many ways on the Francis of his youth. The novel evokes Francis's boyhood, which is closely paralleled by that of Hugh, first in India, then making the long sea-voyage with an uncaring guardian to the England he had never seen, with its rigours of boarding school in term time, and an acute awareness of being an unwelcome guest with begrudging relatives in the holidays. In this autobiographical light, the entire novel mirrors the start of a long quest for human companionship and mutual support. In one early scene, Hugh has to be carried home by the family's Muslim servant, Luchmann, after a near accident while out riding. It becomes clear that the affection Hugh has for Luchmann is passionate, but incomprehending of the racial, class, age, and moral constraints that deny it any further growth and genuine mutuality.

Francis's autobiography, *Yesterday Came Suddenly* (1993), makes clear that for many years this quest was thwarted by missteps, misunderstandings, and unrequited or one-sided longings (expressed most forcefully in *A Domestic Animal* (1970), a novel so highly regarded that more than forty years later it was added to the longlist for the "lost Booker Prize" that was eventually awarded for that year). Even when, in his sixties, he did first achieve the domestic happiness of deep and mutual affection, it was cruelly snatched away, in the darkest days of the AIDS crisis, by the premature death of his much younger partner, David.

Francis's real-life loss is eerily prefigured in the last relationship this *Bildungsroman* of a novel describes. Following on a succession of close relationships seemingly dangled before Hugh, and then denied by social barriers, the adolescent Hugh manages to form a stable, passionate, and mutual bond with a similarly sensitive boy at his prep school. Even here, several of the old barriers threaten to foil the budding friendship. Not only is Chorley from an embarrassingly richer family than Hugh's, but the fact that Chorley's mother, one of the few genuinely warm and generous adults in the novel, is Jewish (signalled by her maiden name, Miriam Aaronson), also brings out a thinly-veiled hostility in some people. But like Francis, young Hugh is remarkably tenacious in his quest, especially once he realises that, despite the school's opposition to "this kind of friendship", the affection is indeed mutual. Hugh perseveres, for part of his emotional maturity is moving toward overcoming his particularly heightened child's fear of irrecoverable loss (surely one of the meanings of the title itself, *Never Again*). This perseverance is all the more poignant because it is becoming clear that Chorley has serious, perhaps fatal, health problems. Francis himself had witnessed stigmatizing illness at close hand and at a young age, when he and his family accompanied his father to the sanatorium in Switzerland where Francis's father was being treated for the TB which may have contributed to his early death. At least one hotel turned the family out when the reason for their visit leaked out. Will the young Hugh in *Never Again*, whom we have seen repeatedly terrorised by the experience of loss, cut and run?

As Francis himself observed to me on a number of occasions in the all too brief six or seven years that I knew him, one of the most important kinds of friendship is that which is prepared to "see someone out" at the end of their life, as painful as this may be. In this he was echoing, consciously or unconsciously, a line in George Cukor's witty 1939 comedy of manners, *The Women*, based on the play by Clare Boothe Luce (Francis and I often went to London's

National Film Theatre to see films of the '30s and '40s, which he
loved.) Is it simply coincidence that a character in that film, played
by Paulette Goddard, has the name "Miriam Aarons"? Indeed both
Miriams, in *The Women* and *Never Again*, combine absolute self-
assurance with genuine warmth and are a source of good advice
and encouragement to the respective protagonists. In the film, her-
oine Mary Haines, played by Norma Shearer, is making a show of
bravado in divorcing the husband she loves, now that he has fallen
into the clutches of Crystal Allen, a hard-as-nails shop-girl played
by Joan Crawford. Unimpressed, Mary Haines's wise old mother
observes, "Ah, but it's being together at the end that really matters."

The key question the novel moves toward, is whether Hugh, by
the closing pages of *Never Again*, now has the strength of character
to "see someone out". We know from real life that despite Francis's
self-doubts, by the 1980s he himself did indeed have the strength
to see David out, as devotedly as could be imagined, in the face of
his partner's protracted and excruciating demise, and amidst all
the prejudice and despair associated with that then nearly always
inexorably fatal illness.

Early in the novel, the naive Hugh, oblivious to the rigid social
structure of colonial India, completely fails to understand why it
is out of the question for the kindly Luchmann simply to be his
friend and accept the watch Hugh wants to give him as a token of
his affection before he leaves for England. Francis is at his stylistic
best when he handles this kind of social comment with oblique
but masterful understatement. Some pages earlier, the young
Hugh, fluent in Hindustani, as indeed the young Francis was, feels
stricken with guilt at having put the servants to particular trouble.
Unthinkingly, he tries to exercise the same good manners with
them that he would with his own race. He wants to apologise,
but the sentence grinds to a halt when he suddenly realises that,
fluent though he is, it had never occurred to anyone to teach him
how to say the simple words, "I'm sorry," in Hindustani. This un-
worldly ineptitude in the face of restrictive social conventions is
what Hugh must struggle with over the entire course of the novel.
First he must come to recognise it for what it is, and then find the
courage to confront it, "doing the right thing" by his natural incli-
nation for affection, and indeed his emerging ethical beliefs.

Yesterday Came Suddenly traced Francis King's own evolution from a socially insecure, well-meaning but incomprehending child, into a young adult with the strength of character to be a conscientious objector during the Second World War; with the self-assurance to acknowledge and accept his own homosexuality at a time of legal persecution and widespread social prejudice after the war, and with the honesty to depict such feelings and experiences from the time of his earliest published novels and short stories. In works as early as *Never Again*, same-sex affection had, of necessity, to be fairly obliquely evoked, otherwise they could never be published. Over the following couple of decades, however, the explicitness of Francis's treatment of this topic consistently outpaced the slow thaw in legal and social attitudes. As Compton Mackenzie laid bare in his campaigning novel, *Thin Ice* (1956), lives of professional people in the public eye at this period, like Francis, teetered on the verge of legal and social catastrophe. Consequently, when homosexual themes were seriously treated, they might require subterfuges. Francis, for instance, published *The Firewalkers: A Memoir* (1956) under the pseudonym of 'Frank Cauldwell', to avoid having his career at the British Council brought to an abrupt end. Nonetheless, he managed to persist with writing that included reference to same-sex relationships, without resorting to a pseudonym again.

In *Never Again*, Hugh must learn to live his life with the courage called for when one's nature, feelings, and beliefs run counter to what society is prepared to accept. As Francis also did, he must find the strength to "see someone out" if necessary. I am so glad that Francis, too, managed for a second time to find someone to return his affection, and this time around to see him out. In this new edition of *Never Again* we can once more appreciate how Francis, in his early twenties, frankly and honestly recalled his own *éducation sentimentale,* and already couched it in the smooth and precise style for which he was praised throughout his lengthy literary career, and which alongside his trenchant themes makes him such a pleasure to read.

ROBERT KHAN
London
April 23, 2013

NEVER AGAIN

"The atoms are in themselves dull, senseless things. But when they touch each other, they strike off eternal sparks."

CONTENTS

Part I

INDIA

CHAPTER I

That night there was a fire on the opposite hillside.

Hugh woke out of a deep sleep, and seeing the crimson flush which spread beyond the window and the figure outlined against it, sat up and screamed. At the noise, Hetty turned to quieten him. "It's only me," she whispered. She came across to the bed, her bare arms and throat gleaming, her silk wrap swishing like water.

"What is it?" he asked. "What's all that red? What's happened? What does it mean?"

"Sh!" There was a shrill note of hysteria in his voice. "Now don't be a silly boy. Nothing has happened. It's the other side of the valley. There's nothing for you to fuss yourself over."

"But what is it?" he repeated, struggling against the arms which would force him back on to his pillow. "What is it? Is it another fire?"

Hetty did not answer his questions. "There, there!" she soothed him. "You *are* nervous, and no mistake. It can't hurt you. It's miles away." She sat on the edge of the bed and put her arms round him. He was trembling with excitement. The touch of her flesh, chilled by the night air, was not unpleasurable, and he leant closer to her, feeling that her massive body was some sort of protection against his fears.

"Silly boy!" She ran her fingers through his hair and down his cheek. She pressed damp lips on to his forehead. "Silly, silly boy!"

They remained there for several seconds, the young boy clasped in the arms of the vast woman, until at last he whispered: "May I see? May I go to the window?"

5

"No, no. There's nothing to be seen. You can see everything from here."

"Please, Hetty!"

"You'll catch your death of cold."

"Please!" he implored again. "I can put the eiderdown over me. Just for a few seconds. Please!"

At first she was resolute; but after he had wheedled her for a short while, she gave in. She usually gave in to him. "First your dressing-gown." The camel-hair tickled his neck. "Now your slippers." She eased them on to his feet; he himself claimed the privilege of pulling the zip-fasteners. Finally she put the eiderdown over his shoulders and lifted him up in her arms and carried him to the open window.

As if in a trance, he looked outwards. The snows of the distant Himalayas bloomed strangely, and above them the sky curved deeper and more red. With each gust of wind that blew Hetty's hair across his face, brilliant granules of fire were shot up into the air and whirled downwards. He had imagined that this must be what a volcano looked like. Beneath, the lake, which had once seemed so friendly, now mirrored the whole scene, making it doubly terrible by distortion.

Yet round their own house, on this side of the valley, everything looked as it had always looked. He was reassured. He knew these nights of the full moon, when everything in the garden appeared either as distinct as an engraving on metal or furred with darkness. There was no compromise between the two extremes. Bamboos leapt out of the landscape or receded in vertical bars of black; leaves lay now in gleaming discs, now in massed clusters; and even the hillside alternated between quick-silver and hollows whose depths seemed full of Indian ink. He took courage from this strange effect, for to him it was not strange; and the house itself, gleaming nakedly in its circle of trees, and the lights from the servants' compound, and the tennis-court and the garden and the paths which he knew so well, brought him a consolation far more potent than the strong arms which held him aloft.

With curiosity now rather than fear, his gaze reverted to the destruction on the hillside opposite him. Although the flames

were many miles away, the sight of them and of the pink snows
beyond them all at once made him prick with heat. Hetty had set
him on the chair beside the window-sill, and hoping that she was
too absorbed to notice, he slipped the eiderdown to the floor.

"Tck, tck!" She hastily retrieved it. "What do you think you're
doing? Do you want to catch another of your chills?"

"But I'm so hot."

"Hot! It's not hot to-night."

"But the fire's so hot——"

"The fire?" She burst into laughter. "You can't feel that. Whatever next?"

So the eiderdown remained round him. Although it made him
sweat, he liked the softness and the way it was so cold on the outside and the noise it made when one scratched one's nails on it.
"That's the third fire this year," Hetty was saying. "It just shows.
One can't be too careful."

"How do fires happen?"

"Oh, I don't know. Someone doesn't put out a cigarette properly. That's the usual way."

"Then we might have a fire. If Daddy were to——"

"If Daddy were to what?" His father had come into the room,
followed by his mother.

"Heavens!" Mrs. Craddock exclaimed when she saw that Hugh
was awake. "I was afraid he wouldn't sleep through it."

"He insisted on getting up," Hetty explained. "You know what
he is when he wants to do something. He's so obstinate."

"Oh, well!" His mother came and stood beside him, placing one
hand on his shoulder. He looked up at her and then, raising his
own hand, took her fingers. Unlike Hetty's fingers, which were
coarse and large and rough, as though she washed them too much,
his mother's fingers delighted him with their smoothness and fra-
gility. He felt for her wedding-ring and turned it round and round.

She was not beautiful, but he was still young enough to believe
that she was. At night, with her hair all loose about her shoulders
and wearing an embroidered wrap, she appeared to him as the
princess in a legend. The sight of her, framed in the window, made
him catch his breath. Her throat was voluptuous in the moonlight

and from her body a warmth seemed to radiate towards him.

His father had fetched his binoculars and was now scanning the hillside. He was still half-dressed, and Hugh asked: "Were you working, Daddy?"

With a gesture of weariness, Mr. Craddock lowered the binoculars and ran a hand over his forehead. "Yes," he said. "I was working. I ought really to be working now."

"You've done enough for to-night." This from his mother.

His father seemed always to be working. Hugh could not see why.

"Have you any idea whose house it is?" Hetty asked.

"Miss Pritt's. I rang up. Fortunately she was on duty at the hospital, but her old mother . . ." He broke off and looked at Hugh.

"What a dreadful thing!" Hetty exclaimed. There was a silence.

Hugh did not like Miss Pritt. She had come to nurse him when he had had rheumatic fever, and as she often told him, she "stood no nonsense." When she smacked his pillows, she did so as if she wished to hurt them; and she called him "Laddie" instead of by his own name. But her mother was a kind old lady. She was very dark, and her face was the lined face of an old ayah; he had often heard grown-ups laugh about it, and he knew that this was the reason why she spoke with that soft, sing-song accent which he was never allowed to use.

As he thought of her, his father's words came back to him. In panic he clutched the hand which he had formerly been caressing. "Is Mrs. Pritt burnt?" he shrilled. "Is she?"

"Hugh dear!"

"My dear boy!"

"Now, don't you begin worrying about that," Hetty said, and with the facile intuition of children he knew that he was right. "She is! She is!" he screamed. The tears rushed from his eyes; he leant forward in anguish, clutching the window-sill.

"I was afraid of this."

"I'll get him to bed, Mrs. Craddock."

"It was my fault. I shouldn't have said anything. Is he all right?"

"He's so impressionable."

Through his grief he heard their agitated, grown-up talk. They put him to bed, and he lay with his mother's hand pressed to his lips. Hetty brought him some hot milk, but he refused it. Slowly the red smear dulled beyond the window. "Go to sleep," his mother murmured. And then he heard her speaking to Hetty: "I'm afraid he'll have one of his 'days' to-morrow. He's been so excited about the cousins, and now all this."

Hetty ticked sympathetically.

Hugh thought of Babs and Zena; but whenever their faces came into his mind, they changed horribly and became the face of an old woman, with sunken eyes and high cheek-bones and a dark, leathery skin. It was Mrs. Pritt. "Tell her to go away!" he exclaimed in his half-sleep. "Tell her to go away!"

"I've told her to go away," came his mother's voice. He clutched her hand tighter.

CHAPTER II

He knew what was meant by "one of his days." At such times his voice became peevish and querulous; however much he tried he could not keep the tears out of it, and when he was told not to whine it only made things worse. Everyone seemed to be set on annoying him; nothing went right.

When he awoke the next morning, he remembered his mother's prophecy and a chill came to his heart. It seemed inevitable. Hetty had agreed with her, and if they both said so it must be true. But he did not want to have one of his days. He did not want to fret and sulk and upset the whole house. He lay for a long time watching Hetty's sleeping face in the bed next door to him, and wondered if there was no appeal against that verdict. If he tried very hard, would he not show them to be wrong? Wrong—Hetty and his mother! He put aside the thought as being treasonable. And already his throat was beginning to ache with the tears which he knew that he would not be able to fight back during the hours ahead.

But it was impossible to remain miserable while Hetty snored so loudly, breathing in through her mouth and out through her nose. This spectacle always made him want to laugh; and so, in

spite of his feeling of impotence and the knowledge that this was
going to be a black day, his spirits rose appreciably. He turned from
Hetty and, kneeling up in bed, attempted to see out of the window
on to the opposite hillside. Everything looked as it always looked,
and for a moment he imagined that perhaps he had dreamed the
happenings of the night. But then he saw the black square which
had once been a house and the black leafless trees around it, and
once more the terror came upon him.

"Hetty! Hetty!"

"Yes?" She did not open her eyes. She mumbled something,
drew the blanket closer to her chin, and took no more notice.

"Hetty!"

He shouted so loudly that she sat up with a start. Her face
was flushed and ugly, and she wore a net-cap over her thick curls.
"What is it?" she asked. "Can't you let one sleep in peace?" She
looked at her watch and then held it to her ear. It was a large watch,
more like his father's than his mother's, and it had a loud tick. "It's
only seven o'clock," she grumbled. "*Chotah hazri* won't be here for
another half an hour. Get back to bed." She yawned and stretched,
showing black shaven patches under either podgy arm.

"But I want to get dressed. I want to go for a long ride this
morning. I want to ride over to the fire."

"No ride this morning." Hetty burrowed into the blankets once
more. She closed her eyes.

"Why not?" There was no answer, and he repeated, in a voice
made sharp by exasperation: "Hetty—why not? Why not?"

Without opening her eyes, Hetty retorted: "Because your mother
says not. Not after last night."

"But the *sayce* will be bringing Robin round——"

"He can take him away again."

"But I *want* to go riding." Again no answer. "Hetty! *Hetty!*"

"Oh, for God's sake!"

"But I want to go riding."

This was the way in which one of his "days" began. In the end
Hetty sent him into his mother's bedroom; she was already awake.
His father had been up and dressed for over an hour. "Mummy,
Hetty says I'm to ask you whether I can go riding to-day."

"Not to-day, dear. You'll be riding down to the station to meet the cousins before lunch."

"But, Mummy, I want to——"

"Now, no tantrums, Hugh!"

All at once he began to cry. The tears ran down his face and he could not stop them. He was overwhelmed with self-disgust.

"Hugh, my dear! What *is* the matter with you?" She tried to take him in her arms, but he pulled away from her. "Well, of course, if you want to sulk. . . ." The tears redoubled. He did not want to sulk and he was hurt that his mother should think that he did. He was only sickened by his own weakness, and for that reason considered himself unworthy to be embraced by her.

As usual his tears had their effect; his mother told him that he could go riding. But it was an empty triumph; he knew that he had appealed to her basely, and for that reason felt his success to be ill-deserved. "Thank you," he muttered.

"Aren't you going to kiss me?"

His lips touched her cheek. He walked to the door with slow, dragging footsteps.

Half an hour later he and Hetty were eating hot buttered toast and drinking tea. Hugh had already changed into jodhpurs, a canary sweater, a tie with hounds on it, and a jockey-cap which he wore even at this moment. He felt happier. He liked the salt, soggy taste of the toast and the lukewarm liquid; he liked the clothes which he was wearing; and even at this moment he thought affectionately of Luchmann, the orderly, who always accompanied him on his rides.

Hetty sat up in bed hugging her knees. She ate noisily and drank her tea black and bitter. Her pink nightdress was creased, her bedclothes rumpled, and some curls had slipped out of her hair-net. Hugh felt sorry for her without knowing why. His mother had taken his side rather than Hetty's, and this made him feel guilty. But the pathos did not arise solely from that cause. He guessed obscurely that it lay in her extreme ugliness, her dark skin, her coarse black hair, her father, who was a subordinate on the railway, and her mother, who was companion to a Maharanee. He put an arm round Hetty and nestled against her.

"Good gracious me! What's the matter with the child?"

"Am I very wicked, Hetty?" He looked up at her with his dark, lustrous gaze.

She did not answer his question, but said with a queer abrupt laugh: "You *are* an odd one and no mistake." She was touched by his affection. She kissed his forehead, and then began gulping the black, scalding tea. Tears appeared in her eyes and her nose reddened. "Get along with you!" she said. "You'll have to hurry if you want to be back in time for breakfast."

He took the stairs in twos and threes, ran across the hall, through the verandah, and out on the tennis-court in front of the house. Robin stood tethered, while the *sayce* and Luchmann squatted together and carried on a conversation. When Hugh appeared they both rose and salaamed him. In his haste he had forgotten his riding-crop, and Luchmann was dispatched for it. While the orderly was gone the *sayce* offered to lift Hugh into the saddle, but the boy made a brief gesture of refusal. It was Luchmann who always hoisted him up in his strong arms.

"All right, sahib?" the orderly asked.

"All right."

They set off at a trot, with the two servants running on either side of him. Luchmann, who had the physique of an athlete, did not weary; but the *sayce*, a small man with a pock-marked face, panted, sweated, and in the end had to fall out by the side of the road. Hugh halted a few yards further on, and for some reason felt acutely disturbed by the sound of the dry phlegm rattling in the man's throat. He turned the horse back, intending to say, "I am sorry": but when he was faced with the man he realised that this was one of the Hindustani phrases which he had never been taught. Instead, he put out a hand and touched the man's wrist, making the wretch draw away in mingled fear and bewilderment. "We'll go slower, now. You're not as strong as Luchmann."

The *sayce* nodded ruefully.

The road which they had taken ran horizontally along the foothills, a few hundred feet above the lake. Below them the ground spun away in ravines, boulder-strewn slopes, and patches of scrub and woodland. The sun was up and the sky was a clear blue; the horse's hooves made a monotonous clop-clop on the dusty surface of the road. They passed some hillmen, squat figures who lurched under great loads or rested together in some shady spot. One of them had an upright piano on his back, and Hugh remembered that Mrs. Timpson had said that she was having her piano sent up from the plains. Mrs. Timpson had complained to the Craddocks because Robin, the pony, had wintered out one season.

It was strange that he should have thought about Mrs. Timpson, for at that moment she appeared round the hillside, astride her thoroughbred. Captain Curtiz was with her.

"Hullo, Hugh." She wore a double-terai hat and blue Aertex shirt. "I've got something for you."

"Something for me?"

"Yes. Guess what it is."

He did not like to guess, for fear that it might be something nicer than the actual thing: so he remained silent, with downcast eyes.

"He's rather a shy little boy," Mrs. Timpson explained to Captain Curtiz. "But doesn't he look doggy in that get-up? ... Well, Hugh—it's those photographs. Don't you remember? You asked me to take Robin——"

"Oh, yes, Mrs. Timpson. Are they—have they come out nicely?"

"Very nicely. If you come back with me, I'll give them to you."

"Well, as a matter of fact ..." He knew that if he called in at the Timpsons he would not have time to cross the valley and look at the fire. Yet he did not wish to be ungracious. Mrs. Timpson, who had no children of her own, was always very kind to him; intuitively he knew that she did not understand children and was afraid of failure with them, and for that reason it was all the more important not to hurt her feelings.

When he hesitated, Captain Curtiz asked: "Do you think he's afraid of me?" He had closely cropped grey hair and spoke in a short, clipped voice.

"Are you afraid of Captain Curtiz, Hugh?"

"Oh, no. Of course not," he mumbled.

"Then you will come back with us? You can have a glass of orange-juice if you like. And Captain Curtiz has brought me an enormous box of chocolates from Simla."

"Thank you, but I really don't think I'd better eat chocolates before breakfast."

Captain Curtiz gave a brief, dry laugh in which Hugh was able to detect a note of derision. "Little prig!" he exclaimed.

"Not at all," said Mrs. Timpson. "The child's been well brought up. More than you ever were."

"I like that!"

Their laborious banter continued until they reached the house. Breakfast was laid on the verandah, and Mrs. Timpson left Hugh with Captain Curtiz while she went within for the photographs. Every object on the table was covered with its own gauze cage, and Captain Curtiz went from one to another, raising the gauze and peeping underneath. "I'm feeling peckish," he said to Hugh.

Robin was cropping grass on the lawn, and when he had finished this scrutiny the Captain asked: "Would you like some sugar-lumps for your pony?"

"Robin does like sugar."

"Here you are." Captain Curtiz took a handful of sugar and extended it towards Hugh.

"Oughtn't we to ask Mrs. Timpson first?"

"Take it or leave it," the Captain said irritably. He disliked this boy, with his precocious manners and his desire to do the right thing. "Do you like riding?"

"Oh, yes. Very much. I want to be a jockey—that is, if I don't grow too much. One has to be very light, doesn't one?"

"Ever done any hunting?"

"I don't think I'd like to hunt."

"Why the hell not?" Captain Curtiz demanded, flushing with exasperation.

At that moment Mrs. Timpson came through the bead-curtain which separated the verandah from the hall, and Hugh did not have to give an answer to the question. The next few minutes were spent in examining the photographs, while Captain Curtiz went in for a wash. One of the snaps showed Hugh on the shoulders of Mr. Andy, a young man who acted as Mr. Timpson's assistant and lived in the house.

"Is Mr. Andy up yet?" Hugh asked.

"I expect so."

"Will he soon be coming down for his breakfast?"

"He has his breakfast in his own room . . . But you've come to see me, not Mr. Andy."

In some way he knew that he had offended her. "You and Mr. Andy are great friends," she said. "But I don't expect he'd bless me if I sent you up to him at this hour. It's in the early mornings that he tinkers with his wireless. He doesn't like to be disturbed."

It was the wireless that Hugh wished to see. Mr. Andy had a room at the top of the house, with a low, narrow bed, a chest-of-drawers, and a large deal table littered with mechanical parts, screws, and fragments of wire. He had a clean, pink face and a clean smell; his face was babyish, with a small tuft of moustache, a turned-up nose, and a chin which was rough to the touch. Hugh liked him.

The bearer came in carrying silver dishes which gave forth a rich fragrance; some were placed on spirit stoves, while others were full of hot water. There were kidneys, brown on the outside but roseate at the centre; fried eggs; bacon which still sizzled; some small birds which Mrs. Timpson told him were teal; fish and curry. Hugh marvelled at the repast.

"Now what will you have?" Mrs. Timpson queried.

"Oh, nothing, thank you. I really must be going. It's getting very late, isn't it?"

"Don't worry about that. I'll give your mother a ring and say that you may be late. . . . What's it to be?"

"I think I'd better go. . . . Well, if I could just try one of those little birds——?"

"The teal?"

The meat tasted dry and bitter, and he had difficulty in getting it off the bone. He felt slightly sick when he thought of the small bird flying hither and thither. "Who shot it?" he asked, between mouthfuls.

"Captain Curtiz. He's a wonderful shot. . . . Why?"

"I just wondered."

"Did you see the fire last night?"

He flushed. "Yes."

"Were you frightened?"

"Oh, no."

"Poor Mrs. Pritt!" She looked at him over her steaming coffee-cup. "I don't expect you knew her. It's very sad. It's the way these houses are built, you know—all wood. It might happen to any of us; it makes me quite nervous."

"I don't think I can eat any more."

"Oh, I hope it isn't going to disagree with you. Perhaps I shouldn't have allowed you to. . . . I don't suppose they let you eat teal at home. You're not feeling sick, are you?"

He shook his head. "I'd better go." He spoke in a precise, grown-up voice: "Please say good-bye to Captain Curtiz for me. And I'm sorry to have missed Mr. Timpson. Thank you for the breakfast. And I should also thank you for these photographs. Good-bye, Mrs. Timpson."

"Aunt Norah," she put in.

"Good-bye, Aunt Norah."

"Aren't you ever going to remember? If you don't like the 'aunt,' you must call me just plain Norah. But I won't be called Mrs. Timpson."

"I don't think I'd like to call you just Norah."

"Why not? 'Aunt' makes one feel so old."

He did not answer. He stood for a moment, twisting his cap, his eyes fixed on the ground. Then, with his flair for what the situation demanded, he went forward and kissed her on the cheek. "Good-bye, Aunt Norah," he repeated. "What a lovely smooth skin you've got."

When Captain Curtiz returned Mrs. Timpson told him of the incident. "He's never kissed me before," she said. "At least, not without being asked to. One can't help liking the child. If only he were not so spoiled!"

"School will knock that out of him."

CHAPTER III

Hugh had often been told that he must walk Robin down hills; but this morning, in his hurry to be back in time for breakfast, he ignored Luchmann's remonstrances and clattered at a brisk pace down the drive. The next thing he knew was that he had a hot, stuffy pain in his head and Luchmann was bending over him. "Hurt, sahib?" Robin had fallen, throwing him over in a somersault.

"I'm all right," Hugh said crossly. This was his first fall, and he felt humiliated. Looking down, he saw that mud was spattered over his jodhpurs. "Come on. Let's get on." He allowed Luchmann to help him to his feet, and clean the worst of the mud off.

But the pony had gone lame. The *sayce* seemed to think that the injury was serious, but Luchmann contradicted him. They began to wrangle; they called each other by names for which Hugh did not know the English.

"Oh, shut up! Shut up!" he screamed at them; and at the sound of the boy's voice the two men fell silent. "I'll have to walk," he said authoritatively. "You take the pony back. . . . Luchmann, come with me."

For a while Hugh trudged beside the orderly; but the sun was now hot, and each footstep raised its cloud of dust; the hills seemed much steeper than when one was carried in a dandy. Hugh wearied. His pace became slower, he dragged his feet, he whimpered with each breath he took.

"Shall I carry you, sahib?"

"Oh, no. I can manage."

But his head was throbbing after his fall; it must be long after nine; Mrs. Timpson had probably forgotten to warn his mother that he would be late. His throat ached with tears of exasperation. At last he broke down.

"I'll carry you, sahib."

Without waiting for his assent Luchmann lifted him up on to his shoulders. Everything looked different from up here: where the road was banked up, he could put out a hand and clutch at ivy and woodbine and the sweet, moist grass. His tears ceased, and he began to sing. From Luchmann's body there came a warm, not unpleasant smell; it was the smell of animals and seemed to have nothing to do with their common humanity. It reassured him, bringing with it memories of the old ayah who had left when Hetty had come. He had not been as fond of her as he was of Luchmann, because she had been ugly and he had all a child's susceptibility to mere physical beauty. But touching the skin of Luchmann's neck, which was brown as hers had been, and smelling that exhalation, he felt a curious tenderness for her, which mingled with the tenderness he felt for Luchmann himself.

Breaking the silence, he asked: "Will you always be my servant, Luchmann?"

"I should like to, sahib. But the sahib will soon go to England."

"I don't want to go to England. Besides, you must come with me. I'm going to ask Daddy. If Daddy says yes you'd come, wouldn't you?"

"Of course, sahib."

"I mean, now that your wife and your little boy. . . . There'll be no one for you to stay in India for, will there?"

Luchmann did not answer. His wife had died in childbirth; but he had been so overjoyed that she had given him a son that he did not at first mourn for her. The servants all congratulated him, and throughout that day he wore a wide and somewhat foolish grin. He brought Hugh some sweets from the bazaar, a sticky mass of them, which Hetty took away. She wanted to give them back to Luchmann, because she thought that it was impertinence for him to make the present. But Mrs. Craddock told her not to be foolish.

Hugh never saw the baby, for it was put in the charge of a foster-mother. But a few weeks later Luchmann wept during the morning ride, and told him it had died. Hugh wept also, not so much from grief as from the shock of seeing a grown man in tears.

When he now alluded to Luchmann's sorrow, he did so naturally and without any of the false restraints of the adult and the civilised. He and Luchmann often talked about it, discussing whether the orderly would marry again.

As they moved on in silence, the boy on the man's shoulders, each of them derived a solace from their actual physical proximity. Master and servant is not the best of relationships; but when on the one side there is an unquestioning assumption of authority, and on the other an unquestioning obedience, it is possible to create a friendship unvexed by slights, excesses, or demands. An equilibrium is achieved; and equilibrium is the secret of all friendship. It is not the best sort of equilibrium, for it is imposed from without, by class or wealth or colour, instead of springing from within. But it, too, has its fruits.

As they crossed the tennis-court, neglected and covered with a thin rash of green, Hugh's grip tightened on the man's neck. He was sweating and the perspiration darkened the collar of his tunic. As they went through the rose-garden, there flowed over them a wave of perfume, so sweet and cloying that the head ached, the senses reeled. Hugh felt vaguely sick. "Put me down," he commanded Luchmann. He went to one of the beds, picked a rose, and held it out to the man. The dew trickled on to his fingers.

"Salaam, sahib." Luchmann took the bloom, and put it in his turban.

As Hugh went towards the verandah, he raised his hand to his nostrils; the scent still clung to it, obstinate and rank.

"Oh, here you are!" said Hetty. They were all seated at breakfast. "Come along. Wash your hands and brush your hair. . . . Heavens!" She saw the mud on his jodhpurs. "What have you been doing?"

All at once he was overcome by lassitude. He explained in a few mumbled words what had happened. He kissed his father on the forehead and his mother on her cheek. Hetty bustled behind him as he went into the bathroom.

When he came back, his father was working as he sipped his coffee. His *babu* stood beside him with a sheaf of papers. At the other end of the table Mrs. Craddock sat behind the silver coffee-pots. She smiled at Hugh, and reaching out an arm, helped him to corn-flakes and cream and sugar. She looked cool and gracious, and he was glad that her lips and eyelids and her finger-nails were not painted as Mrs. Timpson's were.

"Maurice," she said.

"Yes?" Mr. Craddock did not look up.

"I rang up Miss Pritt. . . . I rang up Miss Pritt," she repeated in a loud voice.

"Oh . . . did you?"

"I thought I'd better ask her to come and stay here if she had nowhere else to go. But fortunately Mrs. Sidney has offered to have her."

"That was a lucky escape."

"Maurice!"

"Well, you know you loathe the woman."

"Yes, I know but . . ." Mrs. Craddock began laughing. "Wouldn't it have been awful if she had accepted?" she said.

Hetty turned to Hugh. "Don't stare so. Eat up. You've hardly taken a mouthful."

"I don't feel very hungry. I don't feel I can swallow."

"Well, you can't waste that—all that good cream. There are lots of poor children. . . ." She did not continue; the sentence was too familiar.

Hugh masticated in silence. Looking out from the verandah one could see the lake, iridescent in the morning sunlight. A yacht slurred over it; its sail was very white, the wake was clean as a line in an engraving. Perhaps the far-away figure in shorts was Mr. Andy. On his days off he went sailing; he had wanted to take Hugh, but since the boy could not swim the Craddocks had not allowed it.

Suddenly Hugh turned to his father: "I say, Dad."

"Yes, Hugh."

"About Mrs. Pritt. . . . Do you—do you think it hurt her a lot?"

His father eyed him gravely. Although he was not yet forty, his hair was thinning, his cheeks sagged, his eyes seemed strained and unfocused. Nevertheless he was good-looking. "I don't expect so," he said in his deep, reassuring voice.

"But it *must* have hurt—terribly. When I burnt myself on the electric iron—it was only my finger—I thought I couldn't bear it. And if it was that sort of pain all over her. . . ." He looked white and distraught.

"It's not quite the same thing," his father soothed him. "She was a very old lady, and perhaps she had died from shock before the flames touched her. She did have a weak heart. In any case it must have been quick—so quick she'd hardly have time to notice."

"Anyway, she's happy now," Hetty put in piously. "Do you think I might have a drain more coffee, Mrs. Craddock?"

"I should *hate* to be burnt. Wouldn't you?"

His father laughed. "One has to die sooner or later. Why worry about it?"

"Oh, do let's stop all this talk about dying!" Mrs. Craddock exclaimed. "You're so imaginative, Hugh."

"Could I have some more coffee, please?" Hetty repeated. Her cup was still empty.

CHAPTER IV

When the time came to set off to meet the cousins, it was broken to Hugh that, since Robin was lame, he would not be able to accompany his mother. Tears and recriminations followed.

"Why can't I go in my own dandy?" he asked.

"I've already told you, dear. Babs and Zena are going to come up in your dandy. Aunt Cecil will come up in mine. I shall be riding, of course."

"But it's my dandy, isn't it? It's so unfair! You promised me I could go."

"Now, come along, Hugh. Don't worry your mother." Hetty came towards him with an expression he knew well. Her lips were pressed tight together, her eyes were narrowed. She put out a hand to lead him from the drawing-room.

"Don't touch me! Leave me alone!"

"Come along, Hugh!" She began to pull.

"I won't come! Leave me alone! Oh, why won't you leave me alone?" His voice ran down the whole scale and ended in a groan.

"Now, no nonsense! None of that temper!" Hetty tugged and he tugged. One of her curls slipped forward over her forehead. She became red in the face.

"You'd better leave him, Hetty," his mother said quickly. "I'll speak to him."

"As you please!" Hetty released Hugh, pulled down her cardigan and went out, closing the door carefully behind her.

"Now, see!" said his mother. "We've gone and annoyed Hetty. One of these days she'll give notice and leave us. Then who will we get?"

All at once Hugh buried his face in her lap. "Everything's gone wrong to-day," he gulped between sobs. "It's all that beastly fire. And now Robin's lame, and Hetty's angry, and I can't meet the cousins."

"Quiet, Hugh! *Quiet!*" She shook him gently, until the tears ended in a hiccup. "I'll tell you what I'll do. I'll ring up Mrs. McBride and ask if we can borrow Trixie."

"Oh, would you! Oh, please, Mummy!"

"I don't *want* to ring her up, because I don't want to speak to her again." The two women had quarrelled. "But since it's the only thing that will satisfy you . . . ." She sighed.

She did not intend to spoil him, but somehow she found it impossible to treat him otherwise. He was her only child, and after he had been born she had been told that she would never have another. Her love was very great, and that worried her; she knew that excessive love is the most dangerous of all forces. She knew it, but could not help herself. Even at this moment she drew him towards her and kissed his tear-stained face.

The last twenty miles of the journey up to the hill-station had to be made by car. It was a dusty, precipitous route, with many curves, and Hugh was always sick on it.

Babs and Zena had not been sick. As soon as the car drew to a standstill they jumped out and ran towards the Craddocks. The hot weather had browned their arms and legs, and given them a sallow, jaundiced look. They both had straight black hair, fastened on either side with tortoise-shell clips; their limbs were skinny, their voices strident. Babs was ten and Zena was nine, but they were often mistaken for twins.

"Hullo, Aunt Stella!" They kissed her dutifully, and then looked

at Hugh. It was over a year since they had seen each other, and all
three felt shy.

"Hullo," said Hugh.

"Hullo." They stared at each other awkwardly.

"You have grown!" Babs put in, remembering that this was what
grown-ups said on such occasions.

"Have I? You've grown, too."

"Well, Hugh! Aren't you going to say anything to your Aunt
Cecil?" His aunt was a massive woman; her hair was Eton-cropped,
she spoke in a gruff masculine voice; she had written many books.
"Well?"

"Hullo, Aunt Cecil," Hugh muttered.

"Heavens! Don't say that you're shy of me. We're old friends."

In a moment they all began laughing. She had this effect on
people. Hugh reached up to kiss her, and she swung him off his
feet. "You're still not much of a weight," she said. "Look at you! I
don't believe you've put on a pound since we last met." She pinched
his arm. "Not much meat there! All skin and bone! You are a poor
thing."

Her criticisms did not wound him, as they would have done if
they had come from some other source. Her benevolence was so
obvious, and truth, of itself, without malice, has no power to hurt
a child.

"That's not your pony, is it?" Babs asked, while Mrs. Craddock
and Aunt Cecil were away seeing to the luggage.

"No. We had to borrow her. My pony's called Robin. He's much
prettier—at least I think he is. He has a blaze, you know. . . . Do
you know what a blaze is?"

Babs wrinkled her nose. "Sort of." Then she pointed hurriedly
at Trixie: "But she's pretty, too. Is she easy to ride?"

"Oh, very. She's nearly eighteen. She's a dull old thing."

"Do you think I might . . . on the way home . . . ? I have ridden
once or twice. I don't think I'd fall off."

Hugh bent down and began ostentatiously to dust some of the
morning's mud off his jodhpurs. "I don't think you'd better," he
said. "She's not ours, you see, she's only borrowed. And if something were to happen . . ." He felt ashamed, for this was not the

real reason for his refusal. He much preferred riding himself to travelling in the double-dandy, which seemed to him babyish.

"Oh, never mind!" Babs tossed back a lock of hair. "I just wondered. It would have been rather fun."

The way she said the words made him feel mean and selfish. He knew that Babs' father was not nearly so rich as his own father was; the cousins had few of the things which he had. Hetty was always telling him what a lucky boy he was, with his pony, and his fairy-cycle, and his meccano, and his electric trains. Babs and Zena had spent three hot-weathers in the plains.

He had already mounted Trixie, but now, just as the coolies hoisted the dandy in which Babs and Zena were seated face-to-face, he called out: "I don't think I want to ride after all, Babs. I'm feeling rather tired. Would you like to change?"

"You can't change," his mother put in. "I'm sure Babs doesn't . . ."

"But she *wants* to," Hugh explained.

"Yes, I want to, Aunt Stella. It would be such a treat."

"Well . . ." Mrs. Craddock looked at her sister-in-law. "Do you think it's advisable? Trixie's pretty safe, but if the child's had so little experience . . ."

"Got to learn sooner or later," Aunt Cecil retorted, in exactly the way Hugh knew that she would. "All right, Babs. If you fall off you'll have only yourself to blame."

Babs hoisted herself with difficulty on to the pony. Then they set off, Hugh and Zena sitting knee to knee, too shy to say anything to each other.

CHAPTER V

A certain awkwardness remained through lunch, which the children ate away from their parents, on a verandah on the other side of the house.

They were all careful to pass things to each other, Hugh was punctilious in seeing to the wants of his guests. Hetty, who presided at the head of the table, complimented herself on the way in which she had brought him up.

Only at the end of the meal was there a suspicion of rowdiness, making her remember other visits of the cousins, when behaviour had been less restrained. They were eating mangoes and Hugh seemed to have forgotten the way in which he had been taught to deal with the fruit. He now followed the example of Babs and Zena, who merely sucked, the juice running down their chins and over their fingers, their faces tense and voracious. All at once an accident occurred. Zena was clutching her mango so tightly that the large, slithery stone catapulted out of her hands and landed on the table-cloth. It made a yellow stain.

"Do be careful, Zena." Hetty sent the bearer for a damp cloth. "You know how mango stains." She did not care for the fruit herself; it brought her out in boils, and the turpentine smell was disagreeable. "Zena! Are you listening to me?"

None of the children were listening to her. All three had been convulsed by the accident. "How did you do it?" Hugh asked.

"Oh—just like this. You hold it tight—and then. . . ."

"Zena! *Zena!*"

"Let me try." Hugh's stone leapt feebly into the water-carafe. The plop sent them into hysterics.

"Watch mine! Watch mine!" Babs commanded.

"Zena! Babs! Hugh!"

Stones shot across the table. Hugh's fell under his chair and he went on his knees for it. Zena and Babs whooped with laughter. The bearer remained standing in one corner, his lips twitching with amusement.

Hetty shouted at them: "Sit down! Sit down!" But they took no notice of her.

All at once the door opened and Aunt Cecil came out on to the verandah. "What's all this shindy?" she boomed in her deep, masculine voice. "Well, Zena? What's going on?"

The cousins mumbled something under their breath. Hugh felt sick and frightened. Aunt Cecil was very strict; she thought nothing of beating the cousins.

"If there's any more of this nonsense, I'll give you both a hiding." She took no notice of Hugh. "Understand? I've had enough of this sort of behaviour. I'm warning you."

When she had gone out, Zena tittered; a moment later both she and Babs were giggling uncontrollably. But Hugh still felt breathless; for some reason he did not want to eat now, and his hands trembled without his being able to stop them.

That afternoon Hetty took them for a walk. They went along the road which ended at the Fall. The Fall was a sheer precipice, which fell downwards, many miles it seemed, until far, far away, one saw what seemed to be a measuring-tape drawn over boulder-strewn hillocks, ravines and dark patches of scrub or conifer. There was an iron railing which shut the road off from this terrifying vista, and Hugh felt giddy even when he clung to it and looked over. But on picnics, grown-ups had been known to climb over the railing in order to take photographs.

When they reached this place Hetty, whose feet were a constant source of pain and anxiety to her, sat down upon a rock and undid her strap-shoes. "Don't go too near the edge, children." But the advice seemed superfluous, since nothing would induce Hugh to so much as climb on to the first rung. Babs and Zena appeared to be unimpressed by the drop, but Hugh felt his inside fall away whenever he looked downwards. From the other side of the rock, Hetty's voice came to them again: "Take care, children. Don't climb on to the railings."

"Have you ever been on the other side?" Babs whispered.

"Oh, no," Hugh answered in a shocked voice. "It's supposed to be terribly, terribly dangerous."

"But it's not steep—at least, not at first. One could just walk from rock to rock."

"Daddy did once. But he said 'never again.' One can go for a few yards, but after that it's awful. One might get so giddy that one fell."

Zena made a scoffing noise, and at the same moment Babs had clambered up the rungs and was over on the other side.

"Babs! Babs!" Hugh tried to clutch at her. "Babs!" His voice became a thin wail, which mingled with her laughter. "Come back!"

But she had disappeared. Horrified he turned to Zena. "She'll die," he said.

"Oh, bosh!"

All at once he lost his head. "Babs! Babs!" he screamed at the top of his voice. And then "Hetty! Hetty! Help! Help!"

Hetty appeared with the straps of her shoes still unfastened. "What is it?" she asked wildly. She stumbled as she ran, and her shoes threatened at any moment to fall off.

"It's Babs!" he screamed. "She's killed! She's killed!" He broke into incoherent sobs.

Afterwards when Babs had scrambled her way back and Hetty had said that Aunt Cecil would have to be told about the occurrence, Hugh felt ashamed and rather foolish. The three of them walked without speaking to each other, while Hetty followed behind, her mouth pursed.

"You were a galoot," Babs said suddenly. She spoke without any unkindness. "What did you want to shout like that for? If you always do that we shan't have any fun."

"He couldn't help it," Zena put in, in a grown-up way which made Hugh feel all the more contemptuous of himself.

"Well, he must learn."

After that, Hugh was determined to prove himself to the cousins. On their way home they passed a white-washed shed which stood half-screened by mountain-ash and elder.

"Do you know what that is?" Hugh queried.

"No. What is it?" Zena still spoke in her "superior" voice.

"It's a—you—know . . . I asked Daddy and he told me it was. And then I asked Luchmann, and he told me the same thing."

"What do you mean? What is it? What *are* you talking about?" Babs and Zena were both interested.

"I'll show you if you like. But we'd better hurry before Hetty catches up. Let's hide, and then she'll think we've gone on. . . ."

Shaking with suppressed giggles, they crouched together behind a clump of laurels until Hetty had passed them. Her expression was so comic, half pout, half grimace, and she hobbled so in her large strap-shoes, that it was all they could do not to burst into loud peals of laughter. As she turned the corner they raced up the path, Hugh leading.

The shed was a lavatory. As soon as they entered, Babs clutched her nose. "Phew!" She doubled up with merriment. "Look! Look!" Shouting, laughing, and gesticulating, they explored the place. There were three large earthenware jars of water. Zena put her hand into one and began splashing the others. Babs still held her nose in mock horror at the smell. Hugh began splashing Zena. Babs gave one of the ewers a push and it rolled over on to the floor. Water gushed out. The air was heavy with the stench of ordure.

All at once they heard a voice from outside. "Hugh!" it said faintly. Then, louder, it repeated: "Hugh! Hugh! Are you there?" It was Hetty, who had not the courage to enter the lavatory and see for herself.

Hugh was going to answer, but Zena hurriedly slipped a hand over his mouth. The two cousins were quaking with giggles, until at last Zena burst forth into a loud guffaw. At the sound, they again heard Hetty: "Come out of there, this instant! Babs, Zena, Hugh! Come out of there!"

"Come and fetch us," Zena retaliated.

"Certainly not. I refuse to set foot in . . . in that sort of place. . . . I warn you. If you're not out by the time I've counted five. . . . One, two, three . . ." She reached five but still none of them appeared. Zena and Babs each grasped one of Hugh's wrists.

"Come and fetch us," Zena chanted, and then they both took it up: "Come and fetch us! Come and fetch us!" Hugh felt faint at his own disobedience, the foul smell, and the punishment which would certainly be administered to them. He tried to struggle away from the hands which imprisoned him, but the cousins were stronger than he was; and in any case he made only a half-hearted effort, because he did not wish to be called a coward or a traitor by them.

"Very well," he heard Hetty say, in a voice which made him think that she must be out of breath. "If that's how it is. . . ."

"Yes, that's how it is," Babs mimicked back.

There was a silence. "Do you think she's gone for Aunt Cecil?" Hugh asked. He was certain that at any moment he would be sick. But just as he spoke he heard Hetty: "Hugh! Hughie!" That was him; she was talking to him. Her voice was tearful and coaxing. "Is there anyone in there except you three?"

Hugh was again going to answer, and again the hand was put

over his mouth. "There's a horrible old Indian with a beard," Zena called out.

"I think it's your father," Babs got out between giggles.

She had no sooner said the words than Hetty rushed in, her face red and terrible. She cuffed Babs, and pushed them all out into the open. "Out! Out!" she bellowed. "You'll hear about this! Go on! Out!" As Hugh ran out before her transfigured presence he caught his foot on a stone, tripped and grazed himself. But Hetty did not help him up, as she usually did when he fell, nor ask him whether he was hurt; and for some reason this indifference appalled him far more than her angry torrent of words or her red face or the passionate gestures which she made with her hands.

Babs and Zena still giggled on the way back home. But it was all Hugh could do to drag one foot after another; he felt weak, and his eyes stung with unshed tears of remorse, fear, and guilt. At the tennis-court, Hetty left them and went purposefully into the drawing-room, where Aunt Cecil, his mother and his father could be seen through the french windows with cups of tea in their hands. The children waited. They moved away from the window, because it seemed better not to watch Hetty as she told the grown-ups of all that they had done.

"What do you think will happen?" Hugh asked, licking dry lips.

Zena brought her hands together in three resounding slaps, which had the effect of making Hugh's heart bump against his chest-bone as if it were something sharp. Babs tittered nervously.

"I've never been beaten properly," Hugh said.

"What!" The cousins looked at him derisively.

"Well . . . I've had the ruler on my hand. And Hetty and Mummy sometimes slap my face. Oh, and Daddy once used the slipper on me because I was pulling the cat's tail." His blood chilled as he remembered this incident.

"You'll learn," Babs said. "It's not as bad as all that."

"It hurts at the time, but one soon gets over it."

At that moment the door of the french windows swung open, making them all jump. It was Aunt Cecil. "Babs! Zena!" she said, in a voice which was doubly terrible for being matter-of-fact. "I want you both. Into your bedroom!"

The cousins ran dutifully round the house to the wing where they both slept. Aunt Cecil glanced at Hugh, without any apparent interest, and then turned away.

"Aunt Cecil . . ."

"Yes?"

"Do you want me as well?"

"No. . . . Why?" Her eyes seemed to be twinkling at him.

"Because it was my fault, also. If it hadn't been for me they'd never have——"

"That's not my business," she put in. A smile lingered round her mouth, making him feel that she was laughing at him.

"Oh."

"I expect your mother will speak to you."

"Yes."

Aunt Cecil went in, and he was left to himself, out on the tennis-court. The sun was setting, and the distant Himalayas wore that same bloom which had covered them on the night previously, flushed and roseate. Some sparrows set up a harsh chatter in one of the trees, and from the servants' compound he could hear voices, remote and mysterious in the falling dusk. The dimming tennis-court seemed to expand, as he stood waiting; and it seemed desolate now, desolate and vast and empty of all companionship. He picked up a ball which he had left lying there that morning, and threw it against the banked hillside. It came whirling back to him, and again he threw it. But the next time he let it be. On any other day Hetty would have called him for his tea by now; he wanted to go in, and yet was afraid to go in. He stood in the dwindling light which edged through the branches of the plane-trees, and felt lonely, and hopeless, and miserable.

A terrible whinnying cry shattered the stillness. Three times it was repeated; and then three times again. There was a moment when the whole landscape seemed to wither; his gorge rose; his forehead pricked with a chill sweat. Then he took to his heels. He ran round the house, intending to go in through the nursery verandah; but he was stopped by the sight of a hunched figure which leant over the railings at the far end of the rose-garden. It was Hetty, and she stood at the place where the hillside fell away sheer—a "cud" it was called. Hugh hesitated and then walked slowly towards her. "Hetty!" he called, when he was a few yards away from her. "Hetty!" But she did not turn round.

For a while he stood beside her, and together they gazed at the hills and the lake and the enormous dahlias which bloomed all down the hillside at their feet. A wind blew the scent of the roses at them; and though it was so much colder now, and it was difficult for him to stop the chattering of his teeth, yet the twilight seemed no longer desolate, but calm and beautiful and full of harmony. The lake was edged with streaks of indigo, the birds twittered, and slowly the colour drained away from the Himalayas, leaving them white and immaculate and chill.

"Hetty," he repeated. He slipped an arm into hers. "I'm sorry. I didn't mean it——"

She turned angrily. "Of course you meant it. I thought you cared for me, and you don't. It was so unfair. And all that about my father. . . . It's not my fault if . . . if . . ." She began sobbing in a spasmodic, gulping fashion which he felt must be excruciating for her.

"Hetty! Oh, Hetty! Don't cry! Please don't cry!"

"I'll leave here. That's what I'll do. It's no good my staying. You hate me. You all hate me."

"I don't hate you," he put in.

"Of course you do. You wouldn't have done all those things—or said all those things. . . . And now I don't feel one bit like going out to-night, even though it is my night off, and I was going to the Army dance."

"Oh, but you must go out."

"I don't want to! I don't want to!" she sobbed. "I tell you, I don't want to!"

By degrees he quietened her. He kissed her cheeks, so salt and moist to the taste, and stroked her large, ungainly hands which he could never help contrasting with his mother's. "I love you," he whispered. "I do love you, Hetty. I didn't mean to hurt you. . . . Not really," he added, for truthfulness' sake. "We seem to hurt people most when we don't mean to. I wish it wasn't so. Don't be unhappy, Hetty."

"But I am unhappy."

Unhappy; suddenly, as he ran his fingers over her hair, the word frightened him. It seemed to belong to that world from which he was as yet excluded—the grown-up world. What did it mean? What did it really mean? Perhaps he had never been unhappy; it seemed at that moment that to be unhappy he must suffer more than the disappointments and fears and irritations of his life as he had so far known it. He looked into the gathering darkness. His mind groped forward. And for a moment, in sympathy with Hetty or perhaps in a flash of vision, he felt all life drop out of him, like a gross weight, and he seemed void within, and there were neither tears nor words to ease his heart. Then he knew, momentarily, what was meant by unhappiness. And a second later he had forgotten.

One by one the lights on the opposite hillside flared up. It was dark now, except for the horizon which shimmered like a piece of black water-ribbon where the hills divided and the valley flowed out into the world beyond. "You will go to-night?" he coaxed Hetty.

CHAPTER VI

After Hetty had gone out to the dance, her face caked with powder, her pink artificial-silk dress already creased where she had sat down on it, Hugh remembered that his parents had still not spoken to him about the incidents of the walk. Perhaps Hetty had not reported him, when she had reported Babs and Zena; or perhaps, after he had told her that he was sorry, she had asked his mother to forget his misbehaviour. Poor Hetty! He felt stirring in him once more that same tenderness which he had experienced that morning; it sprang, not from love, but from pity. Her evening-dress had been cut audaciously both in front and behind, so that he had not failed to notice, with his adult sensibility, how coarse and rough was the flesh thus exposed. He knew that the colour pink did not suit her, and that the artificial flowers at her shoulder and her waist looked slack and faded; and the pathos lay, not so much in this drabness, as in her ignorance of it.

"Hugh! Hughie!" It was his mother's voice, calling from the other end of the corridor.

"Yes?" He felt very afraid.

But the clear, smooth quality of her voice reassured him: "Would you mind coming here for a moment, darling? . . . That is, if you're not undressed."

Hetty had left him with his clothes only half off. He did not have a bath on her evenings out; his mother came to tuck him in and turn out the light. Hastily he pulled on a dressing-gown and padded down the corridor to his mother's room.

She sat before her kidney dressing-table, with the light above her gleaming on her bare shoulders and back; she was screwing on an earring, and her head was tilted to one side, her lips faintly smiling in the mirror. Before her were the silver-backed brushes, the heart-shaped casket which held trinkets and hair-slides, the small vials of perfume, the sheen of the satin pin-cushion, and the reflection of her face and arms, glossy in the polished wood.

"Are you going out to-night?" He felt suffocated by her regal beauty, and not daring to approach any nearer, remained standing in the shadows of one corner.

"Oh, no. We've just got a few people coming over to pot-luck. . . . How do I look, darling?"

He was still worried that she might perhaps be going to speak about the afternoon and for that reason found it impossible to criticise her appearance with his usual thoroughness. "You look lovely," he murmured.

"I don't!" She got to her feet, laughing. It was then that he noticed that she was still not wearing the dress which she had brought back with her from Paris when they had last gone home on leave.

"I wish you'd wear the shining one," he said.

It was a blue dress, embroidered with sequins.

"The Schiaparelli? But, darling, that's much too good. That's for some very special occasion."

"The special occasion may never come."

She looked at him for a moment, as if she had experienced some slight twinge of pain. Her brows were contracted. Then she gave her clear, rippling laugh: "What a lot of wisdom there is in that remark!" She slipped her feet into their high-heeled slippers and held out the button-hook for him. "Would you?"

As he knelt at her feet and struggled to pull the sleek thongs over the gold buttons, he heard her say: "Oh, by the way, Hugh, Daddy wants to talk to you about something. You'd better run into the dressing-room when you've finished this job."

Again the old fear descended upon him, making him gauche and heavy-handed, so that the button slipped repeatedly out of the hook and the sweat stood out on his forehead. "Let me try," his mother said, hearing his laboured breath. She raised each foot in turn and, having taken the hook from him, dexterously made the fastenings. "Don't forget about Daddy," she reminded him.

There were different smells in his father's room; not those sweet, feminine smells which his mother shook out of her glass-stoppered vial, but rough smells—leather, boot-polish, tobacco, carbolic soap, and hair-cream. His father was adjusting his bow-tie before the mirror, while the bearer took his suit out of its mahogany press. There was a tin trunk in one corner of the room, long and narrow, and some gun-cases, and the sword which his father wore on ceremonial occasions. In the other corner there was a narrow, monastic bed; he had seldom seen his father sleep in it.

"Well, lad?" His father turned interrogatively at his entrance.

"Mummy said you wanted to see me." In his own ears his voice seemed dry and foreign, as if it belonged to someone other than himself.

"Did I want to see you?" His father frowned in thought. "Damned if I can remember. . . . Oh, yes!" His utterance seemed to take on a clear, official quality; it struck Hugh that he might be giving an order to one of the native servants. "Hetty had a tale about your playing the fool this afternoon. It's got to stop. There's been too much of that sort of thing lately." He paused.

"Yes, father." At such times he did not call him "Daddy."

"It's got to stop," Mr. Craddock repeated. "I won't have it. You've got to behave like a gentleman towards Hetty." The bearer came up behind with his waistcoat, and he slipped first one arm and then the other through the sleeves. The bearer whipped round to the front, and began to do up the buttons. Speaking over the man's head, his father went on: "You must grow up. You're not a baby any longer. I know it was partly the cousins' fault. They're little monkeys. But you mustn't let them lead you into mischief."

"Aunt Cecil beat them, I think."

His father flushed. "Did she? . . . Then you ought to consider yourself damned lucky. I suppose I ought to follow her example. Perhaps a good hiding——"

"I hope you're not being too hard on my boy." It was Mrs. Craddock.

"Hard on him?" His father sighed. "No, I don't think so."

"He looks frightened enough." She put her arms round his trembling body, as if to protect him. "My poor Hugh. Always so nervous."

"I was just telling him that he was lucky not to get off with a hiding——"

"Sh, sh!" Hugh had winced at the word. "Do we spoil him?" she asked. "Do you think we spoil him?"

"Oh, well . . . what does it matter if we do? Childhood's so short that one might as well have all the happiness one can. I think children should be spoiled. In a few months he'll be without us, and then what harm will a little spoiling have done? There'll be time enough for discipline when he goes home to school."

"Don't, Maurice! You'll frighten the child." She held him closer, so that his senses were drowned in her perfume and the nearness of her. "I wonder if I can ever bear to leave my baby. Do you think they'll look after him properly, Maurice?"

"It won't be long. Only a few months until Cecil goes home: then you and she can do turn and turn about. Though how I shall manage without you . . ."

"That's what's so hideous about this life. One's perpetually torn in two. . . ."

Hugh followed their conversation in mute anguish. He had heard them discuss his future before, as if he were not present. He knew that in a few months they would say good-bye to him, and he would go to school, in Hampshire, in England. . . . "Must I go to school?" he asked, as he had so often asked before.

"Must you go to school!" his father exclaimed. "Well, of course, you must."

"But I mean, couldn't I go to Mr. Frobisher's——?"

"Certainly not." Mr. Frobisher was the headmaster of the large boys' school in the station. "I don't want my son to grow up into a *Chi-chi*. In any case, they're going to transfer me to the plains next year, and then what will become of you? You know the doctor said he wouldn't be answerable for the consequences if you spent another hot-weather in the plains."

The logic of this seemed irrefutable. He knew the arguments; and since there were no weapons with which to combat them, he must needs acquiesce. The certainty that his father was right and he himself foolish to question his verdict only made him feel more helpless and miserable. If there were some hope of his doom being averted he could face the future with a less heavy heart. But he knew that the sentence had been passed irrevocably; there was no reprieve.

Seeing the desolation in his face, Mrs. Craddock exclaimed: "Oh, don't let's talk about parting! It's months and months ahead yet. Anything may happen. It's stupid to begin worrying now."

But when she stooped above him to kiss him good-night, he detected an unnatural tenderness in all she did for him. He watched her hands as they smoothed the sheets and drew them under the bed; they seemed to linger over the task, as if reluctant for it to end. Then her lips touched his cheek, and that action, too, seemed to prolong itself, intolerably, since he caught from her the infection of her melancholy.

"Sleep well," she murmured. "I don't expect Hetty will be back until midnight. Call me if you want anything. Good-night." She repeated, tremulously: "Good-night, darling."

CHAPTER VII

That night he had the first of his fire dreams. The blue dress with the sequins had been laid out on his mother's bed, and in his dream he had gone into the room, because she had told him she would wear it that night and he wished to see her in it. But the room was empty; he experienced a strange sense of foreboding. Suddenly his eyes fell on the bed. The dress was burning: it burnt with a dry crackle, not as material usually burnt, but like the bonfires of laurel leaves made each year by the *mali*. The blue smoke filled the room, and he began to choke in it. But he must save the dress. Screaming for help, he tried to beat out the flames with his bare hands. A dry wind scorched his face, the thick fumes were suffocating him. It was useless. The dress, the whole bed, even the curtains were now blazing. There was no more smoke, but everything gave off a sharp, crystal haze, through which he looked at a strangely distorted world in which objects lost their old shape and form, and became things of menace.

Waking, he shrieked: "Hetty! Hetty!" There was an appalling silence. The fire in the grate was almost out, but by its last flicker and by the wan light which flowed from the window he saw that her bed was empty. She had not yet returned; he was alone.

In panic, he leapt from his bed and ran down the corridor. At the top of the staircase he was halted by the bright lights from the hall below, the tinkle of glasses, the sounds of voices and laughter. "Mummy!" he called. But the noises from below continued undisturbed. "Mummy!" Tearful with exasperation, he yelled: "Mummy! Mummy!"

There was a silence; then he heard Mrs. Craddock: "What is it, Hugh?"

"Please come here."

"What is it?"

"Oh, please come, Mummy."

He heard a man say "I'll go, Mrs. Craddock." The door opened into the hall; footsteps rang on the parquet. "Well, old man?" It was Mr. Andy. He wore a dinner-jacket green with age; his cuffs were too long, and his trousers too short. His hair was plastered down with the glue-like hair-cream which Hugh had seen him use. "Well, what's the matter?"

"Nothing." Hugh felt ashamed for having made a scene. "It was just that—that the house seemed so big . . . so empty."

"You'll catch a cold if you stand about without a dressing-gown. . . . How about a piggy-back?"

He bounced Hugh on to his bed, and clumsily straightened the bedclothes. "I've got something for you." He put a hand into his dinner-jacket and brought out three squares of the chocolate fudge which the bearer made so expertly. "Rather sticky, I'm afraid—and not too good for my pockets!" He laughed in his boisterous way, and rubbed his hands together; Hugh noticed that they were stained with grease.

"Who else is there to dinner?" he asked. And when Mr. Andy had told him: "Are you having a nice time?"

Mr. Andy wrinkled his short nose. "Of course I like coming to your house, and I like your mother and father. But I'm not much good at these sort of functions. That's why I offered to come up and talk to you."

Hugh flushed with pride at this admission that Mr. Andy preferred his company to that of the grown-ups. "I wanted to see you this morning," he said. "But Mrs. Timpson . . ." He broke off, because it seemed unchivalrous to say more.

"I know. She's like that. . . . I wish you had come up, because I'd just got America on the short-waves."

"America!"

"It was frightfully exciting."

"I bet it was!"

They talked together in this fashion for what seemed a long time. Hugh liked Mr. Andy. His voice was different from the voices of other grown-ups; it lacked the authoritative ring, and there was no patronage in it. It was an immature, boyish voice, and the words it used were the words which Hugh himself might use.

In a pause in their conversation, Hugh said: "You know, Mr. Andy——"

"Mr. Andy!" He guffawed. "I think you'd better call me Bob."

"You know, Bob. . . ." It came quite naturally; while he would never learn to call Mrs. Timpson Norah or Aunt Norah as she had so often requested him. "I had such a funny dream. I think that's what really frightened me."

He began to describe the dream; but all the time that he spoke

he was conscious of making the wrong effect. Mr. Andy was staring down at his large hands. "Queer," he murmured at the end. It
was as if he thought it a very small thing to be frightened at. He
looked at Hugh: "You must be an imaginative little beggar."

"That's what they all say. Mummy says I'm nervous. She says
I'll grow out of it, though. And Hetty says school will knock it out
of me."

"Oh, well." Mr. Andy seemed stiff now, almost embarrassed.
"I'm afraid I was just a normal little boy. I expect you're very
brainy."

"Oh, no!" Hugh repudiated the suggestion. But then his vanity
got the better of him: "Though Hetty does say she's never taught
anyone who did English better. And I always get more marks than
Babs and Zena."

"Well, you'd better get to sleep now, hadn't you?" Something
had gone wrong: currents of friendship and sympathy no longer
flowed irresistibly between them. Hugh was distressed by this
change, blaming his own childishness which he imagined must
have come between them. It had all been all right until he had
admitted to being frightened by what was, after all, the tamest of
nightmares. Zena had once dreamed that she was being chased by a
bull, and Babs had been captured by pirates. He did not realise that
Mr. Andy had been all at once abashed by a hard core of incom-
prehensibility which he had discovered in the boy. He was not sure
what it was; perhaps it was something which he had got from the
Indian servants. But in his dim, unimaginative way he recognised
in Hugh a quality of spirit not usually discoverable in one so young.
He recognised, and saluted it; he was also frightened by it.

"You'd better get to sleep now." He sounded vexed and irritable.
Hugh lay awake for a long time.

CHAPTER VIII

All about him he sensed mystery. There was the mystery of the
adult world, from which he was excluded, like one shut out of a
room and left to eavesdrop. He often wondered, naïvely, what it

would be like to be grown-up. Of what did grown-ups talk, when there were no children present? Why was it that Aunt Cecil would interrupt her conversation with his mother when he appeared, and murmur "*Prenez garde*"?

Grown-ups spoke of "love," and they seemed to mean something different from the love which he felt for Hetty, Luchmann, his mother, and his father. When they lived in Delhi, Hetty would often take him for walks in the military cantonment; and on such occasions they stopped and talked to a tall man in uniform. Hugh did not like him; his teeth were discoloured, he smelled of perspiration and stale tobacco, and his "joking" was only a cruel form of teasing. But whenever they met this man he could not help noticing the change in Hetty; she seemed pretty, her eyes shone, and she laughed, not gruffly, but with a low, musical tinkle. One day she told him that she thought Bill was in love with her; and it seemed strange and wonderful that this one fact, of having someone love her, should so change Hetty and soften her and make her more attractive. Hugh almost felt jealous. It vexed him; and he sulked when, at their next meeting, Bill put an arm round Hetty, and she said, between giggles: "Don't! The child's watching you! Whatever next!" But as they came back through the cantonment after that incident, the parched sky cooling, the dust settling, the whole landscape loosening and expanding before them, he felt strangely happy and tender; he decided that Bill was not such a bad fellow after all; he took Hetty's hand.

Perhaps, at that moment, the door had opened a chink for him; perhaps he had glanced on the mystery. He could not be certain. But how else explain that exhilaration, that tenderness which brought a pang to his heart? He felt that he had wrested for himself a small share of the grown-up world. He had an inkling, which he could apprehend like music heard from a great distance.

Within the mystery there lay another mystery. It was the Japanese box which lies within a box. Wherever he looked, there moved people whose lives were secret and hidden; not only grown-ups, but young children, with grotesquely distended stomachs, bare limbs, and an air of wonder and entreaty, which disturbed him, he knew not why. He was excluded from this world not because of any limitations within his own self—it was his own limitations which kept him from the adult world—but because everyone seemed to have conspired that he should be excluded.

It was true that he had often made attempts to enter this world, but except for Luchmann and the old ayah, he had always failed. When he had been about five or six years old he had noticed the man who pulled the *punkah* in the drawing-room; he was susceptible to physical beauty, and he never wearied of watching the man as he moved rhythmically to his task. He sat cross-legged, and the sweat rolled down his breast between the squares of his muscles. In the end, Hugh decided to talk to him; he went up and said a few words in Hindustani. By way of answer, the coolie emitted a series of strange, guttural noises, more animal than human. It was terrifying, and Hugh fled in panic. Later on he was told that the man was deaf and dumb.

The incident, so far off now, seemed to be a symbol of all his other attempts. If there were no physical impediments, there were other impediments, far more disastrous. When they drove in the car, through mile upon mile of countryside, they would pass bullock-carts laden with wicker-baskets, bundles, children, and even animals; they would come to places where rough tracks branched off from the main highway; they would pass through small villages, with dogs, fowls, and naked urchins fleeing before their onrush; in the evening the sun would pick out a distant minaret, or reveal a temple or a ruin, shimmering behind trees. But the car whirled onwards; the dust rose behind. And when they did stop, it was before the front-door of some European sub-inspector, who insisted on playing them year-old jazz on a battered gramophone.

Once he went into one of the huts in the servants' compound. The women giggled, and the children stared at him. There was a bowl of goat's milk, and he asked if he might drink some of it. They all conferred together, gesticulating and pointing at him, until in exasperation he raised the bowl and took a sip. The milk, thick and sweet to the taste, made his gorge rise. He ran out. Later Hetty told him how lucky he was not to have caught something. She examined his vest and head under the electric light.

It seemed impossible; it seemed as if this mystery would always be a mystery. On walks, he liked to stop and listen to the hillmen singing their incomprehensible songs. They chanted in a rhythmical monotone; and the harsh sound of their voices made him feel sad, yet happy. Listening to them, his heart was troubled by longings to which he could give no name.

Sometimes even Luchmann became part of the mystery; and when that happened it frightened him. It was as if he had been holding someone's hand in a dark place, and the hand had been withdrawn from him. It happened at unexpected moments; nothing was said, no sign was given, but all at once he knew that Luchmann was slipping away from him; and though he felt lonely and desolate, he could do nothing about it. His father's work necessitated long journeys, and the family often went with him. Then Hugh would lie in the back of the car, his head on Luchmann's lap, because the interminable miles made him feel sick and weary. He would lie there and look up at the fine, serene face; and it was then that Luchmann most often seemed to go away from him, his face changing and becoming secret and withdrawn. Hugh would gaze at it, with love and terror in his heart, as if by some exertion of the will he could bring back the desired sympathy; and perhaps, after a few minutes, as a lamp shows at the window of a dark house, Luchmann would glance down at him and smile; and he would smile back.

But apart from these two major mysteries there were others which baffled him. Pain, death, and hatred were things spoken of, but barely understood. When he had had rheumatic fever he had been in pain, certainly, and he had often cried out with it. But that was a small pain; Miss Pritt told him he was a baby to make a fuss about it. He often thought of the pain which was called agony; he remembered the cousins' whinnying cries when Aunt Cecil beat them, and how they had once picked up in the car a native whom they found by the roadside, and he had groaned and cursed and made strange sighing noises. He had been run over. How much pain could he himself bear? What was pain? Would he always be a coward?

Death troubled him also. Old Mrs. Pritt was burned, and Luchmann's son and wife died. But what became of them? Did they all go to the same heaven? He feared death, and often waking up in the middle of the night he could think that he was going to die; he would have some suffocating dream, and it would seem that he could not breathe and his heart thumped, as though it were going to burst into hot fragments. He screamed for Hetty.

Hatred he did not understand either. He, himself, hated no one, though he did not *like* Miss Pritt, or Captain Curtiz, or Hetty's young man, Bill. For that reason he was bewildered when his father was poisoned and had to go to hospital; and the same day the police called for their cook, Hussein. He had come to them when he was still quite a boy; and apart from his hare-lip, which was ugly and frightening, Hugh had been fond of him. When he iced cakes he made birds and flowers and animals; he used to give Hugh sweets when no one saw him; he had a friendly grin which revealed that his two front teeth were broken. Yet Hussein had tried to kill his father; his mother would not tell him what would happen to him now that he had gone away with the police. "But why?" he asked in his bewilderment. "Why did he want to do it?"

"Not all the Indians like us," his mother said, with a strange, pensive melancholy.

"But Hussein liked us. I'm sure he did."

Mrs. Craddock shook her head. "I'm afraid he hated us."

"Hated us!"

He had heard the word used before, but never of themselves; he had imagined that they neither hated nor were hated. He could not imagine why Hussein should have hated his father, who was so mild and considerate with the servants, and never shouted at them or struck them, as Mr. Timpson did. Yet Hussein had so much loathed his father that he had tried to kill him. Almost in tears, he repeated: "But why? Why did he hate Daddy?"

His mother touched his cheek with her hand.

"Don't worry about it, darling. You wouldn't understand."

"But tell me!"

She considered a moment; then she said one word: "Politics."

She was right; he did not understand. And this incident had shaken his faith in some benevolent presence—it might be God, or the King, or the governor—who watched over their especial interests. Before, it had seemed as if they lived in a charmed circle, where pain, death, and hatred had no power. Others were burned; others were knocked down by motor-cars; others were beaten. But they were safe. Even the presences of those he loved—of Luchmann, Hetty, and his parents—were exorcisms against all danger.

For a while he was shaken; for a while he saw the panic and uncertainty pour through the cracks, like water in a broken cup. But then his faith reasserted itself. For a moment the charm had failed, and there had been disaster; hatred, pain, and death had broken through. But all would now be well again.

When he was nervous, the thought of the affection which existed in the house was sufficient to solace him; it was like another presence, projected from all those whom he loved. His mother's or Hetty's arms, the touch of Luchmann's hand, his father's voice—all soothed the spirit.

Nothing could go wrong.

CHAPTER IX

A few weeks after the cousins had returned to the plains, he found a revolver in his mother's handbag. She had sent him up to her room to fetch her a handkerchief, and since the sachet in her drawer was empty, he had looked in the bag. It was a small weapon and there were carvings on it; he imagined that she had bought it for him, as a surprise; it looked like a toy.

"Oh, darling, this has been used before," his mother exclaimed, when he brought the crumpled square of linen. "It wasn't in the sachet, was it?"

"The sachet was empty, so I looked in your bag. I'm afraid I couldn't help noticing what was in it."

"What was in it?"

He coloured. "You know."

She looked at him for a moment in bewilderment. Then: "Oh, that!" she exclaimed. "You didn't play with it, did you? It might go off. You must promise me never to touch it."

"Then it's—it's not a toy?"

"It's not a toy." She noticed that he was staring at her. "Well?" she queried. "What's the matter?"

"Mummy, why . . . why do you carry a gun?"

"Oh, I don't know," she said with affected casualness. "One might need one. You never know."

"You never used to carry one."

"Daddy gave it to me. He thought it just as well. We might meet a tiger one day, when we're out on a walk. Then I can take a pot-shot at it."

"But you wouldn't use the gun to kill people, would you?"

"Even if I did fire it at anyone, I should be sure to miss."

She had not answered his question. He was so much attuned to her that he knew, intuitively, that she was concealing something. But he said nothing more. Instead he brooded on his memory of the weapon. In his mind it became a thing of menace; he saw it, perfect in every detail, and often he woke from sleep with its report in his ears. Why should she need a revolver? What danger threatened her? He detected a sombreness in her mood; looking at her, when she did not know that she was being looked at, he saw the anxiety which drew her eyebrows together and made her mouth sag. He was more affectionate to her than ever before; he would stop playing at cricket with Luchmann and come onto the veran-dah where she was seated and, putting an arm round her shoulder, he would kiss her forehead and her cheeks. He was afraid for her, obscurely and without reason; he was afraid to speak of his fear. He knew that she would only laugh at him and tell him not to be silly.

When she gave bridge-parties he often came in and was given fudge to eat from the filigree silver bowls which stood on each of the tables. As he entered the drawing-room, on one such after-noon soon after his discovery of the revolver, his mother's friends were all talking together, in a strange, low-pitched buzz. The cards remained neatly in their packs, where he had seen the bearer put them over an hour ago; there had evidently been no play that afternoon.

He caught Mrs. Timpson's voice: "We're none of us safe! None of us!" She made a melodramatic gesture with one hand. Then hearing the click of the door, she stopped. There was a silence.

"Hullo, Hugh," she exclaimed, making a swift recovery. "Come and talk to us."

Miss Pritt, who usually took no notice of him, held out one of the filigree dishes. "I can recommend this lot." They all asked him questions, and there was much laughter.

But when he had left them, anxiety gnawed at his heart. What did Mrs. Timpson mean by those words of hers? The thought of them drained him of all strength. The rains had started, and for a long time he stood out on the verandah listening to the melancholy swish and rattle of water on the corrugated-iron roof. The hills opposite lay draped in mist; the sky was livid. The tennis-court, which a week ago had been parched and dusty, was now covered with a green rash. The water ran over it in rivulets, and could be heard gurgling in the drains. It was a melancholy sound, the swish and gurgle of the water; it seemed to come not only from around him, but from far, far up in the sky and from beyond the hills and from deep in the earth. It seemed to come from within his own self.

For a long time he stared into the rain; although it was still early, the day had become brown and heavy, like a sodden flower. The mud seemed to have mingled with the air, impregnating it and making it damp and thick and slightly earthy to the taste. He picked with a nail at the wooden balustrade against which he was leaning; the timber was rotten and fell to the ground in moist chips; some ants crawled out, and ran hither and thither, looking for the protection which he had taken from them.

What had Mrs. Timpson meant? What was being hidden from him?

The next day the rain ceased for a few hours, and Hetty took him out for a walk. They went to the Fall, and noticed that one of the big boulders had disappeared. They could not see how far it had rolled, for a mist blanketed the whole of the hollow beneath them; it was a yellow mist, and instead of making the drop seem less precipitous, it had the effect for Hugh of turning it into a bottomless chasm from which curled sulphurous vapours. "Let's hope no one was hurt," Hetty said. "It must have been very sudden. One might have been walking along the road one minute, and then the next . . ." She shuddered a little.

"How suddenly things happen," Hugh said. "That rock looked so firm. Zena tried pushing it, and it wouldn't budge. It must have been a colossal weight."

"That's how life is," Hetty sighed. The rain had had its effect on her spirits also, as on everyone else's. It was like the smell of death, insistent and evocative.

On the way home they met Roger Leader and his governess, Miss Graham. He had caught a number of slugs which now squirmed together in a jam-jar. Wherever they writhed they left a scumlike congealed fat. Hugh examined the jar, while Roger, a chubby, flaxen-haired boy chattered about it: "I don't know which of them are hes and which of them are shes. Miss Graham doesn't know either. But I do hope they'll have babies. I wonder what I ought to feed them on. Do you know?"

Hugh had ceased to listen. He was looking over the jar at the two governesses who were talking in that same subdued, yet excited manner which he had noticed at the bridge-party. Hugh could not hear all that passed between them, but certain fragments came to him with awful clarity:

"It makes one quite nervous," he heard Miss Graham say; she was fiddling with the black ribbon which attached her pince-nez to the bosom of her Kashmir jumper.

A moment later, Hetty said: "I couldn't help overhearing what Mr. Craddock said on the telephone. Of course, I didn't mean to hear, but I was knitting out on the verandah. . . . You know what a clear voice he has." Miss Graham nodded vigorously. "Well, he was saying something about General Quincey having said that he wouldn't be happy unless his forces up here were doubled. Doubled! That means they're expecting something big."

At that instant, Miss Graham noticed that Hugh was eavesdropping. She nudged Hetty: "Little pitchers," she murmured.

"Come along, Hugh! We must be getting home before the rain starts. Say good-bye to Roger. . . . See you later, dear," she murmured to Miss Graham. "I've a hundred and one things to tell you about."

As Hetty and Hugh walked on she happened to glance at him: "I hope you're not sickening for anything," she said. "You look a bit off colour."

"Do I?" he said weakly. He almost asked her what she and Miss Graham had been talking about. But she had so often scolded him in the past for eavesdropping on her conversations that he did not dare to. Instead, he muttered: "This rain! I wish the rains were over." He knew for certain now that something was being kept back from him.

The next day the papers arrived from England, and he learnt the truth. *The Illustrated London News* had always been his favourite; and turning the glossy pages, alone, in the drawing-room before a high-piled fire, he saw the picture of a face which seemed familiar to him. He began to decipher the caption underneath, a sense of foreboding already making him feel sick and weak: ". . . Mr. R. O. Davie, superintendent of police at Scila Tal, whose wife and two children were victims of the recent outrage. . . ." As Hugh read on, it seemed as if the blood were draining away from him. A dacoit had run into the compound where the two children were playing, and struck at them with a sword. At their cries the mother had run out, and she, too, had been murdered. Hugh let the magazine slip from his fingers, and for a long time stared into the fire; he stared for so long a time that his cheeks and lips became parched, and his eyes ached. He was trembling all over. Suddenly he leapt to his feet, ran out on to the verandah, and began to vomit over the bal-ustrade. As each spasm took him, the tears rolled out of his eyes.

They put him to bed, and decided that he had caught a chill. Hugh did not at first tell them what had upset him. But that evening his mother and father were going to a dance at the Club, and when they came in, as they always did, to say good-night to him, he clutched his mother: "Don't leave me here! Please don't leave me! Don't go out!"

"But, darling. . . . We've often left you before, Hetty will be here to keep an eye on you. What's the matter? . . . Hugh darling, what's the matter?"

"I'm so afraid," he sobbed.

"Afraid? What of?"

In the end he told them. His father took off his evening-coat and his silk scarf: "We won't go," he said. He said it with a smile, as if it were no disappointment to them. Then he sat down on one side of Hugh's bed, while his mother sat on the other. He talked to Hugh, explaining that the man who had killed Mrs. Davie and the two children was a madman; there were very few madmen, and it was unlikely that such a thing would happen again, for a long, long time. In any case, Luchmann was always near Hugh, and he would look after him. There were people in India who did not like the British, and they sometimes did stupid or mischievous things; but they had not done the murder; they did not want to hurt women or children. The man who had done it might just as easily have been English as Indian.

His father spoke with quiet, reassuring logic; he held Hugh's hand. "You must learn not to be frightened. Terrible things do happen. But it's no use worrying about them. You can't alter life, so you might as well enjoy it, instead of filling it with worries about things that certainly will never happen to you."

The voice went on; and from the fingers which clasped his there seemed to flow strength and love and courage. He became drowsy, and at last fell into a deep sleep, his cheeks still damp with tears.

There was a drizzle all the next day, with the sun appearing at intervals, round and orange and very close, just above the hills behind the house. His father had the day off and suggested that Hugh should go out for a walk with him. "Put on your gum-boots," Hetty commanded him before they set off.

"But I don't want to wear gum-boots. I can't walk in them. They're so tight."

"Put on your gum-boots," she repeated inexorably.

"I won't!"

"You will!"

"I won't!"

Mrs. Craddock made a sign to Hetty without Hugh noticing her. Hetty sighed and pursed her mouth: "All right. You can wear shoes. But if you come back soaking, don't blame me."

Hugh enjoyed going for walks with his father. He pointed out all the birds to him and told him their names. He could imitate birds, so that they called back to him. They walked to the top of one of the hills and stood for a while, on the summit, and looked about them. All round them there curled a yellow mist, obliterating the whole valley, the lake, and even their house. Out of these scarves of vapour the hills rose, and above them the sky was a rinsed blue. Mr. Craddock touched Hugh's arm, and pointed; together they stood breathless and tense. For a moment a cheetah was outlined against the hillside; then it plunged downwards into the fog. As they descended the rock-strewn path, its surface channelled and pitted with rain, they met Mr. Sumajee. He was a Hindu, a lawyer, who dressed in immaculate European clothes and had a soft, persuasive voice without any trace of an accent. He was picking his way up the hillside in an attempt not to get his feet wet. But just as he neared them he stumbled and splashed mud over his shiny galoshes and creased trouser-leg. "Damn! Damn! Damn!" he exclaimed, smiling up at them. He had a round face, and his hands were so chubby that they dimpled at the knuckles.

"Well, Maurice!" He and Mr. Craddock were old friends. They had both been at Balliol. "What weather!" He turned to Hugh: "You've got yourself nicely wet, young man." He pointed with his umbrella at Hugh's squelching shoes. "You'll have to change when you get home. Have a glass of whisky with some lemon in it. Eh?" He chuckled richly.

They remained talking on a dry patch in the centre of the path. All round them the dark, glossy trees lisped as the rain fell off them on to the grass beneath. The air was laden with the odours of corruption; there were great puff-balls, which exploded into an orange dust when one's hand touched them; festoons of bindweed trailed from bush to bush, like wet string. The moss on the boulders seeped a fluid which smelled rank yet vaguely disinfectant.

"Terrible business, that murder," his father was saying.

Mr. Sumajee looked in Hugh's direction. "Have you told the boy?"

"He found out for himself. I think it's as well to discuss it quite openly. The most powerful thing in life is mystery. Nothing is as terrible as one imagines it to be. That's how religion gets one."

Mr. Sumajee shrugged his shoulders. "You know best. . . . Yes, indeed—what a terrible thing! It's the worst thing that could have happened to our cause. A few fanatics alienate the sympathy of half the world. Everywhere this outrage is being associated with

Congress's policy of Civil Disobedience. Oh, why, why, why? Why do they do these things? What point is there? What good do they achieve?" He spoke in tearful exasperation. "They're ruining our cause. This is just the sort of thing your Press is looking for. One act of barbarism. . . ." He made an eloquent gesture.

"We suffer from the same thing. Over-zealous officials—bullies—fools and scoundrels. . . . A mere handful of them can bring contempt on the Government. Causes are always judged by their worst elements—never by their best."

The two men fell silent. They looked mournfully into the fog, while Hugh's gaze travelled back and forth from one to the other of them. Their mood of hopelessness and exasperation communicated itself to him also. He kicked out at one of the puff-balls, and particles of the orange dust clung to his damp shoe; other particles drifted upwards, pricking the nostrils with a foul stench. His feet felt cold and heavy, and once again he had that sensation of the blood draining out of him, leaving him faint and weak. The sky had become livid again; and as they walked away, leaving Mr. Sumajee, the rain began. It fell endlessly out of a black sky; it stung his bare face, ran off his hair in rivulets, and trickled down his neck. Its impetus split leaves open and levelled nettles with the ground. It ate into the heart, like an incurable malady, sapping all youth and joy and life.

It was almost dusk when they reached the house. He felt dazed and giddy. Hetty took him into the nursery where a great fire blazed; she sat him down on a chair and, kneeling on the floor beside him, began to pull off his shoes and stockings. There was no light in the room and the fire threw her crouching figure on to the wall opposite, making it leap and shudder like a wild animal. The heat of the flames made Hugh feel sleepy and rather sick.

As she pulled off the second sock, Hetty gave a hard scream. "Look at you!" she exclaimed. Then she began calling: "Mrs. Craddock! Mrs. Craddock!"

Hugh looked down. His bare legs were smeared with mud; and on each were five or six things which looked like knotted and swollen veins. "What are they?" he asked. "What's happened?" He felt faint, and the fire's roar seemed to become louder and louder,

drowning his own voice and Hetty's answer and the endless hiss
and rattle of the rain.

His mother came, and held his hand; he heard the word
"leeches"; the light was put on, but at intervals the room seemed
to go black again. As in a dream, he felt Luchmann carry him up to
his bedroom. They were putting salt on his legs; then, when that
failed, his father held his cigarette against each of the blue, swollen
things in turn.

"There! There! It's all over!" It was his mother, holding a cup of
something hot to his lips. He drank it, and it made him cough; it
burnt his stomach. He heard the roaring once more; his mother's
voice changed and became indistinct. "I'm going to die," he thought.
"I'm going to die."

"Of course you're not going to die." He opened his eyes and
they were all standing round his bed. He felt better. He lay back
against the pillows and smiled at them, faintly. "What happened?"
he asked. "Have I been ill?"

"You've lost a little blood—that's all." Again his mother's voice,
tender and solicitous.

"Did someone . . . did someone try to murder me?" He could
not remember very easily.

"Of course not." His father was laughing at him.

"The things the child thinks of!" Hetty's face looked down at
him, stern yet oddly white and anxious.

He closed his eyes; he wanted to go to sleep. But even as he lay
there, he could hear their conversation:

"Poor child!"

"I'm afraid that business has made an awful impression on
him."

"Perhaps we ought to send him away for a while. At any rate,
until all this trouble blows over."

"Send him away!" That was his mother.

"It might be wiser. One never knows what this civil disobedience may lead to. He can go and spend a few weeks with Cecil.
You could take him, Hetty, couldn't you?"

Send him away, send him away, send him away. . . . He seemed
to hear the words over and over again; but he was too weak to

protest; he could not even open his eyelids. "Send him away." It became part of the fabric of his dream: a dream of fire, and of parting, and of anguish. It became an incantation which had power of life and death over him. He turned over, put out a hand, and moaned. He thought of the swollen lumps which they had had to burn off with a cigarette. The fire of the cigarette became the fire in the grate, whose roar drowned all other sounds.

Send him away, send him away, send him away.

CHAPTER X

They motored the twenty miles down to the railway station. At intervals they had to stop the car so that Hugh could get out and be sick. It was still raining, and the road, which wound downwards in a series of hairpin bends, was slithery under their tyres. They had to drive carefully, for on one side of them there was a sheer precipice.

Uncle Mark was an official on the railway, and for that reason Hetty and Hugh were to travel in the saloon which he normally used. There was a kitchen, a lavatory, and two bunks with a table between them. Hugh was so delighted that he forgot his misery at being sent away. While Luchmann brought on board the suitcases and the rolls of bedding, Hugh opened cupboards, examined the shelf of books, and turned on the tap in the lavatory to see if it really gave hot water. His mother and father remained seated on one of the bunks; they smiled at him, with a hint of melancholy. He noticed how his father's hand rested on his mother's. But there was so much to be examined, it was all so exciting: he had no time for home-sickness.

The train did not start until late in the evening. They ate a meal together, which Luchmann had prepared. Hugh ate voraciously; but Mrs. Craddock pushed her food to one side, and sat with her chin resting on her hand. She looked out of the streaming window on to the station, where the light was grey and figures passed carrying lanterns.

When they had done, she told Hugh to prepare for bed. Hetty

began to undress him, but then she herself took over. She said nothing; her hands were cold when they touched him, and often he found
her looking at him in a way that he was not used to. "There!" she
said in a soft voice when she had finished. "When the train leaves,
you must promise me to be a good boy and go straight to bed."

Far away they could hear a jackal. It was a weird, melancholy
noise. Some Indians were arguing outside their window; one of
them coughed as he spoke, and spat frequently, with a dry rattle of
phlegm. The rain still fell with what seemed to be an unwearying
malevolence. It came through the roof of the station and fell on
to the pathetic shapes huddled along the platform. For two hours
now the same people had waited in the same places; they looked
no different from the crates and packing-cases stacked between
them. They made no sound, unless it were to cough and expecto-
rate. They suffered the rain, mutely and without opposition.

A whistle blew a long, shrill gasp, and Mr. and Mrs. Craddock
climbed out of the train. Mrs. Craddock drew the hood of her
mackintosh over her head, so that her face was in shadow; Hugh
could no longer see it.

"Good-bye, Hugh." His father kissed him, and smiled reassur-
ingly.

His mother said nothing. She stood by him, clutching his hand
to her mouth. Her silence and immobility brought panic into his
heart; he could not understand why she did not kiss him or speak
to him, and the thought entered his mind that perhaps, in some
way, he had had cause to offend her. He tried to see her face, but it
was impossible: nothing was visible except the unnatural gleam of
her cheeks and eyes.

The train jolted, and he heard Hetty behind him exclaim:
"We're off! We're off!" He tried to take his hand from his mother's
grasp, but she would not let him. "Hugh, my darling! My darling
boy!" The agonised words broke at last from her: and at the same
moment her face came into the light, and he saw that it was bathed
in tears. "Hugh! Hugh!" she called wildly. Now she was running
beside the train, still clutching his hand. She ran from under the
station roof and the rain fell on to her face and on to their clasped
hands and in through the window from which he leant.

Where the platform ended, she let go of him. His last glimpse of her was standing bowed and desolate, the rain falling all about her. She raised one hand in a salute. He saw it fall, and then he saw no more.

He was happy enough at the cousins. Every other day the post-man brought a letter. Hetty would read it to him, because he could not decipher his mother's writing. In the first of these she apologised for "behaving so foolishly at the station." The words brought an ache to his throat. He could not put out of his mind the image of her hand raised in that last farewell. It seemed more terrible than her anguished cries or the way in which she had run after him.

During the day he could forget: he and the cousins were riding on ponies borrowed from the Maharajah's stables; Aunt Cecil read *Treasure Island* to them; they discovered that Luchmann was a wonderful jumper, and never wearied of seeing him clear the obstacles they put up for him. It was only at night that Hugh felt home-sick. He had dreams from which he woke up in tears. It was often the old dream, of the blue dress which had caught fire; it had many variations—sometimes he poured water on it, and some-times he attempted to beat out the flames with his hands. But always he failed; the dress was destroyed. Once, he dreamed that his mother was wearing the dress, and as it burned, he heard her screaming: "Hugh! Hugh, my darling boy!" in the same anguished voice which she had used at the station.

He became afraid of going to bed; for however happy he had been during the day, the night invariably brought its terrors. Hetty became worried and consulted his aunt; his aunt consulted the doctor. After that he was given a mild sedative before going to sleep. The drug had the effect of giving him an unbroken rest from night to morning; Hetty was no longer troubled. But he awoke peevish and headachy; and there seemed to be lurking in the recesses of his mind terrible memories which he could not bring out into the open. He only knew that they were dreams of intense light or heat.

At last the day came to return home. In a week's time it would be Christmas. There was a whole box of presents to be taken back, and he himself had bought a gift for his mother. A Chinese box-wallah had come to the door, and Hetty had purchased a pink kimono for herself, a lace table-cloth for Aunt Cecil, and some slippers for his father. She suggested that he might like to spend some of his pocket-money. He examined many things—handkerchiefs, silk night-dresses, embroidered cushion-covers—but what chiefly lured him was the tray of jewellery. There were necklaces of seed-pearls, rings of Indian gold, bangles, jade charms, and ashtrays inlaid with turquoise. Among all this bric-à-brac he saw a brooch shaped like a blue-bird; it was studded with artificial jewels, which glinted when one held them to the light.

"Vellee nice," the Chinaman murmured. His face was pock-marked, and he sat with his legs crossed, revealing ankles grey with dirt.

"You don't want that," Hetty put in. "It's shoddy."

"It's not shoddy! Look at all those stones!"

"They're not real."

"They are real. . . . Anyway, what does it matter even if they aren't real?"

"It's just a waste of money. Your mother won't want a thing like that."

"Of course she'll want it. She can wear it on her blue dress."

The Chinaman listened to their altercation, his head on one side.

"Well, what's all the argument about?" Aunt Cecil pushed aside the chick and came out on to the verandah at the sound of their heated voices.

When Hugh showed her the brooch, she shook her head: "In England you could buy a thing like that for sixpence at Woolworth's."

"But I want it," Hugh said sullenly.

"He's so obstinate," Hetty put in. "He just hates to be contradicted."

"Well, of course, if you want it, it's your own money. But I really think you'd do much better to buy one of these turquoise brooches. They're really pretty."

"But I want this," Hugh repeated.

The brooch was bought. It now lay in a matchbox which he had then wrapped in tissue paper, at the bottom of his suitcase.

Once again, the journey was to be made at night. They all kissed each other good-bye, and Zena, who had fallen in love with Hugh, began to cry loudly. Then the train started. Hugh lay in one bunk and Hetty lay opposite him; he could hear her snoring. But though he lay still for a long time, he could not get to sleep. In spite of the comfort of being in a room which was his private property, with bed-clothes, a dressing-table and a light-switch above him, he was kept awake by the incessant jolting of the train, the sudden squeal of a whistle or the dull roar as they passed over a bridge, and always in the centre of all this, something which he at first imagined to be excitement, but later knew to be an obscure anxiety for which he could find no reason. He was worried; he could feel the dark all round him, like a presence which refused to be exorcised. He shivered and turned over restlessly.

At intervals they stopped at wayside stations; and then all the sounds that he seemed to have heard vaguely, as from a distance, converged into hoarse cries, the patter of feet, conversation, and later, like the breathing of an asthmatic, the hiss and pant of the engine. Lanterns shone through the worn blinds, their glow betraying the passing of an official or a search for lost luggage. Lights fluttered like moths. *"Pân! Pân!"* The venders yelled with a sad insistence.

But at last he was lulled into a state of drowsiness. He became less and less conscious of the halts; he seemed to be moving through the noises of the train, the rattle and scream of the engine, the knock of points, to a hard core that thudded in the centre, like a heart. He sighed and was asleep.

When he awoke, he had once more had the Dream. The memory of it made him feel chill and hopeless. It had never been so clear before; he could recollect every detail. He remembered how the sequins had coruscated in the fire, and he could still smell the dense and choking fumes. It had been more terrible than any dream he had ever had before; and now, looking back on it, he could not be certain that it really had been a dream. He lay back, exhausted, and the tears trickled from under his closed eyes.

After a long while, he put out a hand and raised the blind. The tears still falling down his cheeks, he stared outwards at the dawn countryside. They were moving through the desert, and in that light it looked unearthly and foreign. It might have been part of the moon's surface, touched as it was with a strange blueness. Their swift passage made tumuli and dwarf trees scurry across the pane like living things.

Then the sun rose; as from a wound, the red light burst upwards from the east, tingeing his hands and Hetty's sleeping face and the white linen on their beds. A bloom seemed to settle on the countryside, like the down on a peach. He watched it deepen, from rose to amber, and then to red. He seemed to be in a trance; and somehow the whole vista put him in mind of that night when he had sat at the window and watched the fire. He shivered slightly, but did not think of putting the eiderdown about his shoulders. He wanted to wake Hetty, yet did not wish to speak to anyone. He did not know what he wanted. He knew only that he was alone, alone utterly.

CHAPTER XI

Mrs. Timpson need not have worried so much about telling him. She said that she had come to fetch him, as his parents were so busy; she put an arm round his shoulders and led him to the car. Meanwhile, Mr. Timpson was telling Hetty.

They all sat silent in the car. Hetty, dry-eyed but gulping, did not dare to look at Hugh. Mrs. Timpson was going to break the news to him as soon as they got home. She went over the words in her mind, as she had gone over them all that morning. She felt afraid; she could have told an adult, but children frightened her. There seemed to be no way of getting into touch with their inmost feelings.

For once Hugh was not sick during the journey. With white face and eyes dazed, as if from migraine, he stared past Mr. Timpson's bald head on to the road ahead of them. Winter had come, and the trees were leafless. The wind clashed their bare branches together, and though he could not really hear the sound, he imagined it, in all its mournfulness. Everything that had happened to him since the Dream was unreal. Mrs. Timpson was unreal, and the car, and the wintry landscape through which they were now moving. All that was real was his memory of the Dream, the sequins flashing and his hands beating at the dress and the stench and hopelessness of it all. Otherwise he seemed to exist without feeling and beyond the reach of words. He could not be sure that anything had really happened to his parents; and, terrible thought, he no longer cared. He cared about nothing. Everything seemed insignificant and small. He did not know what was the matter with him—something was certainly amiss; and the thought came to him that this must be what death was like. Perhaps he was dead. Perhaps! But even that thought could no longer frighten him.

In the late and wintry afternoon the dandies carried them up to the Timpsons' house. They went by a way which made it impossible for Hugh to see the desolation of his home; and Mrs. Timpson was surprised that he made no protest at being taken by an unaccustomed route to a house not his own.

Before a high-piled fire, clasping and unclasping her hands, she told him the news. As she spoke the words the tears started from her eyes and smeared her cheeks. He sat straight and silent, gazing past her at the stuffed head of a tiger which Mr. Timpson had shot on their honeymoon. She slurred over the tragic details. There had been a fire; his father and mother were both dead. She did not tell him that his mother had lived for six hours in the hospital, her face burnt out of all recognition; nor that she had died calling for him.

When she had finished she went up to the sofa where he was seated, and put her arms round him. She sobbed uncontrollably. But Hugh was stiff and resisting in her arms; he seemed to suffer her caresses only for politeness' sake; and this resistance at such a moment shattered her far more than all the other events of the day. Then she saw with ghastly clarity that she would never understand children, and they would never love her. The realisation made the tears flow faster. "Hugh! My poor Hugh!" she choked, in grief for herself, not him. "My poor motherless boy!"

In a flat, tranquil voice she heard him say: "Then I'll never see Mummy or Daddy again?"

"Never again." She released him with what was almost hostility. Taking a handkerchief she began to dab at her eyes.

"Never again?"

The words clanged together in his mind, and then reverberated, on and on, interminably. They seemed to express a sorrow beyond all tears; they seemed to hold the essence of all partings. They were irrevocable. Ordinarily, there was always the hope of some reunion, somewhere, at some time; but "Never again" sundered him for ever from those whom he loved. The two words passed like a sponge over memory, erasing the whole past, its small fears and its great happiness.

"I think you'd better go to bed now. Don't you?" She was uneasy in his presence; and resentful that he should make her feel uneasy.

He considered a moment. "May I see Luchmann?" he asked.

"Luchmann!" She was taken aback. "Well—of course. . . . But he's gone home—I mean to your home. . . . The servants' compound wasn't touched, you see . . ."

"I see." He knew that she was lying; he knew, obscurely, yet with all his nerves, that Luchmann was sitting out on the verandah, waiting, in case he could be of some service to him. But he did not care even about that. He shrugged his shoulders.

Hetty came into his room to undress him. It was a strange Hetty, tender and motherly. She made him weep a few burning tears. "There, there! my precious!" Her own face was hot and red. But her hands, usually so coarse and rough, now seemed smooth and gentle; it was as if his mother were touching him, not her.

When she had gone, he noticed that it was snowing. The white flakes drifted past the window; and through them he could see the desolate garden beyond. His teeth chattering, he watched them fall endlessly out of a black sky. They drifted like petals on the wind; they heaped themselves into the corners of the window-panes; some forced their way into his room, and dissolved on the floor. As they fell, each one of them seemed to make a thud; they fell, slantingly, and the sound of their falling was like a muffled drum. They fell on his heart, and on his hopes, and on his whole childhood. They thudded as they fell; and the thudding was within his own self.

CHAPTER XII

He had been forbidden to visit the ruin of his old home; but on his walk with Luchmann, the next morning, he saw it from a great distance, the charred refuse black against the white snow. He stood with his bare hands resting on some railings which fenced off the precipitous pathway; the snow had melted and then congealed to them, and they were smooth and icy to the touch. He felt the cold enter his fingers, making them ache like a disturbed tooth. The wind was chill, also; at intervals it blew up a hail as fine and gritty as sand. It brought tears to his eyes, and at its impact, his face became numb and hard and scaly.

All round the house the trees were grimed and blackened; the roof sagged inwards; beams, fragments of clothing, and scraps of furniture littered the tennis-court. The heat of the fire had melted the snow in the near vicinity; there was a circle of devastation, and then the vast, obliterating whiteness. It softened the boulders and lay heavy in the forks of the trees; it covered the roofs in the servants' compound; it gave off a tingling brilliance which dazed the sight.

Like a flotsam washed up on a lonely shore, the pathetic scraps seemed to have been long abandoned. Yet two days ago all had been safe, and as he had remembered it. The hail struck his face with sharp malevolence, and he raised both hands as if to shield himself. Luchmann, seeing the gesture, touched his sleeve:

"Come away, sahib."

They returned to the house where, behind closed doors, endless discussions were held about his future. In the end, Mrs. Timpson called him to her and told him that he would be accompanying her to England in two weeks' time. She would leave him in the hands of his relatives.

"But can't I go to Aunt Cecil?" he queried.

Her mouth hardened. "No, Hugh. We've been into all that. I've had long talks on the telephone with both your uncle and your aunt. Your aunt isn't going home for another eight months. That would mean another hot-weather in the plains for you. You know the doctor said . . ." She looked at him with a mixture of pity and hostility. She felt sorry for the child—who could help feeling sorry for him?—but his coldness and lack of all emotion brought a chill to her heart. Being herself over-demonstrative, she could not understand reserve in others.

"I should have preferred to go to Aunt Cecil," he said simply and resignedly.

Nettled, she retorted: "Well, I'm afraid it's impossible. You'll have to put up with me. I'm going home in any case. I'm sorry if these arrangements don't suit you, but in the circumstances, they're the best that can be managed." When she had spoken, her own asperity made her feel ashamed. "Did you have a nice walk?" she asked in a voice that was now gentle and modulated. "I hope you'll be happy here. I want you to . . . to . . ." She meant to say "I want you to look upon me as your mother"; but knew the unworthiness of the appeal before she had time to formulate it. She felt angry with the boy and yet, obscurely, she wanted to draw his head on to her own aching breast. "Will you . . . do you think you will be happy here?"

"Oh, yes . . . I expect so." He spoke in a crisp, non-committal voice. ". . . Was there anything else you wanted?"

Her head bowed, she said: "No. There was nothing else." She sat for a long time, alone, in the unlit room, staring into the fire: the logs were green, and they hissed and steamed and gave off an aromatic smell. Mr. Timpson came through the bead curtain with a loud clash, and leant over her; his hands, corpulent and stained with nicotine, caressed her neck. "Oh, don't!" she exclaimed tearfully. The sap oozed from the logs and fell into the hearth.

The next day Hetty told him that he must put on his best suit as he would be going to the funeral. He did not answer, and she went up to him and put an arm round his shoulders. "You must be brave," she said.

"For whose sake?"

"For whose sake!" She looked at him in astonishment. "What do you mean?"

When his father had been poisoned, Hugh had been taken to the hospital to visit him; his mother had gone in first, leaving him in the waiting-room with some frayed and out-dated magazines. Mr. Pillbury, the vicar, had come in soon after, having finished his round of the ward. He was a massive man, with large hands whose backs were covered with coarse, red hair. He spoke to Hugh, telling him that he must be brave, "for his mother's sake." The phrase had impressed him, and he had done his best.

"What do you mean?" Hetty repeated.

"Oh, nothing. . . . Just that there's no one left to be brave for—is there?"

There was a hint of bitterness in his voice. Hetty found herself at a loss for an answer. "A funeral's not too bad," she said. "Don't worry."

He thought for a moment. "I don't think I shall go."

Hetty gaped. She was astonished, not so much by the refusal, as by the calm way in which it was expressed.

"Not go to the funeral? But . . ."

He shook his head. "I don't think so," he said gravely. "I don't think I want to." Then all at once his voice broke. "Oh, Hetty!" he cried. "It must be horrible—horrible!"

She, who had been bewildered by his self-possession, now ran to him. "There, there!" she crooned. "Don't cry, my chicken. You needn't go. Of course you needn't go." She was all motherliness and solicitude. "You're far too young—far too young."

He was doing a jig-saw puzzle in the drawing-room when they all set off. Mrs. Timpson came to say good-bye to him, and for once she seemed beautiful: she wore little make-up on her face, and when he looked into her eyes they were sad and tender and like his mother's. For a moment he loved her; he forgot that she would never understand him, and the innumerable ways in which she had gained his disapproval; he forgot that she was vain, shallow, and frivolous. He did not know what had changed her; he did not realise that the memory of his own mother had, for that day, cast its gracious and transfiguring shadow over her uneasy sparkle.

He did not know, yet acknowledged in her some revelation of the dead woman. He took her hand and kissed it.

"Thank you, Hugh. . . . Oh, thank you." At any other time the gesture would have made her gush over him; he would have loathed that. But now she merely smiled, faintly, humbly, and with great love.

"I hope you'll be all right. Mr. Andy will be back from work in about half an hour. . . . You'll like that, won't you?" She could even afford not to be jealous.

Hunched over the jig-saw puzzle his thoughts returned to the funeral. However much he tried he could not put it out of his mind. It seemed terrible, to throw earth upon those whom one had loved. He could hear the rattle of gravel on the wooden lid of the coffin; he saw the mourners, shivering in the wind which blew off the Himalayas; he heard Mr. Pillbury's voice, rich and valedictory. . . .

"Well—Hugh." It was Mr. Andy.

"Hello."

He came and knelt beside him, and helped with the jig-saw. When they had finished, he looked at his watch: "I was going down to the Club for a game of squash. Never mind. Too late now. . . . What would you like to do?"

"Oh, please don't worry about me. I'll be all right."

Mr. Andy guffawed by way of answer. "I don't believe you've seen my yacht yet. I don't mean my real yacht—you've seen that often enough. This is a model I've made. I'm rather pleased with it."

He took Hugh up to his room and showed it to him.

"It's wonderful. . . . Couldn't we—couldn't we sail it?"

"Sail it?"

"Oh, do let's." He ran to the window. "Look! It's thawing. It's been thawing all to-day. We can sail it from the orchard right down to the reservoir." All about Mrs. Timpson's orchard, channels had been made for irrigation: they flowed artfully, bringing sustenance to the great rose-beds, the crown-imperials, the massed hydrangea-bushes, at a time when the drought had turned the gardens of others into a wilderness.

Mr. Andy hesitated. "Do you think . . . I mean . . . ?"

"Oh, come on! Of course we can do it." Hugh supposed that his uncertainty sprang from doubts as to the possibility of using the channels for navigation. "I've often sailed boats there."

"I didn't mean that."

But Mr. Andy did not explain what he did mean. He was as excited as Hugh. They ran down the stairs and out across the lawn, Hugh clutching the model yacht in both hands. "Look out!" The paths were covered in slush, and Mr. Andy slithered, lost his balance, and just failed to come a cropper. "That was a near thing!" he exclaimed. His breath wreathed outwards on the chill air.

The water swirled brown and deep along the channels; they had to run fast in order to keep up with the yacht, and there was always the danger of falling over. Their cheeks became hot and red, their breath came short, and there was a delicious tingle all over their bodies.

"Hoorah!"

Mr. Andy yelled as the small boat shot across the reservoir and collided with the bank on the other side. "I beat you!" he shouted over his shoulder; Hugh had arrived a few feet behind him.

"Let's do it again," Hugh shouted. "Oh, let's do it again!"

"Let's do it again!" Mr. Andy took up the cry. He jostled past Hugh and began to leap up the terraced rose-garden.

"Hi! Wait for me!" Hugh bent down and scraped some of the snow into a ball. It was sharp and crunchy to the touch; the water ran down his wrists. Raising it above his head, he hurled it at Mr. Andy.

"You little devil!" The missile caught him in the back. He, too, began to scrabble in the slush. One snow-ball missed, but the second exploded on Hugh's chest. They fought with shouts and laughter and schoolboy curses. They dashed behind the rose-bushes; the thorns tore their clothes and grazed their faces and their hands. Hugh tripped over one of the hydrangeas, and there was a loud crack. A branch hung broken.

"I'm winning! I'm winning!" he shouted.

"Oh, no, you're not!"

There was no animosity in their contest; they fought as young animals fight, snarling and yelping and rolling over each other. It was the seal to their friendship; for friendship, like love, must, sooner or later, be consummated by some physical act.

"I'm winning! I'm winning!"

There was a silence; Hugh looked round.

"Bob!" Her face bleak with rage or astonishment, Mrs. Timpson stood at the french windows. "What are you both doing?"

Neither of them spoke for many seconds. Then Mr. Andy shambled towards her: "We were having a snow-ball fight," he faltered. His hands and face were blotched and smeared with dirt; his hair was tousled.

"A snow-ball fight!" She stared at him, in incredulity. "A snow-ball . . . Oh, how could you? How could you?" Her eyes travelled past him, and rested on the rose-bed. "My beautiful malmaison! . . . And the hydrangea . . ." She went from one to the other, making vain attempts to join the snapped branches. Mr. Andy stood sheepishly behind her.

"How could you let him do such a thing?" she demanded. "He's only a child. . . . You knew, didn't you? It's—it's so heartless. . . . Bob, I just don't understand."

"It wasn't all Mr. Andy's fault. It was my fault really. I suggested sailing the yacht—and I threw the first snow-ball."

For the first time, she fixed her eyes on him. There were patches of mud and water on his immaculately pressed suit; his face was that of a street-urchin, grimed, flushed, and somehow insolent.

"Your clothes!" she exclaimed. "Your suit! And look how wet you are! . . . Run upstairs immediately. You must have a bath. I'll send Hetty up to you."

"But . . ." He hesitated. "You do see that it was my fault——"

"Run upstairs!" Her voice was peremptory.

He went in through the drawing-room, where he saw that the bearer had set out a tray of drinks and sandwiches. On the staircase, he met Mr. Timpson, who wore a black pin-stripe suit, obviously too small for him. He had a detective novel in one podgy hand, while with the other he patted his moustache. Catching sight of Hugh, he exclaimed: "Great Scott! What have you been doing with yourself?" But Hugh ran on past him.

Soon after he had got into the bath, Hetty banged on the door. "Open, please!" Dripping water, he got out and pulled back the bolt. Her mouth was set in a thin line; as she loomed up at him, through the fog, she seemed terrible and strange. She had rolled back her sleeves, and the muscles in her forearms had never seemed so big. He lay deep in water, looking up at her.

"Well!" she snorted, taking up the loofah. "That was a nice way to carry on, I must say. That was fine! . . . Come on, sit up, sit up. You can't expect me to scrub you like that. Sit up!"

He did as she had told him. But as she leant over his naked body he suddenly threw both arms round her neck. The water seeped through her overall. "Hetty," he murmured in terror. "Hetty. Am I terribly wicked? Am I?" In spite of the warm bath he shook with an uncontrollable ague.

CHAPTER XIII

A few of his parents' possessions were rescued from the fire. Mrs. Timpson went through them, with Hugh to help her. "If there's anything you want to keep," she told him, "you must remember to tell me." But since it was impossible to keep everything, he thought it best to keep nothing. He could not differentiate between so many old friends.

He watched with a rising sense of panic, as Mrs. Timpson placed one object after another in the heap which would go to the auctioneer's. There were the silver filigree sweet-dishes, some towels which he remembered that his mother had herself embroidered, odds and ends of furniture, a water-colour of the Ponte Vecchio which his father had called "insipid" and ordered to be taken from the drawing-room. These objects, and the many others like them, had the power to bring tears to the eyes. When the tide had swept in, and swept out again, bearing with it so much that he had loved, it had left these pathetic remnants, not as a consolation, but as a goad to memory: and as he touched them, it seemed to him that there clung about them a bitter odour, the smell of burning, which could raise up the dead in all their agony.

While he mused, Mrs. Timpson had picked up a matchbox.

"These are the things you brought back with you—the Christmas presents." She opened the matchbox, and tittered. "Oh, Hugh! What's this?" She held the preposterous ornament between two lacquered finger-nails. "How did this get here?"

"Give it to me!" He snatched it away from her. "It's . . . nothing."

She realised that she had wounded him; and clumsily she attempted to undo the hurt. "But it's lovely," she said. "It's so beautiful. It's a bluebird, isn't it? I do like it, Hugh."

"Do you?"

"Oh, yes. Rather!"

"I bought it for—her."

She came close to him and said: "May I have it, Hugh? Will you give it to me?" She looked at him, coaxingly, her lips parted.

"No!" he exclaimed. "No, no!" He clutched the brooch in one fist. "No one can have it. No one."

Mrs. Timpson decided that Hugh was selfish, mean, and obstinate. She shrugged her shoulders. "Very well," she said. "Though God knows what use it will be to you." She picked up another of the objects strewn before her, and then put it down again. All at once she felt tired and disheartened. She knew that if, at that moment, the devil had taken her up into a high place and shown her all the kingdoms of the world, she would have demanded only one thing of him—the brooch.

"Of course you'll keep this," she said, a few minutes later. She held out his father's silver pencil.

Hugh hesitated. "Take it," she said. "Clip it into your pocket. Or get Hetty to pack it for you, if you think you might lose it."

"I don't want it."

"Don't want it!"

"No. . . . What should I do with it?"

"Well—write with it. Use it when you get to school."

It would be useless to explain to her. He could never use his father's pencil for the day-to-day business of doing sums or making notes; if he kept it, it would only be a relic; and young though he was, he knew the danger of relics. But even if he had been able to put all this into words, she would not have understood his attitude. It would have either irritated her or seemed to her "quaint."

Silently he took the pencil, and put it alongside the brooch in his trouser-pocket.

That afternoon Luchmann took him for another walk. They walked up to the summit of one of the hills; and on their way down, Hugh halted where the water from the melted snow gushed black and swift between the two banks of a nullah. As it fell, with a hoarse threshing, it worked itself into a lather; there was a perpetual clink-clink of the stones which were sucked downwards by its force.

Hugh took the brooch from his pocket and, with Luchmann watching him, threw it, in a wide arc, downwards, into the foaming water. For a while their eyes followed it; then it sank, and disappeared.

Hugh turned to Luchmann, smiling. He felt relieved. "And this is for you." He took the silver pencil from his pocket and held it out to him.

"No, no, sahib."

"Take it," Hugh commanded.

"No, sahib."

They argued for many minutes. Hugh, unused to disobedience from the servants, became angry. "If I tell you to take it, you take it."

But the man still shook his head. "You can sell it," Hugh expostulated. "It's worth an awful lot. You can do what you like with it. It's yours."

Still Luchmann refused, until, in a fury, Hugh shouted at him: "If I tell you to take it, you take it. Otherwise, I shall never speak to you again. Understand! I shall never speak to you again."

The man put out his palm. His face was passive and humble under his khaki turban; he raised his other hand in a salute.

The next day Mrs. Timpson returned the pencil to Hugh. "I got this back from Luchmann," she said. "What were you thinking of?" She was shocked by what she regarded as the boy's callousness. This was the only memento he possessed of his dead father, and he gave it away to an Indian—a servant!

Breathless with anger, Hugh demanded: "How did you find out that I'd given it to him?"

"That doesn't matter." Her own bearer had told her; but she was ashamed of admitting that her servants gave her information. "I must confess to you, Hugh, that I was astonished to hear it. I know that you're fond of Luchmann and he's been an excellent orderly, but really. . . . Don't you understand? That pencil belonged to your father. It's something special, to keep and treasure."

It was she who did not understand. After she had gone, he went out on to the verandah to find Luchmann. An uneasy mist was wafting upwards from the lake; it was chill and damp, and one could not see more than a few yards ahead of one. The geraniums which had hung round the trellis were all dead; but the air was still musty with their odour. A large spider ran from under the door, as he opened it; he put out a foot, to squash it, and then stopped himself. Instead, he stooped downwards and cupped it in his hands. It wriggled, and pressed its hairy legs against his skin; when he at last released it, it left a fine rash over his fingers, like a nettle-sting.

Luchmann sat cross-legged at the other end of the verandah. His home was in the plains, and he was not used to such excessive damp or cold. His face was grey, and he was shivering. Hugh held out the pencil to him.

"Why did you give it to Mrs. Timpson?" he asked. "It was nothing to do with her. The pencil belonged to me, and I gave it to you. Keep it."

But Luchmann shook his head mournfully. "It is impossible, sahib. It cannot be. I told you it was impossible. You cannot give it, and I cannot take it."

He began coughing, because the mist was getting into his lungs. They were further away from each other than they had ever been before.

CHAPTER XIV

Christmas came and passed. Hugh knew that the Timpsons were angry with him, because his presence in the house put a curb on all gaiety. They spoke in subdued voices, even when they were telling jokes, and at Christmas dinner they seemed to offer up a mute apology for each cracker pulled. They did not give their usual party, and Mrs. Timpson wore a black evening-dress to the Club Dance.

It was only when Hugh went to bed that the restraint seemed to fall from them. Lying awake, in the dark, he would hear Mrs. Timpson's voice, shrill and clear and frivolous; there would be a guffaw from Mr. Timpson; Mr. Andy would say something. The sound of their merriment made him feel alone and out of things. Hetty was living with friends, Luchmann was in the servants' compound; no one thought of him or wondered if he was all right. It was almost a pleasure to brood on his loneliness; self-pity would well up in his breast, intoxicating him like a heady wine.

After Christmas, there were preparations for departure. Mrs. Timpson was leaving her husband behind. "The doctor says I must get home as soon as possible. I don't know how poor Claud will manage. It quite worries me." Hugh heard her using these phrases, time after time. They made him feel sorry for Mr. Timpson, who did simple card-tricks, drank a great deal, and obviously loved his wife.

The day they left was the first day of spring. Going into the garden, Hugh noticed the small spurs on the apple-trees, the crocuses, and the sweet smell of grass. The air was soft and warm, yet somehow autumnal. It brought an added sadness to the heart; it spoke of hopes which would not bloom afresh, of dead memories and dead desires.

As they drove beside the lake, glittering and trembling in the sunlight, and so moved outwards and downwards into the plains, Hugh did not say the words which he had always said on other such occasions: "Good-bye lake. Good-bye hills. Good-bye shops. Good-bye home." It all seemed childish now. But looking back through the window of the car he saw, for one brief moment, the charred beams and leafless plane-trees; he saw the tennis-court and the rubbish that lay about; he saw the shell which had been his home, and his spirit went out in one long, last farewell. Good-bye home. Good-bye, for ever. For he knew that he would never return there again; it was all finished and done with.

Mr. Andy met them at the station in the plains. He had gone down there for a police case a few days before. Since the day of the snow-ball fight, he had shown a certain uneasiness in Hugh's presence. But now, for these few last minutes, the old intimacy grew up again. "How I envy you!" he told Hugh. "You are a lucky beggar— going back to Blighty—with your schooldays before you!"

"I suppose I am lucky."

"Of course you are. They'll teach you how to play footer, and there'll be cricket in the summer. You'll like that, won't you?" There was a note of wistfulness beneath the hearty phrases.

He had brought Hugh a good-bye present. It was the model yacht which they had sailed together. He had packed it in ravelled paper, and there was a card with Hugh's name on it, written in his childish, slanting script. He watched Hugh's face as he raised the lid of the box and pulled aside the wrappings; and when he saw the boy's face become for a moment radiant and transfigured, he was overwhelmed with an emotion which found him unprepared. Like most adolescents his feelings tended to play him up; it was the inevitable result of going through life as if feelings did not exist. He often had these sharp reminders, and then he lost his head; he was frightened of emotion, and did not know how to deal with it. So now, when Hugh said to him: "Thank you. It's wonderful. Thank you, so much," he turned away mumbling some incoherent words.

Mrs. Timpson had been watching the scene. She took no notice of Mr. Timpson, who stood beside her, his lower lip sagging, his hands trembling. They had spoken nothing to each other for several minutes. For six years they had lived without saying anything of importance to each other, and now it was too late. Once Mr. Timpson began: "Dora—you know, I shall miss you confoundedly . . ." but he broke off, clearing his throat. She eyed him with derision.

At last the time came for leave-taking. Mr. Timpson took his wife clumsily in his arms, but as soon as their lips met, she began to pull away from him. "You'll ruin my hat," she expostulated. Mr. Andy and Hugh shook hands solemnly. Luchmann was travelling with them as far as Bombay, so only Hetty remained now.

"Good-bye, Hetty." She raised a face which was red and blotched, yet young and almost pretty; grief had transfigured her, as love had long ago in the military cantonment. The quickening of her spirit under pain and parting brought vitality to her. She held him close to her, his head on her breast; and he heard her whispering through her tears: "Be happy! Be happy always!"

He could say nothing. A whistle blew, and they were moving outwards. Hands waved; Mrs. Timpson sat down and took off her hat; the cluster of people on the platform diminished, became as small as pin-men, and at last could be seen no more. The train gathered speed, and the night drew close around them.

He could not eat throughout the long journey. Luchmann prepared all his favourite dishes—baked eggs, sardines on toast, tinned sausages—but as soon as he took a mouthful he felt that he would suffocate. "Eat, sahib," the orderly coaxed him. "Eat a little, sahib." But he shook his head mournfully, and pushed aside the plate.

He sat at the window for many hours on end; but now all the mystery seemed to have gone out of the countryside through which they passed. His heart no longer stirred when he saw a group of nomads, trudging beside the railway-line, nor when, at evening, he saw the distant fires of a village, pricking the late haze. Such things had lost their power to excite him. He became aware of a monotony in what he looked at. There were always the rice-fields, the paddy-fields, the bullocks, and the black natives. There was always the untidiness, and the sense of nothing being completed; there was always the vastness. It made his head ache. As they neared Bombay there was a change in the scenery. They passed, not isolated villages, but endless vistas of mills, factories, huts, and tenements. Above them there hovered the birds of the city, their wings affording the only shade in a place without trees. Luchmann, who had never seen such buildings, hung far out of the window, making childish exclamations of wonder. But Hugh remained indifferent.

Night came on; and with it a pale glow from the distant city swept upwards and outwards, grading the sky from jet to dove-grey and azure. The glow intensified. A white heat seemed to be rising, like the film of vapour which comes off a great fire; and through this uneasy gauze everything appeared hard and yet faintly distorted to the eye. It was as if the lights, the outlines of buildings and even the colours in the sky were all being viewed through binoculars, from a great distance. To Hugh, the effect was that of a nightmare; but Luchmann never ceased to exclaim: "Wonderful! Beautiful!"

They drove through the city to their hotel. Hugh felt dazed and sleepy; his long fast gave an air of hallucination to everything he saw. There were many lights, and he had an impression of people jammed together in huge masses. Water glittered in the far distance, and an aeroplane throbbed overhead. The Indian chauffeur turned round and grinned when Mrs. Timpson asked him some question, and Hugh saw that his teeth were crowned with gold.

They went up some steps into a vast hall; it was like a cave, and the atmosphere was hot and clammy. They stood at a desk, Mrs. Timpson filled in some forms, and then they shot upwards in a steel cage. His pillows were cold under his burning cheeks. There was a stiff place where the initials of the hotel were embroidered on them. He began to shiver; he was very tired; he fell asleep.

The next morning Mrs. Timpson had to reprimand him for spending so long in the lavatory; it had made them late for breakfast. "What on earth were you doing in there?" she asked.

"Oh, nothing," he answered briefly. He did not wish to tell her of his fascination with the flush-closet. He had never seen such a thing before. Spell-bound, he had listened to the gushing of the water; then, when the tumult had subsided, he had given the chain another pull. Nothing happened. He went on pulling, the exertion making him sweat and pant, until at last the tank refilled and he was rewarded by another rush of water. He could not understand why he had had to wait so long; there must be some knack to it.

When they went into the dining-room, he was astonished to see Captain Curtiz. But Mrs. Timpson walked straight to the table where he was seated, took one of the chairs herself with a murmured "Good-morning, dear," and motioned Hugh into the other. Captain Curtiz looked up at him from over his newspaper, and said "Hello" in a crisp, unfriendly voice.

Hugh was puzzled; but he was sufficiently tactful not to ask questions in Captain Curtiz's presence. It was not until he and Mrs. Timpson were alone once more that he ventured: "How funny our meeting Captain Curtiz! I thought you said that he had already sailed for England."

"I never said that."

"Oh, yes, I'm sure you did. I remember distinctly. Mr. Timpson asked you what had happened to him, and you said——"

"Yes, yes. I remember now. . . . He didn't sail when he thought he would. He has friends in Bombay. They persuaded him to wait for the next boat." She lied carelessly, imagining that it was no hard matter to deceive a child. "Of course, I knew nothing of this change of plans. As a matter of fact I rather lost touch with Captain Curtiz after he left the station. You know how it is."

"It'll be nice for you to have him on the boat with you," Hugh said innocently.

Mrs. Timpson flushed. "Oh, yes. It's always nice to have someone one knows."

"Particularly an old friend."

She looked up at him, wondering whether he was being simple or extraordinarily subtle. His face reassured her; it was without any trace of guile. But for a moment she had felt uneasy.

That afternoon Luchmann was sent upstairs for the luggage while she paid the bill. He found Hugh standing at the window of his room, with one hand on the sash-cord. As he entered, the boy jerked round as if he had woken from a dream. "I've come for the luggage, sahib."

"Is it time already?"

"The memsahib has sent for the car." He picked up the suitcases and was going out of the door, when Hugh called him back.

"Luchmann . . . will you—do you think you will forget me?"

"Of course not, sahib."

"I'll write to you. And you must write to me. You will write? You must get a *babu* to write for you."

"I'll write, sahib."

"One day I shall see you again. I shall come back again. I shall come back again." He uttered the words, as if he were seeking for conviction from them.

All at once the Indian went down on his knees; he put his arms round Hugh's legs and pressed his face against his body. "Come back, sahib!" he said in a strange, hoarse voice. "Come back!"

"I shall come back." But he did not believe the words. "I shall come back, and you shall be my servant." All faith went out of him, leaving him helpless and alone. He put out one hand and then the other, and touched the Indian's tear-stained cheeks. They remained thus for many seconds.

"What have you been doing? Get a move on, Luchmann!" Mrs. Timpson came in, followed by Captain Curtiz.

No further words passed between Hugh and the orderly. A conventional good-bye would have been impossible after what had gone between them; and there could be no other sort of good-bye, once they had moved back into the world to which they had been trained. Their revolt had been intuitive; it had lasted for a few minutes, and the minutes had sufficed. Now they would conform once more.

Hugh and Mrs. Timpson and Captain Curtiz stood on deck as the boat left the harbour. Hugh watched Luchmann; he watched Luchmann, and saw nothing else. He watched him until his eyes began to sting and water, and he could see no more of him. The shore receded, and with it the stench of petrol-fumes, and tar, and bilge. The town shimmered through the noonday heat; for a moment it looked beautiful; its very remoteness made it seem desirable. Then it, too, faded.

Mrs. Timpson exclaimed: "Good-bye, India! Oh, good-bye!" She spoke with joy.

Part II

ENGLAND

CHAPTER XV

At first Mrs. Timpson and Hugh got on well enough together. He was neither boisterous nor ill-mannered, he had a natural tact, and it was unnecessary to talk "down" to him. She could almost persuade herself that he was an adult. It pleased her that he was so much of a success with her own friends; they all told her how charming he was, and envied her her good fortune in having the care of him. In particular he won the favour of a Miss Amberley, an American missionary who was returning to the States after thirty unbroken years in India. She was a large, dowdy woman, who always carried a bag with silk tassels hanging from it; her arms were freckled and she wore bangles on them. She spoke in a gruff yet kindly voice; she smelled of perspiration, and her hair was drawn into an untidy bun from which hair-pins continually fell out on to the deck.

She played draughts with Hugh, told him stories, and treated him to iced drinks. He liked her, except when she fondled him; then he was revolted by the damp and fleshy touch of her, her smell, and the wisps of hair which grew round her mouth. He was ashamed that these things should disgust him; he remembered how often his mother had chided him for judging people by appearance. He knew that if Miss Amberley had been less unprepossessing he would be feeling, not affection for her, but love. He found it impossible to love those who were ugly; but beauty thrilled him and destroyed his critical faculty.

"My! What wonderful blue eyes you've got! And such a milk-and-roses complexion! You're as pretty as a girl."

Hot with shame, he turned his face away from her, squirming in her grasp. "There now!" she exclaimed. "I've made you blush." She gave a deep, rumbling laugh and ran one hand down his cheek. He struggled away from her, making her laugh still more.

"I'm just crazy about that child," she later told Mrs. Timpson.

"He is rather sweet, isn't he?"

But sweet or not, his continual presence became irritating. She had to share her cabin with him; he sat with her up on deck; he was always asking questions. Already guilt was nagging at her like the sting of a broken tooth, and Hugh too often jagged the raw place without realising it. She began to devise means of ridding herself of his company. Miss Amberley was useful, of course, and so were one or two other of the passengers. Eventually, she did not need to tell him to go elsewhere when Captain Curtiz joined them; Hugh would get up and leave of his own accord.

Captain Curtiz complimented her on this. "You've trained the boy well." For much of the day he wore only a pair of bathing-trunks and gym-shoes. The sun had cooked his body to a hue of purple, his hair had become dry and bleached. He was several years younger than Mrs. Timpson, and for his sake she played deck games which made her weary and breathless.

As they sailed through the Indian Ocean a fancy-dress dance was given. Hugh was delighted with the costume which Mrs. Timpson intended to wear; she had brought it from India with her. It was the costume of an Indian dancing-girl: there were small red slippers, embroidered with gold thread, the toes pointing upwards; there was a *sari*, shot with rainbow colours, and a gold tunic; there were ornaments, great gold necklaces, with belts and coins and lucky charms, bangles for wrist and ankle, ear-rings, and a pendant for the forehead. When Mrs. Timpson was out of the cabin Hugh liked to run his hand over the materials; they were sleek and soft and almost diaphanous.

While she was dressing she sent him out of the cabin, and he went along to see Miss Amberley. She was writing letters, with a large, thick-nibbed fountain-pen, but as he came in she closed the pad and beamed at him. "I thought you'd be in bed by now."

"Well, I am half undressed." He was wearing his dressing-gown.

"Mrs. Timpson is just putting on her costume. Oh, it's wonderful; you ought to see it."

"I shall see it." She gave a slightly wry smile.

"What are you going as?"

"Me? . . . I'm going as myself."

"Yourself?"

"I'm too old to start dressing up."

"Oh." He was disappointed. Gallantly, he said: "But you're not really as old as all that. You can't be much more than ten years older than Mrs. Timpson."

"Much more than that, I'm afraid. But thank you for the compliment."

"Well, I'd better be getting back."

As he walked down the passage he once again reproached himself. Miss Amberley was far kinder than Mrs. Timpson and he had thought himself fond of her; yet all the time he had been talking to her he had felt impatient and ill at ease. He had wanted to get away as soon as possible and return to his own cabin. Beauty was a stronger lure than either love or goodness.

Captain Curtiz was lying on the lower bunk, dressed in a toga, while Mrs. Timpson did up the small engraved buttons of her tunic. He scowled as Hugh entered. He felt uncomfortable in his costume, which Mrs. Timpson had made for him out of some old sheets; he did not mind wandering about all day in a pair of bathing-trunks, but it embarrassed him to go into dinner with bare legs.

"Really, Norah!" he exclaimed. "Do you allow the little beggar in here while you're dressing?"

"I've nearly finished. . . . In any case, what about you?" Her eyes were unnaturally bright as she fixed first one pearl ear-ring and then the other. "Get off the bunk," she said. "The child can't climb up to his."

"He can wait."

Hugh put out a hand to one of the buttons; it was engraved with the head of a lion. "Oh, look!" he exclaimed.

"I can't understand how you can let him maul you about so."

"He's not mauling me about, Dick! Don't be so silly!" She gave a titter, burdened with suppressed excitement.

At last she was ready; as a final adornment she took a small vermilion circle and Captain Curtiz stuck it on her forehead for her. His hands were trembling, and she looked up, her lips parted, her breasts rising and falling beneath the gold tunic. Hugh, in his bunk now, gazed down on the pair of them. He knew, in his heart, that he disliked them; yet at that moment they had the power to enchant and inflame him, so that if they had told him to do anything for them, however difficult, he would have performed it, without question.

"Good-night, Hugh." She did not turn her head as she went out, with Captain Curtiz following her. He could still hear the diminished tinkle of her necklace long after she had left him; and as he lay awake, in the dark now, with the sky close and starry through the port-hole, the thought of her, in her gold tunic, with the vermilion star on her forehead and the pearls swinging from her ears, returned to him and again filled his soul with all the unreasoning exaltation which he had felt in her actual presence. She seemed an enchantress then, more terrible and beautiful than she could ever possibly have been; and Captain Curtiz, in his toga, became a stern Olympian deity, in whose hands were thunder and lightning and the four winds.

He fell asleep, and was woken many hours later by the sound of their return. They had switched on the light, but outside the port-hole he could see one star, burning red and large and bright.

"Sh!" It was Mrs. Timpson. She took the *sari* from her hair and shook out her curls. "We don't want to wake the child."

"Oh, blast the child!"

"Sh, Dick!"

"He's a damned nuisance."

"Oh, I know, I know." She sighed. Hugh saw Captain Curtiz place his hands on the gold tunic; they seemed very large there, and for the first time he noticed that he bit his nails. "Don't, Dick. Not here! I tell you, the child . . ."

"He's asleep. I tell you he's asleep."

He leant forward, pressing his lips on her lips so that she could make no further protest. They swayed together; Hugh turned over in the bunk, away from them, so that he could see no more. He

felt afraid; he felt excited; he knew he ought to give some sign that
he was awake, yet did not dare to. Mrs. Timpson seemed more
beautiful than she had ever seemed before, and he wanted to look
at her; but shame and revulsion filled him. He lay trembling, his
palms pressed against his hot cheeks.

"My dearest." Captain Curtiz spoke the words. Then there followed a long-drawn sigh which seemed inexpressibly mournful
to Hugh. The light went out, and he turned over again. From
below there came the sound of voices whispering incomprehensible things. There were long silences, when he heard nothing but
the ticking of the clock on the dressing-table and the sigh of the
waves, and then the whispering would begin again. Listening to
it, he was overcome with terror. It was a terror which made him
rigid and speechless and brought the sweat pricking in cold beads
through the skin of his forehead. He had no conception of what
was going on beneath him, but all his nerves cried out that it was
something nameless and horrible and evil. Even the whispering
had the power to strike panic into his soul. It was unlike any communication which he had ever heard before. If he had been told at
that moment that Mrs. Timpson was a witch, he could not have
been more terrified.

It was impossible to tell how long he lay there. His teeth were
chattering, and he felt that he would vomit. The star seemed to
draw nearer and nearer, until it hung just beyond his left shoulder,
a tight ball of fire. Beyond, far, far beyond, the sky curved in a long,
bluish arc.

At last someone went out and the door closed. The light was
put on, and he shut his eyes, as Mrs. Timpson always told him to
do, when she was undressing. He heard her humming to herself,
and then, a few minutes later, it was dark again. Once more he
heard that strange, melancholy sigh; then her bunk creaked, and
the star began to move away from him, and slide into the blue
beyond. It was nearly morning.

CHAPTER XVI

The next day he felt uneasy in their presence. The thought obsessed him that they knew that he knew their secret. But what was this secret? The memory of what he had seen could still unman him. Yet to his eyes, so little had happened—some whispered phrases, a sigh, and Captain Curtiz's large hands resting on the gold tunic. Once again he learned the power of mystery. All that is just beyond the reach of the understanding and has to be groped for, through imagination, exerts a double lure. The unknown is stronger than the known, the shadow than the substance.

He avoided them all that day. When he was in their company he imagined that they were scrutinising him; they seemed to be enjoining silence on him. He felt that he was their accomplice in something discreditable. Perhaps it was merely that, being so suggestible, he had caught the infection of their mood. They both felt guilty and embarrassed; and yet they also felt a joy which was stronger than all qualms.

Unwittingly, Hugh again jabbed at the abscess which festered in both their minds. The three of them sat beside the swimming-pool. Captain Curtiz had just executed a series of brilliant dives, and now he lay wet and flushed and panting at Mrs. Timpson's feet. He had been showing off for their benefit, and had obviously impressed both of them. Time after time, they watched him flash through the air, straighten, and slice the water. Between dives he floated on his back and smiled up at them, his teeth gleaming under the small, military moustache.

"That was wonderful," Hugh said. It had been wonderful: the sight of the nude body, falling over and over in the sunlight, had brought a strange pang to his heart.

For the first time, Captain Curtiz gave Hugh a kindly look. He took a towel and began to rub himself.

"The child's right," Mrs. Timpson said. "It was wonderful. Absolutely wonderful."

Captain Curtiz made a derogatory noise in the back of his throat. "Swimming's not really my sport," he said.

It was very hot. The eyes were wearied by the dazzle of the waves, and the sun sapped initiative. The heat had a curious effect on the horizon; it seemed to bulge inwards, livid and swollen, like a balloon. Mrs. Timpson gazed down at Captain Curtiz; he smiled up at her. Hugh watched them, and was drawn into the circle of their enchantment.

"Is it to-day or to-morrow we reach port?" he asked.

Mrs. Timpson sighed, and looked away from the body at her feet. "To-morrow," she said shortly. She began to fan herself with the copy of *Vogue* which she had been reading.

"I suppose there'll be a lot of letters waiting for us."

"I suppose so."

"I wonder if Hetty has written to me. . . . There are sure to be masses of letters from Mr. Timpson for you, Auntie Norah."

Her mouth tightened. "I daresay."

"I expect he misses you terrible. It can't be much fun to be alone like that."

She gave a short dry laugh. "He'll be all right." She seemed now to be avoiding Captain Curtiz's gaze.

"Oh, I'm sure he's all right. I didn't mean that. It's just that it must be lonely sometimes——"

"Oh, for God's sake stop this chatter! It's too hot for it." She spoke in sudden temper.

"I'm sorry," Hugh said. A moment ago he had felt himself to be one of them; he knew now that it had been an illusion.

"You talk too much," Captain Curtiz said viciously. "Haven't you ever heard the saying, 'Children should be seen and not——'"

"Oh, yes. Hetty always said I was a frightful chatterbox. She said I'd make a good member of parliament——"

"There you go again! Can't you hold your tongue for one minute on end! We're not the least bit interested in what Hetty— whoever she may be——"

"Hetty was my nurse."

"Blast Hetty! We don't care whether she was your nurse or the sweeper's daughter. We don't care!"

"Dick!" Mrs. Timpson chided him. "Don't be so hard on the child." She ran her fingers through his wet hair.

"He's such a blithering idiot. Why doesn't he go away and play? Hasn't he any friends of his own age? He ought to take some exercise."

His throat burning with unshed tears, Hugh picked up the cricket-ball which Hetty had given him and moved off along the deck. At the far end he came on a group of Australian children, whom he had always avoided sitting next to at meals. They spoke in loud, ringing voices, and grabbed at the food set before them. Their faces were red, their hair was cut short, and their bodies were brown and sinewy. He often saw them playing rough games among themselves, the girls and boys wrestling together, shouting, laughing and tearing each other's clothing. As he hesitated a few yards away from them, one of the girls caught sight of him and let out a piercing whistle. She began to clap her hands together, calling out: "Catch! Catch! Catch!" Since he obviously did not understand what she meant, she shouted out: "Oh, throw the ball, you fool!"

He hesitated, but again she commanded him: "Come on! Come on!" He lobbed the ball towards her, under-arm.

They all burst into howls of contempt. "Can't you throw a ball properly?" one of the boys yelled at him.

"I can throw a bit harder than that."

"A bit harder!" They clapped their sides, and doubled over in mirth.

"I thought it might go over the rail, if I wasn't careful."

"Don't you know how to throw over-arm?" The girl who had caught the ball began tossing it up in the air, as if she were juggling with it. Her nose was peeled with sunburn, and she had a thick face and neck.

"I've never been taught," Hugh said.

"You don't have to be taught," the girl answered derisively, and at the same time two or three of the others chanted: "We'll teach you! We'll teach you!"

"Could I have my ball back, please?"

"Not until you learn to throw over-arm."

"It's my ball."

"Dear, dear!" She bent down and threw it between her legs. One of the boys caught it with a loud smack.

"See if you can stop this," he shouted at Hugh. He hurled the ball at him. Hugh put out both hands to shield himself, there were catcalls and yells of laughter; the ball struck his chest, making him stumble backwards and giving him a sulphurous taste in the mouth.

"Oh, jolly good! Jolly good!" They clapped and cheered ironically.

"You hurt me," Hugh said.

"Did we? Did we really? . . . Bad luck, sir! Oh, jolly bad luck, sir!" They tried to imitate his English accent.

"Well, try this one! . . . Ready, steady——"

The boy had again raised his arm to hurl the ball, but this time Hugh made no attempt to stop it. He watched it as it shot over the deck-rail and landed in the water. There was a splash, and then nothing.

For a moment the children fell silent; this was more than they had intended. Then the eldest boy said: "Oh, beat it!"

"I want my ball."

"You can't have it. Don't be a bloody fool. How can you have it?"

"You lost it for me."

"You heard! Beat it! Scram!"

"I'll tell Mrs. Timpson!" he threatened, already on the verge of tears.

"Boo-hoo!"

"You'll have to get me another."

"Baby! Baby! Baby!" They all began chanting together. He took to his heels and ran back to Mrs. Timpson and the Captain.

"My God! Back already!" Captain Curtiz flicked at Hugh's legs with his bath-towel. "Didn't you hear what we said?"

"Yes, I know, but——"

He poured out the story to them. At the end, Captain Curtiz looked up at him; his blue eyes seemed peculiarly hard and brilliant.

"Well?" he asked.

"That's all."

"And what do you expect us to do?"

"I . . . I don't know," Hugh faltered.

"Haven't you ever been told not to sneak?"

"Sneak?"

"Yes, sneak. Don't repeat every word I say. A sneak's the lowest form of animal life. I don't like sneaks."

"They took my ball."

"And so you have to come crying to mummy."

"Dick!" Even Mrs. Timpson was shocked.

Captain Curtiz flushed. "That's the way little girls behave. Men don't behave like that. . . . You're not a girl, are you?"

Hugh shook his head. He could not trust himself to speak. At that moment, the memory came to him of how Miss Amberley had told him that he was as pretty as a girl.

"Be a man, for God's sake! Fight your own battles."

"There were six of them. And they're much bigger than I am."

"Well, what of it? It doesn't matter if they beat you up. You can't go through life giving in to everyone who is stronger than you. Have you no pride?" He got to his feet, and pinched Hugh's arm just above the elbow. "Took at you! There's not an inch of muscle there. You're flabby. You're soft."

"Yes," Hugh said in complete humility. Before Captain Curtiz's nude body, he knew himself to be skinny, puny, and weak.

"Yes!" Captain Curtiz exclaimed. "You know it then? You know it! But what do you do about it? Do you ever take any exercise? Do you ever try to improve yourself? I don't believe you can swim, can you?"

"I've—I've never tried."

In India, they had been far from the sea, and there had been no swimming-baths; and now that he had the opportunity, he had been afraid. Captain Curtiz was right: he was not a man. Self-disgust overwhelmed him.

"Well, it's time you did try. I've never heard of such a thing. I've never heard of a boy of your age who didn't know how to swim. Why, when I was your age, I could do a swallow-dive."

"He's not had the chance," Mrs. Timpson put in.

"He's got it now, hasn't he?"

"Of course, if you would teach him——" she concurred.

"I'm perfectly willing. I've dealt with his sort before. . . . What do you say, Hugh? Eh?"

Abjectly, yet with great gratitude, he murmured: "Oh, please! I'll do my very best. Really, I will."

"That's more like it." He pulled Hugh's ear with what was meant to be affection. "We'll begin this afternoon. Meantime, you can run down to my cabin and fetch my cigarette-case."

Hugh set off at the double. For a few moments it seemed vitally important to learn how to swim and become like Captain Curtiz. He was full of good resolutions. The next morning he would go to the Children's Class in the gymnasium; he would learn how to box; he would try to get himself sunburnt, as Captain Curtiz was, even if it did mean peeling and having his back sore. These thoughts so much filled his mind that he could hardly swallow any lunch.

But once he was faced with the element, all his resolutions came to nothing. Mrs. Timpson had bought him some bathing-trunks, and he stood waiting for Captain Curtiz, by the pool, his thin, white arms crossed over his chest, his hands under his arm-pits. In spite of the heat, he was shivering, and his small nipples were blue with cold. Captain Curtiz strode towards him, kicking off his plimsolls.

"All set?" He eyed Hugh, and then guffawed. "You do look a shrimp! . . . In you go."

Hugh hesitated. Between chattering teeth, he asked: "Where shall I get in?"

"Where? Anywhere!"

"Mightn't I get out of my depth?" He knew the ignominy of asking such questions, yet could not help himself. Once again self-disgust rose up in him, like a sour vomit.

"You won't get out of your depth this end. No shilly-shallying. Jump in and duck."

It was horrible. The shock of immersion took his breath away; he stood gulping and gasping, while Captain Curtiz shouted at him: "Duck, duck, duck!"

"I can't! I don't know how to."

"I'll show you," came the muttered answer. A few seconds later a hand descended on Hugh's neck, another caught one of his legs, and he had done a somersault into the water. He came up spitting, coughing and rubbing the water out of his smarting eyes. Captain Curtiz flexed arms on which the veins intercrossed like ivy on the branches of a tree. He laughed. "Now you know," he said.

It was a poor beginning. Hugh determined to do better. But whatever resolutions he himself made, his body let him down. When Captain Curtiz told him to lie flat on the water, one hand under his stomach, he would find himself involuntarily squirming round and throwing both arms round his neck. All their attempts ended in this. He loathed himself as much as Captain Curtiz did: it seemed that he had no control over himself—his arms flew out, of their own accord, his legs shot down to the floor of the swimming-bath, and his face was against Captain Curtiz's chest.

"What the hell do you think you're doing? Is this a love-scene?" Captain Curtiz demanded, when, for the hundredth time, Hugh was festooned round his body. "You're hopeless. I've had enough." He pushed him away from him with such violence that he fell over backwards into the water.

Hugh clambered out after him, and took up his towel. He had swallowed a great deal of water, which made him feel sick yet thirsty. "I'm frightfully sorry," he gulped.

"What's the good of being sorry? You're just a rabbit. You just funk the water." He moved away from Hugh, to the other end of the swimming-pool, as if he disliked his proximity.

Following him, Hugh pleaded: "Won't you give me a second chance? Please, Captain Curtiz! I know I'm a coward——"

"No, no, no!" In sudden fury he put out a leg and shoved Hugh with it. The boy tottered backwards, swayed, clutched the air, and disappeared from sight. There was a loud splash.

Captain Curtiz grinned; then hearing the muffled cries which came from the water, he dived after him.

"Stop struggling, you fool!"

"Let me go! Don't touch me!"

They churned about together. Captain Curtiz clutched Hugh's arm, but he slithered away from him. He tried to knock him unconscious, but only made another great splash, his fist striking water. Hugh thought he intended to murder him; he was filled with loathing and terror. When he felt his grip on his shoulder, he kicked, bit, and scratched. Water had filled his mouth, and he spat it out into Captain Curtiz's face. Then, wonderfully, he found that he could swim. He could do a sort of dog-paddle, which took him to the side. He clambered out, and, looking over his shoulder, saw that Captain Curtiz was just behind him. It was like a nightmare; and as in a nightmare, he rushed off, hearing the feet of his pursuer only a short distance from him. The whole scene had become unreal; his panic was the panic of dreams, and it was a dream-world through which he hurtled. He ran across the slippery surface of the bar, through one lounge and then another; water dripped from him, and he saw, with strange clarity, the astonished faces of the other passengers. He bumped into a steward, but ran on. His chest was aching now, and his bare feet seemed numb and leaden. He tore down innumerable passages, the lights flashing past him, above his head: on either side he was followed by the reflection of a nude boy running deep in the glossy wood.

Then all at once he halted. He was alone; no one was following him. He took great gulps, which were also sobs. Suddenly he began to retch.

When that was over he continued at a jog-trot until he had reached Miss Amberley's cabin. As on many other occasions, he discovered her on her knees, in prayer.

"Jiminy!" She was astonished at his appearance. Half-naked, dishevelled, his face white and tense, he stood in the doorway with one hand pressed to his side.

At the sound of her exclamation, he rushed to her and threw himself into her arms. "Miss Amberley! Oh, Miss Amberley! Save me! Save me!"

"What is all this? . . . There, there!" She soothed him. "You're quite safe. Just calm down and tell me what's happened."

"They'll kill me," he said.

"Who'll kill you?"

"Captain Curtiz, and Mrs.——"

"Captain Curtiz! Now don't be silly. Captain Curtiz wouldn't touch a hair of your head. You've got over-excited——"

"But you don't know what I did."

"What did you do?"

"I scratched him, and kicked him, and then—then I ran away."

"Here, wait a minute. We don't want you to catch pneumonia." She fetched her towel and wrapped it about his shivering body. "Now—explain yourself. I can't make head or tail of all this."

He told her the whole story; as he recounted what had happened, his behaviour seemed more and more unpardonable. The memory returned to him of how he had tugged at the hair of Captain Curtiz's chest, and had then dug in his nails. He began to cry softly as he went over it all.

Miss Amberley sat on the bunk, with her hands clasped; she seemed kind and reassuring, and as he looked at her, it struck him that she might even be as strong as Captain Curtiz was. She had a magnificent jaw and chin, and he had seen the muscles in her calves when he had walked behind her.

"That doesn't sound very terrible," she said when he had finished. She smiled at him, got up and began rummaging in her cabin-trunk.

"Oh, but it was. He was terribly angry with me. I don't know what he'll do. He's sure to try to kill me, or beat me."

She was pouring some amber liquid out of a silver flask into a tooth-mug. "Sip some of this," she commanded.

It was hot on his tongue, and, as he swallowed it, tears streamed from him; he was doubled up with coughing. The thought flashed at him that she was on the side of Captain Curtiz, and the drink was poison. But a moment later he experienced a strange, delicious warmth; his teeth ceased to chatter.

"Nothing's going to happen to you," she said. "You must go back to your cabin and get some clothes on."

"Oh, I couldn't! I couldn't do that. He's sure to be waiting there."

"I tell you, no one is going to hurt you." But he remained unconvinced. Whatever she said to him, he shook his head and cowered into a corner. "Very well!" she said at last. "I'll go along and speak to Mrs. Timpson—and to Captain Curtiz, if he's in the cabin."

"What'll you say?"

"Oh, I'll explain things."

"Explain things? But what can you explain?" He became tearful once more.

"I'll tell them that you're not to be punished. Trust me. I'll make everything all right. I know how to deal with this sort of thing. Believe me, I've had lots of practice. . . . Now you hop into my bunk, and keep warm, until I get back."

There was a yeasty smell about her sheets. He pulled the bed-clothes up to his chin, and stared at the ceiling. In spite of all her assurances, he still felt afraid. Of course she was strong, and she was old, and she was a missionary; but what could she do against someone like Captain Curtiz? She and he together were no match for such an enemy; and apart from her, who else could he enlist on to his side? The warmth of the spirits was leaving him, and once more panic flooded back into his soul. He considered the possi-bility of taking refuge on the Captain's bridge, where passengers were not allowed to go; or he might be able to hide in the hold.

"That's all right." Miss Amberley was beaming. "Nothing's going to happen to you. Mrs. Timpson has promised. . . . Now get along with you—quick march!"

"It is really going to be all right?"

"That's what I said."

"Oh, thank you." For the first time he kissed her. "Thank you. Thank you so much."

She was touched by a warmth which he had never shown on any other occasion. She returned his kiss, and for once he did not try to squirm away from her. When he had gone, she went down on her knees once more.

Mrs. Timpson lay in her bunk with a novel, resting, as she usu-ally did in the afternoon. She said nothing when Hugh entered. He looked at her, his heart beating wildly, but she gave no word or sign. She put out a hand and took the glass of water which she always placed by her bedside; as she sipped at it, her eyes rested on him.

"I've . . . come back," he mumbled.

There was no answer. She put the glass down on the table with a click, patted the pillow, and lay back once more. Her hand propped the novel on her chest.

He might not have been there. Indeed, he would have doubted his own existence, if it had not been for that glance which she had fixed on him when he first entered. Miserably, he began to pull on his clothes. When he was dressed, he asked her: "Is there anything you want me for?" He waited in a silence which seemed heavy and charged with thunder.

In the end he left her and went on to the deck. Far away he thought he could see the shore. Something white was trembling and fluttering like a wing; the whole atmosphere seemed to be vibrating. The air was salt and parched, and the other horizon, from which they travelled, still bulged inwards: it was criss-crossed with red and blue veins.

He walked on, the heat exploding up at him from the wooden deck, until he reached a place where he could look down at the swimming-bath. He stood there in a haze, through which moved giant, naked figures. The light seemed to distort not only their bodies but their voices also. It tinged their flesh with a greenish pallor, and rubbed out all that was definite in contour or in line. The sounds they made—laughter, conversation, the splash of water—all merged into a noise like waves heard from far off on a day of storms.

Someone was looking up at him. He screwed his eyes together, and made an attempt to bring the face into focus. It was Captain Curtiz. He was eyeing him in silent loathing. Across his bare chest there were three livid scratches, and three more on his shoulder. The noise seemed to grow louder. But still they stared at each other. Hugh felt the sun above him, like a bright avenging spirit, devouring the substance of his brain. His legs felt weak, and the deck seemed to be pressing up at him. He tumbled sideways, out of range of Captain Curtiz's gaze. He lay for many seconds in the shade; then he dragged himself on his hands and knees towards the companion-way.

The silence lasted throughout that day. Whatever he said to Mrs. Timpson, she made no answer. He went down to Miss Amberley's cabin, but she was not there. He went down a second time, and the stewardess told him she was visiting in the sick-bay. He had never felt his isolation to be so great before. Anything might happen to him, without a soul caring. He went into the lounge where a friend of Mrs. Timpson's, old General Cranston, was playing chess with another man. His heart rose; but when he approached the board, the General said with a hint of testiness: "Not now, Hugh. Not now. This is a serious business." Hugh turned away, imagining that the words held some secret animosity.

As he undressed that night, he decided to make one last effort. If it failed he would do away with himself. He was not accustomed to such loneliness; he had never been ignored before. He did not mind threats or recriminations, but to be treated as if he did not exist was too much to bear.

When Mrs. Timpson came in, he began: "Mrs. Timpson?"

There was no answer.

"Why won't you speak to me? What's the matter? What have I done?" All at once he broke down: "Why, why, why?" he sobbed. "I can't bear it."

She stood for a moment, eyeing him with distaste. "I don't think I very much want to speak to you," she said at last.

"But why?"

"It's quite obvious why."

"I know I was wicked this afternoon. But I'm sorry. Truly, I'm sorry."

"It's not only this afternoon. Anyway, I shouldn't have minded about that. . . . But don't you see what a nasty, mean thing it was to take shelter behind Miss Amberley? And just after Captain Curtiz had spoken to you about sneaking. I've no use for that kind of behaviour. It makes me sick."

"But I was . . . afraid. I thought anything might happen. I thought . . ." The words died at their source. He knew she would never understand.

Inexorably she continued: "We've done our best with you. It's been hopeless. I can't tell you how tired I am. I just can't be *bothered* any more. I just don't care. I wouldn't have gone on so long, if it hadn't been that your mother . . . we were such great friends. I must admit to you, Hugh, that it's not been easy. If you'd only tried to co-operate! You've been so unhelpful—as if you'd gone out of your way to make things difficult for me. I know you've been through a grim time, but you must try and look at it from my point of view. It hasn't been much fun having you always tied to me. You have such a knack for getting in the way. You're so talkative, too. As Captain Curtiz said. . . ."

Eloquent now, she paced up and down the small cabin, clasping and unclasping her hands. She voiced to him all the small grievances which had been nagging at her mind. It was typical of her that having for so long repressed her annoyance with him, she should now go further than she had ever intended. He was defenceless against her; he sat cowed and shivering on the bed, his head lowered as if to ward off some physical onslaught. She did not realise how deeply she was wounding him; or if she realised, the pleasure was too great for her to stop herself. More than once she spoke of his dead parents, and then he felt a strange, lurching collision inside himself, as if a blow had been struck up through his vitals.

"I'm not going to bother about you now. You must go your own way. Captain Curtiz agrees with me. You must go your own way." White-faced and trembling with her outburst, she sat down before the dressing-table, took off her beads, and unscrewed her ear-rings. "Now get along to your bath," she commanded. "I must dress for dinner."

At first he could not weep. But the hot water seemed to melt something deep inside himself. He felt all resistance dissolving, and the bitter tears poured from his eyes. It was a relief. He lay in the hot water, and his grief became a subtle mixture of hurt and pleasure. He cried effortlessly and without sound; and as he cried, he seemed to be floating outwards to the sound of invisible lamentation, over a dark river. He seemed to catch a far music, answering to a note within his own self. It was slow and mournful and spoke of parting and martyrdom and death.

The facile tears still running down his cheeks, he began to wash himself. He lathered himself with the fresh-water which the steward had set in a basin alongside the bath. Then, when he had done, he absently tipped it in with the other water. It was only when he began to clamber out that he realised his mistake. The salt water had made his whole body sticky; Mrs. Timpson had often told him to keep the basin of fresh for a last rinse.

He wrapped a towel round himself, and went out to the wash-basins, where he had seen a steward scrubbing the floor when he had entered. "Could I have some more fresh-water, please?" His voice was harsh and cracked with weeping, and his lips felt swollen.

"Please?" The man was small, with a bald patch, the size of a penny, on the back of his head. He seemed horribly ugly to Hugh; his chin was a greenish-blue colour, he had a hooked nose, and two of his front teeth were missing. There were raw patches on his hands where he suffered from eczema.

"Some more fresh-water, please."

"Fresh-water! Right-ho. Jolly good." He was a foreigner, Hugh realised. He took the basin and filled it with alacrity.

"I can manage it," Hugh said.

"No, no. Too heavy. Damned sight too heavy. You let me."

"Really, I can manage it."

But as he went into the cubicle, his feet slipped on the wet lino-leum, the basin shot out of his hands. Water streamed outwards, soaking his pyjamas which he had placed on the floor. His own arm was bruised, he was badly shaken, and once more he began to cry.

The steward, hearing the crash, had come to see what had happened. He helped Hugh up, murmuring condolences in a lan-guage which the boy could not understand. He smelled of cheap tobacco, and his white uniform was blotched and stained.

"I've made such a mess!" Hugh sobbed. "And look at my pyja-mas! Oh, what will Mrs. Timpson say? What will she say?"

"Don't worry," the man reassured him. He was an Italian. "I see to everything. Everything will be damned fine." He fetched a cloth and began mopping the floor. Hugh watched him. Half-way through he stopped, picked up the pyjamas, and went off with them. "You wait a moment. I put them dry." He brought Hugh some more fresh-water and while he rinsed himself, went on with the mopping.

"Thank you so much," Hugh said at the end.

The man grinned. "For nothing."

Hugh would have said something more to him, but he had already gone.

The cabin was empty on his return; he climbed into his bunk and switched off the light. He lay there, and for a few moments Mrs. Timpson's words came back to him, like some bitter odour which clung to everything. It seemed to foul the whole atmosphere of the room. She had been cruel and unjust to him; she hated him. He was very miserable.

Then he thought of the steward, who spoke in so quaint and incomprehensible a way. He had been friendly; and the recollection of it seemed to purge the room of that other exhalation. It was as if a fog were slowly dissipating; wisp after wisp of it snapped and vanished. The room was growing clearer, and now, looking across it, he could see out of the port-hole on to a sky of stars.

He climbed down out of his bunk again and went to the port-hole and looked out. It was a warm, serene night; the ocean and the sky above it both seemed to have been released from some bondage; they expanded and met and mingled. The stars mingled with the flashing of the waves; the blue above partook of the blue below; there was reconciliation, and peace.

He stood there for a long time.

CHAPTER XVII

In the days that followed, Mrs. Timpson and Captain Curtiz both treated him with the same bleak politeness. They only spoke to him when he spoke first; and though the words were courteous enough, there was a dry, repelling quality in the tone they used. As they passed through the Mediterranean, he was unfortunate enough to suffer from a long spell of sea-sickness. When he had been ill at home in India, there had always been his mother and Hetty to fuss over him. Now, no one bothered. He knew that Mrs. Timpson was disgusted by the stale stench of vomit; she resented having him always lying in his bunk; and, since she knew, in her

own heart, that she was failing in her duty towards him, her irritation was yet further aggravated.

He used to lie for many hours on end, alone, his eyes fixed on
the wall; for if he looked out of the port-hole and saw the heave
and pitch of the waves, he would at once start retching. At mealtimes the stewardess came in, carrying Bovril and water-biscuits.
She, at least, was sympathetic: but many other of the passengers
were also ill, and she could not spare much time for him. If Mrs.
Timpson came down to the cabin, she asked him how he felt and
whether he wanted anything; but he could not help noticing how
she wrinkled up her nose, and her voice was still pitiless.

After Marseilles, he felt better. Wandering about the ship, he
found his way into the cabin of the Italian steward. The door was
half-open and he saw the man, sitting on his bunk, inside. He lingered there, until the man looked up and said, "Hullo."

His name was Gabriel. He was wearing a grubby singlet, and
his forearms were tattooed with fish and snakes. He asked Hugh
in. There was a rancid smell, the bedclothes lay in a heap; on the
walls were pinned glossy photographs of women film-stars.

"You remember me? Yes?"

"Of course I remember you."

The man smiled: many of his teeth were discoloured or broken.
"We friends."

He shut the cabin door, and then patted the bunk where he
himself was sitting. "Please." Hugh sat down on grey sheets and
rumpled blankets. They were very low down in the ship, and the
sea kept hurling itself against the closed port-hole. It was not so
much a cabin as a cupboard. There were drawers underneath the
bunk, and by putting out his feet from where he sat he could touch
the wall opposite.

"You English? Yes?" Hugh nodded. "Me Italian. But wait one
moment, please. I learn your English. You tell me if I learn right."

He produced a much-soiled book in which there were pictures—a cat, a table, matches, cigarettes—with the names written
in block letters under each, in English. He covered the writing, and
made Hugh go through them with him, telling him his mistakes.
They sat close together, with the book balanced between them, so

that Hugh's hand sometimes brushed Gabriel's vest; it was sticky with perspiration.

"Good! Good!" Gabriel clapped his hands childishly. "Oh, jolly good! Oh, damned fine! Only one mistook."

Hugh liked him. He examined the tattoo-marks on his arms and chest, and asked him about the crucifix he wore. He was a Roman Catholic. The man told him about his home in Italy, in Carrara, where the marble came from; and Hugh told him about his home in India. Neither of them understood much of what the other said. But they grinned at each other, and nodded their heads. And at intervals the Italian made one of his absurd exclamations.

Hugh often returned to the cabin, until, in the end, he came to regard it as his own. He went in there, even when the man was out. He did not tell Mrs. Timpson, because he knew that she would forbid his visits, and she was so little curious about what he did that she never found out.

In many ways Gabriel reminded him of Luchmann. He did not possess Luchmann's physique or looks; he was small and puny and even now his ugliness had the power to repel Hugh. But like Luchmann, he was easy to talk to; there was no condescension, no patronage.

On the day before they reached Tilbury, Hugh gave Gabriel the silver pencil. Gabriel had already given him a lucky charm from his home-town—a bronze figure of one of the saints, he was not certain which—and a glass slide which showed the Leaning Tower of Pisa when one held it up to the light.

At first Gabriel refused the pencil; Hugh had to coax him.

"But what about the lady who looks after you? She will be angry."

"She won't know. I won't tell her."

"But of course she will know. She will say: 'Where is your silver pencil?' And you will say: 'I have given it to my friend.' Oh, damned good!" The exclamation was an ironical one.

Hugh explained that Mrs. Timpson no longer cared what he did. Reluctantly, Gabriel was won over. He took the pencil, and put it in one of the drawers under the bunk. "I shall always treasure it," he said sentimentally. "I shall look at it, and I shall remember my great, great friend. *Si!* I shall always remember you."

The tears shone in Hugh's eyes. Gabriel took one of his hands and rubbed it against his cheek; it made a dry, rasping noise.

That evening, as he went into his own cabin to prepare for bed, Mrs. Timpson exclaimed: "Oh, there you are, Hugh!" He had been playing patience with Miss Amberley, and had returned late. "I've been waiting ages for you. I've just had a message—the purser wants to see us."

"Oh." He began to pull off his tie. He did not imagine that "us" included himself.

"What are you doing? What is the good of beginning to undress when I've just told you that we've got to go along to the purser's office? Come on, hurry up! You'll make me late for dinner."

He followed meekly after her, asking in his astonishment: "Who is the purser? What does he want us for?"

"How should I know?" she snapped.

As he trotted behind her, he struggled with his tie. He had just succeeded in knotting it before they reached the office. Mrs. Timpson knocked, and someone called a cheerful: "Come in!" Hugh followed after her.

The first thing he noticed was the silver pencil. It was held between two podgy hands. He fixed his eyes on it: it was so like the pencil that he had given to Gabriel that he began to sweat with panic. He must be ill; it must be a delusion. He could see his father's initials on it, and there was the same dent in one corner. The pencil twirled round and round between the thick fingers.

"Do sit down, won't you?"

"Sit down, Hugh," Mrs. Timpson commanded. He lowered himself on to the edge of a leather-covered chair which creaked whenever he shifted in it. His gaze travelled from the pencil, upwards, to the red face. This must be the purser; he had sandy-tufted eyebrows, and hair grew out of his ears.

He looked at Hugh, and smiled: "Do you recognise this?"

"I . . . think so." He still seemed to be moving in a world of hallucination; nothing seemed real.

"You think so!" The man chuckled.

"Yes, it is," Mrs. Timpson put in. "It has his father's initials. Was

it found somewhere? He's so terribly careless with his belongings——"

"Yes, we did find it somewhere. But I don't think you can blame
the young man this time." His eyes twinkled at Hugh. "It was with
a lot of other stolen property."

"Stolen!"

"One of the stewards." His voice was grave. "He had some
cock-and-bull story of the boy having given it to him. It was the
pencil which put us on to the scent. He was fool enough to wear
it in his waistcoat-pocket—our head-steward saw it—examined
it—and there you are! He told me, and we carried out a search.
You should have seen our haul. All this voyage I've had passengers
running in here with tales of things 'disappearing.' Most of them
turned up in the bloke's cabin."

"Well—that's one story with a happy ending! Take your pencil,
Hugh."

Hugh clutched the end of the purser's highly polished table.
Looking down he saw a white and agitated reflection of his own
face. It only increased his sense of nightmare. "But I did give it to
him," he said. "I did. It's quite true. It's quite true what he says."

The purser shook his head, smiling as he did so. It was more
terrible than any words.

"Don't be silly, Hugh! You've never seen the man in your life.
Why should you want to give your pencil away to him?"

"But he was my friend."

"Your friend!" The purser guffawed, pressing both hands against
his ribs. Sobering, he said: "You must be a very kind-hearted boy.
And really quite an ingenious one. But you know, it isn't just your
pencil that's going to send this man to prison. He's done all sorts
of other things."

"Prison! You can't send him to prison." His voice became shrill
with panic. "He didn't steal it. I tell you, I gave it to him. I gave it to
him."

"We mustn't waste any more of your time." Mrs. Timpson
picked up the pencil and dropped it into her bag. They took no
notice of Hugh's outburst. "I'm really very grateful to you."

"We'll see that the man gets what he deserves."

"But I tell you, he didn't steal it, he didn't! Oh, why won't you listen to me?" Tears began to pour down his cheeks.

"Come along, Hugh." She turned to the purser. "I'm afraid that once he gets an idea into his head. . . . Yes, terribly imaginative. He reads so much. That gives him ideas."

One of the plump hands rested on Hugh's head. "When you're older, you'll understand that wickedness has to be punished." He spoke not unkindly. "I'll tell the man that you stuck up for him. It may give him some hope."

Hugh knew himself to be powerless; he said no more. The nightmare had moved onwards, into its second phase. After the terror and misunderstanding, there was the lying still, unable to move or speak or make a sound. Yet sight and hearing took on a double clarity.

The purser murmured something to Mrs. Timpson, and her voice came to him: "No—not my own. . . . An orphan. I'm taking him back to his relatives in England. It makes things rather difficult. . . ."

They spoke a little longer; then the purser reached for Hugh's hand and shook it vigorously.

"You were silly," Mrs. Timpson said when they got out into the passage. There was no answer, and she continued: "Whatever came over you? I just don't understand. It was so absurd to go on like that. It's not as if you could have saved the wretch. He'd stolen all sorts of things. . . ." A sob broke from Hugh. "Oh, do stop snivelling! It's time you grew out of being such a cry-baby." She glanced at her watch. "Heavens! Look how you've delayed me. It's past seven, and I promised to meet Captain Curtiz for a drink before dinner. . . . Hurry along to your bath."

Instead of going straight to the bathroom, he first went to Gabriel's cabin. The door was locked. He rattled the handle, and knocked many times. Then he stood outside, waiting for he knew not what. He gazed into the white paint of the door, as if he might see Gabriel there.

He found it impossible to believe all that they had told him; and yet it must be true. Gabriel was a thief. "Gabriel is a thief": he repeated it over to himself. "Gabriel is a thief." The words seemed

102102102

---

to lose their power to hurt and shock. Each time that he said them, they seemed to matter less. He stood, appalled; he must be very wicked.

His mother had often told him that goodness was the most important thing in the world; she had scolded him for always caring about how people looked. It was strange, and it was terrible: he had met someone who was neither good nor beautiful; he had met a thief; and yet of all the people he had known since he had left India, he had cared for no one half so much.

What did it mean? What had come over him? Why did he not feel disgusted with Gabriel?

He put out a hand and had one last forlorn knock at the door. Then he turned and walked away.

CHAPTER XVIII

"I hope Hugh's been a good boy during the voyage."

"Oh, yes, I think so." Mrs. Timpson turned away from the relatives with a sigh of weariness. She had treated them as if they both bored her unutterably.

Looking after her with evident hostility, his tight lips pursed, Uncle Kingsley put in: "We mustn't forget all that she has done for Hugh." He touched Hugh on the shoulder: "I think you might have shown a little more gratitude. You seemed very casual."

Hugh did not answer: he felt shy in the presence of these two strangers. They were both big, overpowering people; they had the same long, horse-like faces, red complexion, and vast noses. Their skins looked as if they had only just scrubbed them. His aunt wore a check skirt, a shapeless red jumper, and a necklace of large amber beads; her grey hair stuck out in wisps from under her straw hat, and when she had kissed him, strands of it had stuck to his lips. His uncle had shaken hands with him so hard that he had winced. Just level with his gaze he wore a gold chain which looped from one waistcoat pocket to the other; it had a seal attached to it, a coin, and a locket.

They got into one train and travelled up to London, where Hugh was astonished to see houses joined to each other. He wanted to sit in front in the taxi, but Aunt Megs shook her head. There was an argument with the driver at Liverpool Street Station, which culminated in the man throwing a silver threepenny-bit down on to the pavement. Uncle Kingsley stooped and picked it up; his face was hot and flushed.

After they had travelled for many miles in the second train, they once more changed, this time into a carriage without a corridor. There was another woman seated in it, who said "Good afternoon" to the relations in a soft, respectful voice. Then she looked at Hugh, and smiled. She had a large basket of groceries in her lap, and a string bag bulged beside her. Her face was kind.

"I meant to tell you, Mrs. Jones. The milk you sent yesterday was quite off. It really is too bad. My poor sister is meant to be on this milk-diet, and she really shouldn't touch anything else. I hadn't another drop in the house, and it meant that I had to send Mona on her bicycle into the village." Aunt Megs spoke in an aggrieved voice.

"I'm very sorry, Miss Colegrave. But I don't see how it could possibly have been sour. It was fresh that very morning."

Uncle Kingsley looked up from over the *Spectator*. "It was sour," he said. There was a silence.

The train had moved out of the wooded hills through which they had been travelling, and now ran high above a great sheet of water. In the wintry light, the estuary looked yellow and indeterminate, its further side shrouded in a mist from which gulls hovered up towards them with thin shrieks of pleasure.

The sight of the water made Hugh rush to the window. Pushing over Mrs. Jones' knees, he leant out; the wind was cold and kept blowing his hair into his eyes. It was then that he first smelled a smell with which he was to become very familiar. It was a smell of salt and mud; the smell of rotting seaweed, and water at low tide. At first it did not seem unpleasant to him; it was rather jolly; it reminded one that one lived only a few miles from the sea. But then, as he stood there, looking out, it seemed a melancholy kind of smell; he could not explain it, but somehow it brought with it melancholy thoughts. In the failing light, he stared down the estuary; the gulls seemed very large, the fog was thickening, and gradually, yard by yard, the water vanished into it.

"Hugh! Hugh!" A hand tugged at his shoulder.

"Yes?"

"Come away from that window. You really must not be so disobedient. You must answer when I call to you. . . . Now sit down, and try to be a good boy."

"Please don't worry on my account," Mrs. Jones said, pulling down her skirt where he had rumpled it.

"It wasn't that," Aunt Megs said coldly. "I was afraid he'd get a cinder blown into his eye. And there's such a draught with the window open."

Her voice oppressed him; he had taken a liking to Mrs. Jones, and he did not know why his aunt should speak in that tone to her. His uncle got up, and began methodically to pull down the blinds.

"Is it worth it?" Aunt Megs asked. "We'll be there in a few minutes." But he went on with the job. He spent a long time adjusting each blind so that it was not in the least crooked.

Mrs. Jones put her hand into her shopping basket and brought out a green fruit of a kind unfamiliar to Hugh. She held it out to him, inquiringly.

"What is it?" he asked.

"A fig. Try it. Go on, try it. It won't hurt you. It's from my brother's garden."

"It's very kind of you, Mrs. Jones," Aunt Megs put in, just as he was about to take it. "But he'll be having his supper as soon as he gets in. I don't want to get him into the habit of eating out of mealtimes. And figs are such indigestible things."

Mrs. Jones shrugged her shoulders; Hugh had already taken the fig from her.

"Say thank-you, Hugh, and give the fig back to the lady."

"But I want it," he sulked.

"Well, you can't have it."

He clutched the fig in one hand. "Why can't I?"

"Because I say not."

All at once, he saw that Mrs. Jones, whose face was turned away from them, was smiling faintly to herself. He wondered what had amused her. He was so absorbed in this question that he did what he was told when his aunt repeated: *"Give it back, Hugh. Give it back."*

"I see you have one or two things to learn before we go much further." His uncle crackled *The Times* as he began to fold it. "We don't like disobedient little boys." He pulled a large watch out of his waistcoat pocket; it had a gold cover which opened with a loud, metallic "ping!" "Ten minutes late! It really is too bad. We shall have to complain."

"Oh, may I see! May I see!" Eagerly Hugh tried to snatch at the watch.

"T-tt!" His uncle raised it into the air where he could not get at it. "Where are your manners, young man?"

"May I see?" Hugh repeated humbly.

"No, you may not." The watch was restored to the pocket. "Another time, learn to be rather less boorish." His uncle leant back in his seat, folded his arms, and closed his eyes.

The house in which Hugh was to live was high and narrow. It stood in a hollow, among slopes of conifers, and when he first saw it, in the twilight, from the road, it seemed to him that it leaned ever so slightly to the right-hand side. As the night fell, the mist always rose towards it, creeping between the hills and making the air damp and chilly. Uncle Kingsley had built the house twenty years ago, when they had first come to the place, and ever since they had talked of leaving. Aunt Megs complained that the damp made it impossible to keep the woodwork polished; Aunt Frances objected on the grounds of health. But their efforts at selling the place were only half-hearted, and nothing came of them. They stayed put.

Hugh shivered as they entered a cold, brightly-lit hall. "These servants!" his uncle exclaimed. He put out a hand to the light-switch. "You really must speak to them, Megs. They waste the electricity so. It's quite enough to have the stair-light without this one as well." They were now in semi-darkness. An oil-stove had been placed in the centre of the hall, and, while he waited, Hugh stood by it, his hands outstretched. The heat made his fingers itch and tingle; there was a faint reek of paraffin.

"Come along, Hugh!" Aunt Megs said impatiently. "I'll show you your room later. You'd better have some supper, and then straight to bed. It's been a long day for you."

They went into a high-ceilinged room, with leather armchairs and dull hangings. A desk stood in one corner, the flap closed. Aunt Megs went and pressed the bell, and Uncle Kingsley laid some knobs of coal on the fire: he had first put on a velvet glove so as not to soil his fingers.

"Yes, M'm?" A girl of about sixteen, in uniform, stood in the doorway. She had a plain, cheerful face; her hands and lips were chapped.

"Bring Mr. Hugh his supper. We shall dine at eight, as usual. . . . Oh, and Mona—tell Cook I shall come and make my sister's Bengers' myself. She doesn't seem able to get the lumps out—I don't know why. I'm sure I've shown her often enough."

"Yes, M'm."

Mona returned with a tray which she set on a small table beside Hugh. Aunt Megs had taken up some crochet; it was very fine lace-work, and she had put on glasses in order to see better. The lace made her hands seem even larger and rougher than they actually were.

"Begin, begin!" his uncle exclaimed, seeing that he sat before the meal, waiting for some sign from them.

"I don't know that I feel very hungry."

"Oh, nonsense! You haven't had anything since lunch-time."

Hugh picked up his knife and fork and began on the cold bacon before him. There was a little heap of potato salad on one side of the plate and a pickled onion on the other. Two slices of thinly-buttered bread lay on another plate. As he ate, he knew that Aunt Megs and Uncle Kingsley were both watching him. Her raw hands hurried over the lace with amazing dexterity; he lay back in an arm-chair, his eyes half-closed.

"You're not eating the fat." There had been a long silence, broken only by the crackling of the coal in the grate. His aunt paused in her work.

"I don't like fat."

"You must learn to like it. Eat fat and lean together."

"I can't!" he said peevishly.

"There's no such word as 'can't.' Now be a good boy and eat it all up. It's very good for you."

"I never used to eat fat at home."

"Eat it, Hugh." His uncle's sombre voice could not be argued with.

One by one, he gulped down the mouthfuls of salt, vaguely rancid fat. Often, he thought that he would choke or vomit. Although they were so slithery on the tongue, the morsels always stuck half-way down his throat. There was a beaker of milk on the tray, and he took repeated drinks from it.

When he had at last finished, he sat with his eyes fixed on his plate; he had not thought it possible.

"Good!" Aunt Megs put her crochet into a bag, and then rose to her feet. "I think he'll learn," she said to her brother. "I'm afraid poor Stella always rather spoiled him."

"He'll learn."

She had gone to the door. "Bed, Hugh! Say good-night to your uncle, and then I'll show you the way."

"Good-night," Hugh murmured dejectedly.

"Say it properly," his aunt commanded. "Say 'Good-night, Uncle Kingsley'."

"Good-night, Uncle Kingsley."

"Good-night, Hugh."

As he followed his aunt through the hall, in the semi-darkness, he knocked into a bronze bowl which held a pot of bulbs. There was a loud crash, which brought his uncle out of the sitting-room.

"What have you done?" his aunt exclaimed. "Oh, the mess! The whole hall is just strewn with it——"

"I'm terribly sorry," Hugh said, in loud agitation. "But I don't think any of the earth has fallen out. Look—it's quite all right."

"Sh—sh!" she hissed. "Don't make such a noise. You'll disturb your poor Aunt Frances. Do try to be more considerate—and less clumsy. Just look where you're going."

"But I can't see," he protested.

"Of course you can see."

They went up three unlit flights of stairs; half-way up the next there was a door into a small, bare room. There was only one picture—a sepia reproduction of a Greek building. There was a low bed, with a wicker-chair beside it, a chest-of-drawers, and a wash-hand-stand.

His aunt hesitated. "Ought I—can you—can you undress yourself?"

"Oh, yes, thank you."

She was relieved. "That's good. I thought I'd better ask you. It's so long since I've had anything to do with little boys. . . . Then I'll leave you, shall I? I'll come back in about ten minutes and turn out the light."

She showed him where the lavatory was, and then went out. His teeth chattered as he undressed himself; his pyjamas felt cold and stiff. But when he jumped into bed, he was pleased to find a hot-water bottle; it was comforting and friendly, and he held it pressed against his stomach.

"I hope you're not cold," his aunt said when she came back.

"Oh, no. This hot-water bottle is absolutely ripping."

"Hot-water bottle! I don't remember. . . . Let me see."

He showed it to her, and her face set in a number of hard lines. "That's Mona's bottle," she said. "At least, it's not one of ours. I never told the girl. . . . What cheek!"

"It's awfully comfortable."

"I daresay," she said drily. "Oh, well—since you've got it, you might as well keep it."

She went to the window and opened it, above and below. "Good-night," she said.

This time he knew how he was expected to say good-night. "Good-night, Aunt Megs," he enunciated in a precise grown-up voice.

"Would you like me to kiss you?" she asked. She seemed to be embarrassed.

"Mummy always did."

Her lips brushed his forehead; then she hurried out.

There was mist outside the window; he could see nothing but it. With each gust of wind it spiralled into the room; it seemed to settle on everything—the sheets, the walls, his own face and hands—making them moist and icy. It brought with it that strange pervading odour; it brought the cries of gulls. It seeped up the valleys, and seeped through the house. It seeped into his very bones.

That night he had a strange dream. He was crawling on his hands and knees, in a dim light, through a tunnel. At first it was easy enough; but with each yard that he advanced forward, the tunnel seemed to narrow and descend, until it became impossible for him to move without brushing against its roof and sides. The surface of the tunnel was slithery and cold, like wet rubber, and if he pushed hard against it, he could force it back for a few moments. The light thickened; panic seized him. He felt that he would suffocate. He tried to turn round or to move backwards, but the tunnel had closed behind him, and he could only travel forwards. He began to struggle, hitting out at the walls on either side of him, gasping for air and at the same time dragging himself along in the only direction in which movement was still possible. Yet in his heart, he knew that in a few seconds more the tunnel would meet and close in front, as it had already met and closed behind. He would be sealed in; he would never get out into the light of day.

Waking, in the raw dawn, he lay panting with mingled terror and relief. The mist was dissipating; outside his window he could see the nude branches of a tree; someone, perhaps Mona, was moving about in the attic above him. He did not go to sleep again.

After breakfast, Aunt Megs told him that his Aunt Frances wished to see him. "Now remember to talk quietly. And don't knock anything over." He followed her into a room, larger than any other in the house, with a bed beside the window and walls distempered pale green. There was a faint, sickly smell in the air. His aunt lay propped against a mountain of pillows, a tray on her knees. She was quite unlike either her brother or her sister; her features were small, and the skin seemed to have been pulled tight over them. She had a mole just above her lips, and another on the right temple. Her eyebrows were drawn together, in perplexity as it were, making two harsh vertical lines down her forehead, and countless others at the corners of her eyes.

She had just cut the top off a boiled egg and, as she looked at Hugh, she began to scoop the white out of the small piece of shell. "This is Hugh, is it?" She spoke in a soft, vaguely sing-song voice.

Aunt Megs shoved him from behind. "Go and kiss your aunt."

Aunt Frances suffered him to press his lips against one of her cheeks; it felt dry and dead, and he was overcome with horror. "Well? What have you got to say for yourself?" He gazed down at the carpet, and she turned to her sister: "How like Stella he is! He's quite a *pretty* little boy." She put out a hand: "Look at me, Hugh."

He forced himself to look up into her eyes; the lids were red and inflamed, and though there was nothing as obvious as a cast in them, he was struck by a certain, indefinable crookedness. "Do you think you will be happy here?"

"I . . . I think so," he mumbled.

"Only think so? . . . We're all anxious to do what we can for you. Isn't that so, Megs? You've been through a lot for a mere child. . . . Do you say prayers at night?"

"Most nights. When I remember."

"You should always remember. You must do that for your mother's sake. . . . Have you been confirmed?"

"Confirmed?" He had not heard the word before.

"Oh, no, of course not! That'll come later. When I'm better we must have a long talk about all these things. At the moment, I'm not at all well."

"I hope you'll be well soon." His terror made the words sound stilted and conventional.

"I don't know about that. I've had three operations in the last two years. You know what an operation is?"

"Ye—es." He knew vaguely.

"They cut you open and take things out."

Put in this way, the idea all at once nauseated him. He began to sweat and tremble.

"Three operations is a lot," she said. She sighed: "Of course one hopes. One hopes. And one believes. That's the great thing. That's why it's so important that you should say your prayers now. . . . My egg's got cold." She pushed it across the tray. All at once she looked peevish and sullen; she pouted.

"I'll get Mona to boil you another," Aunt Megs conciliated.

"I don't want another. I don't feel hungry." She turned over and drew the bed-clothes half-way up her face.

"I shouldn't have brought the child in. You're not strong enough yet."

"I'm quite strong enough. But now I feel tired." Her voice was muffled by the eiderdown.

"Come along, Hugh."

"Megs . . . I wonder if you oughtn't to get Dr. Phipps to take a glance at him when next he calls in to see me. He seems to have such a high colour. You know he had that rheumatic fever."

"The boy's quite sound. Don't start putting ideas into his head."

"It's not a case of putting ideas into his head. It's just common sense. Rheumatic fever means only one thing—heart-trouble. It won't do any harm to get Dr. Phipps to give him a thorough overhaul."

"Perhaps you're right," Aunt Megs sighed.

"Well, look at me! If mother had taken a little more trouble with me when we were children, all this might have been avoided."

"Say good-bye, Hugh," Aunt Megs told him.

"Just pick those two papers up for me first." An emaciated and bare arm emerged from the voluminous bed-clothes and pointed down to the floor. He went on to his hands and knees and scrambled under the bed; and all at once the night's dream came back to him. He was overwhelmed with terror. He grabbed for the two papers, scrabbling their pages as he did so, and at once pulled himself to his feet.

The two magazines were the *Tatler* and the *Bystander*. As the thin arm received them, his aunt exclaimed: "Oh, Hugh! Look how you've spoiled them!" She emerged once more from the bed-clothes; with an exasperating clicking of her tongue against her teeth, the pages were flattened back. She was so absorbed in this task that she made no answer when Hugh said good-bye to her. But as he went out, he heard her call after him: "Don't forget your prayers, will you? Every night, Hugh! Every night!"

For a while he obeyed her injunction; then he began to forget on certain nights. In the end he ceased to pray altogether. In India, when he had said his prayers over to his mother, the words, though meaningless to him, had nevertheless held a mysterious power. They were incantations, and when he spoke them, his heart thrilled; he seemed to derive from them a supernatural protection and authority. He never doubted that, when his own voice repeated them after his mother's, some presence listened and took note. He believed; and when for some reason he forgot to say them, he felt afraid.

But now all force had gone out of them; they no longer induced a mood of piety or wonder. They were utterly dead for him. Perhaps it was merely that he had at last begun to apprehend their literal meaning. "Pity my simple city" had changed into "Pity my simplicity." As the words were divested of their mystery, so too they lost their former hold on him. They became trivial and even rather dull. When he said them, neither reverence nor wonder descended upon him; however hard he tried, he only felt bored.

At first he was horrified at this change. Perhaps God had withdrawn from him, because of all his wickedness. Or perhaps— terrible thought—there was something wrong with his own self; perhaps he was no longer capable of that thrilling of the heart. Perhaps he would never know it again. It seemed then as if invisible gates had clanged together before him; there were angels, with flaming swords, who barred his way. He was exiled; he was blind to their vision; he was deaf to their music.

Every Sunday morning he was taken to church; but now the ceremony effected in him nothing more than an overpowering *ennui*. In India he had felt breathless with wonder when the organ had sounded its stern, vibrant note for the responses; the altar-cloth, embroidered with gold lilies, the chill, unearthly music of the boys' choir, even the padre, formidable now in his strange robes—all had had the power to lift his heart until it seemed that it would choke him.

The ritual was the same in the village church; but there it all seemed flat and rather silly. He noticed how the choir-boys tittered and nudged each other while the lessons were being read; the sound of Aunt Megs singing the hymns, in a gruff, husky voice, always made him want to giggle; during prayers his knees began to ache, and he would turn his head unobtrusively sideways in order to peep at the watch on the wrist of the old man next to him.

He felt no exaltation; the nearest he came to it was when they filed out of church, and the estuary glittered before him. There were crocuses embedded in the grass round the tombstones; gulls wheeled overhead; the sun shone. Was it only relief that he felt? Or did his heart go out to meet some unseen presence? He could never be sure.

After talking with some of the neighbours for a few minutes, they went back to their Sunday dinner. On his first Sunday with the relatives, Hugh asked: "Is it difficult to carve a joint?"

"It's difficult to carve as well as your uncle does. He makes the meat go twice as far as a bad carver would." Hugh saw the point.

Sundays or week-days, he was at first bored and lonely. On the day after his arrival, he had found his way into the kitchen. It seemed much more cheerful than the rest of the house; Cook gave him a spoonful of cake-mixture to eat, and he sat behind the cooker, where it was snug and warm. He felt a momentary twinge of conscience when he heard Mona and Cook discuss his relatives; he put his head round the cooker, and seeing him, Cook laughed and used Hetty's old phrase about "Little pitchers."

When his aunt asked him where he had been that morning, he saw no reason for not telling her the truth. But she flushed angrily: "I really must ask you not to wander in and out of the kitchen at all hours. It interferes so with Cook's work."

"I'm sure she didn't mind my being there."

"I'm sure she didn't," she said drily. "But I do. In any case, the influence of servants can often do a great deal of harm. One never knows what you mightn't hear them say."

He thought she had guessed what they had said about her and Uncle Kingsley; he became hot with embarrassment and shame. Misinterpreting his discomfiture, and imagining that he was angry, she said: "I'm sorry, Hugh. You may think I'm being unnecessarily snobbish. But one day, you'll learn—as I've learnt—that familiarity breeds contempt. It's an old saying, and it's a true one. . . . I don't

expect your mother allowed you to be with the Indian servants all
the time."

"There was Luchmann—the orderly. . . ." He hesitated. "And
the ayah."

"I'm sure she never allowed you into the kitchen except on special occasions."

"N-no. But that was rather different, wasn't it? The cook was a
native."

"I don't see what difference that makes. In India you don't mix
with the natives: in England you don't mix with—well—with the
lower classes. That's not snobbishness; it's just sense."

He accepted this judgment, and his visits to the kitchen ceased.
But there was so little to do. So far, he had made no friends, his
guardians did not like him to go out of the house by himself, and
he was always being told not to make so much noise. Aunt Frances
was still in bed. He began to read; he read anything—the labels
on the empty patent-medicine bottles which were brought down
from the sick-room, advertisements, old newspapers, and even
the parish magazine. Once he began on one of the books which
Aunt Megs had got from Boots' Library; it was *Sorrell & Son*, and
when Aunt Megs found him with it, she told him he was a wicked,
morbid boy.

There was a shelf of books in the dining-room; Uncle Kingsley
had ordered the set after reading an advertisement in the Sunday
paper. They were classics, in shoddy, imitation-leather bindings,
with gold edges. In spite of his disgrace over *Sorrell & Son*, Hugh
took down one of these volumes when both his uncle and aunt
were out to tea with the vicar. At first he was confused by what
he read; he could not understand many of the words, and the
sentences were chopped into short lines, printed one below the
other. But when he had gone through a whole page, and begun
on a second, a curious thing happened. It was as if he were once
more kneeling with his head buried in his mother's lap, and repeat-
ing after her the prayers she spoke for him. All the excitement and
the wonder swept over him once more; there was the mystery,
and the wish to look behind the mystery; there was the vision of
the unattainable, just beyond his reach, and the incomprehensible,

just beyond his understanding. The angels with the flaming swords parted a moment, and he saw into a space beyond words.

Two lines, in particular, had the power to give him that exaltation. However often he said them over to himself, their spell never failed. He did not know what they meant, but they could make his throat ache with tears. Like a formal incantation, he murmured them:

> "The bailey beareth the bell away,
> The lily, the rose, the rose I lay."

There was sadness in the lines; and yet they conjured up no picture for him. If there was sadness, it was in each word in turn: it was in the sounds, and in the repetition of the word "rose". For what could it mean? He puzzled over it; he knew the meanings of all the words except one. Who was "the bailey"? The bailey must be the clue. If he could discover who the bailey was, not only would the angels part for him, but the gates would be thrown wide open.

He asked his uncle one meal-time: "What is a bailey, please, Uncle Kingsley?"

"A what?" His uncle looked up at him over his plate of beef. He did not encourage Hugh to talk at table.

"A bailey, uncle."

"Bailey! There's no such word. You must mean a bailiff." Hugh said nothing. "Well—do you mean a bailiff?"

"I don't know."

"What do you mean—you don't know? It must be bailiff that you're thinking of. Where did you come across the word?"

He felt a jolt of terror; at all costs he must not reveal to his uncle the source of the word. Intuitively, he knew the danger of such a course. "I don't know," he mumbled.

His uncle had already got up from the table and gone to the bookshelf. Hugh was afraid that he had discovered that he had been reading the book of poetry; but when he came back, it was with a dictionary. "Here we are," he said. "Bailiff. Sheriff's officer, land-agent, steward . . ." He read out the whole definition, and then snapped the book together.

"Well, what do you say?" Aunt Megs asked Hugh.

"Thank you, Uncle Kingsley."

His uncle picked up his knife and fork. "Do you know what book this is?" He indicated the dictionary. "It's a dictionary. It tells you the meaning of any word you don't understand. It's a very wonderful thing. If you have a little book this size, you can understand everything that you see written in English—that is, if you know how to use it."

But Uncle Kingsley's explanation had not helped in the least. As he ate, Hugh said the lines over once more; they were still incomprehensible. Perhaps he was too young to understand them; perhaps they were not meant to be understood. Perhaps, when he was grown-up, he would learn how to use a dictionary, and then he would know the meaning of the lines. But in his heart, he wished that day would never come. He preferred not to know; he preferred to strain after the mystery rather than to gaze into its heart.

A week later it was his birthday. He had lost count of the days, and it was not until tea-time that his uncle had exclaimed: "Good Lord! I do believe it was your birthday to-day, Hugh."

"I'm afraid I forgot all about it," Aunt Megs said. "Oh, that is too bad. What can we give the boy as a present, Kingsley?"

His uncle took out his wallet and looked at it. He fingered a ten-shilling note and pushed it back into place once more. From his pocket he produced two half-crowns, which he set down, one after the other, before Hugh's plate.

"Are these for me?"

"Yes, they're both for you."

"What shall I do with them?" He had never been given so much money before. People had always chosen his presents; he preferred that. As he touched the coins they seemed cold and hard and useless. It was as if his uncle had set two pebbles before him.

"What shall you do with them? Spend them, of course."

"Or save them," his aunt put in, "I think you'd better give them to me, Hugh—for the time being. Otherwise you're sure to mislay them. When you've decided what you want to do with them, you can ask for them back. . . . I don't believe you've said thank-you yet."

Mona, who had been bringing in some hot water, overheard

part of this conversation. The next afternoon, when his uncle was out at work, and Aunt Megs was resting, she pushed her head round the green-baize door which separated the hall from the servants' quarters, and whispered: "Mr. Hugh!"

"Yes?" He knelt before the oil-stove, reading. The drawing-room fire had not yet been lit.

"Cook's got a surprise for you." Her plain, kind face grinned at him.

"A surprise?"

"Yes—in the kitchen."

"I'm not allowed in there, I'm afraid."

"She won't know. Come on."

"She'll be awfully angry if she finds out."

"She won't find out. Come on, do!"

He gave in reluctantly to her cajoling. An iced chocolate cake stood on the kitchen table, with ten candles round it. Cook beamed: "Many happy returns, Master Hugh. I know it's a day late. . . . Come and light the candles." She mistook the expression on his face for shyness or incredulity, and urged: "Come on! It's your cake."

"You shouldn't," he said in horror. "Did she tell you to make it?"

"Not her!" Mona exclaimed derisively.

"How could you!" he gasped. "You know how angry she'd be."

"I bet she'd be angry!" Cook chuckled. "But what the eye doesn't see. . . ."

"Then you were going to deceive her!" Without realising it, the tone in which he spoke exactly reproduced certain inflexions in his aunt's voice. "But that was very wrong of you. And you know I'm not allowed in the kitchen. She told you so. I've a jolly good mind to tell Aunt Megs."

Cook smiled at him, with a gentle sadness which made him feel uneasy. "We only did it to cheer you up, like. Perhaps we did wrong."

"But think of all the things you've wasted—sugar, margarine——"

"Cook bought all those things with her own money," Mona put in hotly.

But Cook put a restraining hand on her arm. "I'm sorry, Master Hugh," she said, with that same smile lingering at the corners of her mouth. "It seems we made a mistake. You'd better run along now, before your aunt catches you."

He hesitated a moment, and she continued: "If she finds out, we'll take all the blame. And if you think it's only right that you should tell her. . . ." She raised her shoulders.

When he picked up his book once more, he felt that his behaviour had been exemplary. Even Aunt Megs could not have found fault with it. She had so often preached loyalty to him; he would like her to know how well he had heeded the lesson. If he went and told her, she would of course realise just how noble his conduct had been; he flushed as he thought of the way in which she would compliment him; there would be generous praise from Uncle Kingsley when he came home that evening. But hadn't Captain Curtiz told him that there was nothing so vile as a sneak? No: he must keep silent about the whole incident, even if it meant that he could not claim the credit due to him. This resolve made him feel even nobler.

But all at once his heart sagged. He knew that he had been priggish and silly; three months ago he would never have behaved in such a fashion. He had caught from his relations the infection of their high principles. The thought filled him with dismay. It seemed that without realising it, one's conduct could be influenced by those with whom one lived. He sat for a long time staring at the stove before him; there was a small red square of cellophane behind which the flame burnt, meagre yet persistent; thus it had burnt throughout his stay. On a sudden, the sight of it filled him with oppression; he drew in his breath, and doing so, made a new resolve. He would never become like them; they were the Enemy; he hated and repudiated them.

He leapt to his feet, and hurried into the kitchen. There was a veiled hostility in the glances which he received from Cook and Mona. "I'm sorry," he said. "I was stupid. I didn't really mean what I said just now. . . . I—I've changed my mind."

Cook stared at him for a moment, in incredulity. Then she gave a deep chuckle: "That's the way!" she exclaimed.

She went into the larder and came back carrying the birthday cake. "You must cut it," she said. "And as you cut it, you must wish." She put a knife into his hands, and told him to wait until she had lit the candles. Then she and Mona stood motionless on either side of him, while he gazed at the cake. Waxen drops trickled down the candles, like tears; there were ten of the candles, and they were burning away to nothing before his eyes. Time, the consuming fire, melted and dissolved his ten years. He thought, suddenly, of the gutted shell of his old home, and the words came back to him: "Never again! Never again!" His eyes began to ache with staring at the flames.

"Blow!" he heard Cook tell him. "Go on, blow!" He gathered his breath within him. "Blow!" she repeated. One by one, he saw the flames shudder and go out. The two women sighed, and at the same moment the reek of smoke filled his nostrils. Decisively he plunged the knife into the heart of the cake. He felt a strange relief, now that the flames had all been extinguished. He was glad that there still remained more than half of each candle. He had, for a moment, stayed the advance of the consuming fire; Time had been arrested.

Mona giggled, her face and hands smeared with chocolate icing. "This is a bit of all right," she said.

CHAPTER XIX

The next day, Doctor Phipps called to see Aunt Frances, and was asked to examine Hugh as well. "Not much wrong with this young fellow," he assured them. "All that he needs is plenty of fresh air and exercise. And good wholesome food. Well, I know he gets the last commodity." Aunt Megs smiled at the compliment, fingering her large amber beads. "But you want to encourage him to be out of doors as much as possible."

"Oh, we do!" Aunt Megs sighed. "He's such a book-worm. It's read, read, read, the whole day through. I'm so afraid he'll ruin his eyes, doctor."

"A book-worm, eh?" The doctor pinched Hugh's naked arm.

"Plenty of time for that later on. You take my advice, Hugh. I've seen too many young boys crock up because they overdid things. It's not worth it. Don't worry about books yet awhile. I tell you, examinations do more to ruin the health of our boys and girls than any other factor. And where do they get you in the end? You find yourself in a sanatorium or a looney-bin at the age of twenty, and that's that."

Aunt Megs was becoming restive. "I daresay there's a lot in what you say, doctor. Of course we do want Hugh to get a scholarship to his uncle's old school. Otherwise I don't see how we can possibly . . ."

"Well, of course, of course, naturally." The doctor pushed his instruments into his bag with quick, flustered movements. "Fresh air!" he exclaimed. "That's my prescription. Fresh air, and more fresh air. There's nothing like it. . . . When's the young man going to school?"

"Next term," Aunt Megs put in. "Frimley Towers." There was a note of pride in her voice, as she spoke the name; obviously she expected the doctor to have heard of it.

"Good school?" he asked vaguely, as he hunted through his pockets for a handkerchief.

"Oh, yes!" Aunt Megs exclaimed. "Forty acres—only three miles from the sea. His father and his uncle both went there. I believe it's very highly spoken of."

"I'm sure he'll be happy. No days like one's schooldays." The doctor gave Hugh a benevolent pat on his head.

As a result of the doctor's plea for more fresh air, Hugh was made to accompany his uncle down to his office each morning. His uncle was a solicitor. Hugh always left him at the door of a building in the narrow High Street, the front window of which was half covered by a brown screen with gold lettering on it: "Colegrave, Brasted, and Brasted, Solicitors." He only once went inside with his uncle, when he had to pick up something for his aunt. He stood and waited in a small, square room which smelt of dust and boot-polish, while his uncle went upstairs. An old man sat at a desk in one corner, writing; as he wrote his pen scratched and his tongue stuck out of one corner of his mouth. Hugh went over and watched him. He wrote with beautiful flourishes, making letters that were round and large and even.

"Well, Hugh!" his uncle exclaimed heartily as he came down the stairs. "Is Mr. Gurney letting you into the secrets of the business?"

The old man looked up for the first time, and his thin lips twitched into a smile. Turning his eyes up to Hugh's face, he said in a high-pitched, quavering voice: "I expect that one day I'll be going to you for my orders." His face became suddenly grave, as if an unexpected thought had come to him: "Unless I'm dead before then," he added.

"That's the way, Gurney!" Uncle Kingsley exclaimed. "We'll have to change this." He tapped the brown screen. "It'll be Colegrave, Brasted, Brasted and Craddock." He rolled the words off his tongue, and as he did so the old man nodded his head rapidly, as if it were on a spring.

"Is that me?" Hugh asked.

His uncle nodded. "Yes, that's you. If you're a good boy, and learn your lessons, and do as you are told."

"I don't think I want . . ." Hugh began. But he broke off, fearing to seem ungrateful. It was fortunate for him that his uncle had already begun to busy himself with other matters and had not heard.

Noticing that Hugh still stood at Mr. Gurney's shoulders, he said: "You'd better run along, Hugh. Old Gurney has a lot of work on his hands."

It was with relief that Hugh hurried out into the spring sunshine. It was like leaving church on Sunday; everything seemed brighter and more definite than when he had left it; the air tasted sweeter. Since his aunt had told him not to hurry back, he did not take the direct route back to the house, but turned down a path which ran beside the estuary. The tide was in, and for a few hours the smell had vanished. He hated the smell: he associated it not so much with the estuary as with the house. The very food seemed to taste of it, and when he kissed Aunt Megs good-night, he imagined that her skin gave off the same odour. He smelled it in his sleep, and when they went into Cambridge for a day, he thought that it followed them there also. It oppressed his spirits, and in the end he came to look upon it as a malignant yet invisible presence, hovering about him. Now that the warmer weather had come there was little mist; but the smell grew worse.

He was walking through the water-meadows. All through the winter they had been submerged; and at the end of February, when there had been a cold spell, people had skated on them. They skated with a wonderful freedom which he envied, on and on beside the glittering estuary, on and on, for many miles. But now the meadows were dry once more; a herd of bullocks grazed in one of them, and a foal was being suckled by a mare. The first grass was a bright, emerald green—an unreal colour: the sallows rattled together with each gust of wind. He was glad to be away from the house and away from his uncle's office. He picked up a handful of stones and began to skim them, one after another, over the water. The sound of the stones plopping in the water was restful and satisfying.

In one of the fields that he walked through a girl and a boy were attempting to coax a pony with a trug full of bread. The pony, a sturdy little animal, would come close to them and even allow them to place their hands on its mane; but as soon as the girl raised the halter, it pulled free and scampered away from them. The girl was obviously older than the boy; he was squat and plump, and wore riding-breeches which were too baggy for him.

Hugh went and joined them. "Can't you catch him?" he asked.

The girl shook her head. She had straight flaxen hair and a slightly tilted nose: her body was strong and full; her hands brown. She wore rubber boots, a shapeless mackintosh, and a black beret.

"You told Pa you'd catch 'im for me," the boy complained. "Pa said 'e'd come and catch 'im."

"Shut up!" The girl made a decisive gesture with one hand. "That's just like him," she said to Hugh. "He's always out to blame someone else for what goes wrong."

Hugh asked if he might make an attempt to catch the pony. The girl eyed him doubtfully: "You might hurt yourself," she said. "Do you know anything about horses?"

"I can ride."

Obviously she did not believe him; or if she did, she imagined that he was one of the riding-school boys who were taken out each Sunday on a leading-rein. "I suppose you can try if you want to," she said grudgingly.

"Have you got some string?"

She was suspicious. "What do you want string for?"

"I'll show you."

She pulled a grubby handkerchief and a catapult out of her mackintosh pocket; a length of string followed.

"Thanks. Now some bread, please."

He went up to the pony, as he used to go up to Robin, speaking gently to it and holding out a crust. They edged nearer to each other; the pony stretched out its neck and took one piece of bread; it took another. He could put his hand on its mane without its veering away from him. Deftly he put the string round its neck, made a loop, and tightened it. "Now you can bring the halter," he said. "He won't get away."

He was glad that he had been able to do it so easily. Since he had been with the relatives, he had come to doubt his own skill. He had knocked over that pot of bulbs on his first night in the house, and ever since he had acquired the reputation for being clumsy and impracticable. He had pinched his finger in one of the doors, a cup had been broken, a cake-stand upset. After each of these accidents, he became more and more nervous; yet his very nervousness and the exasperation of his relatives made certain of a repetition in the near future. "Oh, you are clumsy!" was an exclamation to which he became so used that in the end he accepted, as they did, the imputation that he was quite useless with his hands. His heart had sunk when he had first held out the crust to the pony; he had remembered Uncle Kingsley's sarcasms at his many failures in the small jobs assigned to him. The thought of them had filled him with mistrust. He was afraid of once more appearing as a clumsy fool to this girl and her brother.

But as soon as he had touched the pony's mane, he had known that he could do it. It seemed as if the old confidence had flowed back into him from the animal; he had felt it mount through his finger-tips and so along his arms, into his breast.

"That's an old dodge," he said to the admiring girl. "You don't want to let him see a halter. If he thinks you haven't got a halter in your hand, he comes right up to you. He doesn't see the string."

"You know a lot about horses," she said.

"I had a pony of my own—once."

"Well, we'd better get along. Come on, Tibby. You can take him." She handed the boy the halter.

"Where are you going?" Hugh asked.

"Back home—to saddle him."

"Where's home?"

She pointed to a farm-house on the brow of a hill. "Ash Farm."

"Then you're Mrs. Jones's daughter?"

"That's right. . . . How did you know?"

"I knew she lived there. I travelled in the train with her once—when I first came here. I'm staying with my aunt and uncle . . . Mr. and Miss Colegrave."

The girl's mouth hardened at the name, but she said nothing. "May I walk part of the way with you?" Hugh asked.

"If you like." The blood mounted under her fresh healthy skin. "Come on, Tibs!"

The boy went ahead of them, leading the pony; his legs were short, and he puffed and grew red in the face. The girl told Hugh that her name was Ruby, and asked him his. They talked together until they reached the farm, a low white-washed building with some tumble-down sheds round it, a yard where hens scratched about a haystack and a number of lean dogs who barked furiously until Ruby silenced them. "Well, I suppose I must get on with my work," she sighed. Tibby had already disappeared with the pony.

"What work is that?"

"First, there's the pigs. I haven't mucked them out yet. Then I have to feed the hens. Then I have to take a cart-load of hay round to the cow-shed."

"Do you think I might help you?"

"If you like."

At first the pigs frightened him; they seemed so large. They pushed against him and almost knocked him off his balance. But when he saw the business-like way in which Ruby used the broom to rap them on their bottoms, he was reassured. She set

him to guard the doorway, while she heaved fork-loads of steaming manure into a cart which she had drawn up outside. Then
she told him to fetch her some buckets of water from the tank;
these they flung against the walls and down the floors. The pigs
rushed squealing from one side of the sty to the other; Hugh and
Ruby began to laugh at them, and so became very hot; the water
splashed up into their faces and on to their clothes.

When they had finished with the pigs, he helped her load the
cart with bales of hay. She seemed to have no difficulty in lifting
the heavy bales, but he lurched and staggered under them and
became breathless. The hay had a sweet smell, like good tobacco,
and wisps of it stuck to his coat and to his hair. As they wheeled
the cart together into the cow-sheds, Hugh behind, Ruby in front,
Mrs. Jones met them, a basket full of eggs over one arm.

"Hello," she smiled.

"Hello. . . . You remember me, don't you?"

"Of course I do. Giving Ruby a hand?"

"Yes. I've never done farm work before."

Mrs. Jones hesitated, looking down into the basket of eggs. "I
suppose Miss Colegrave gave you permission to come up here?"

"Oh, I'm sure she won't mind. I didn't actually ask her—I just
met Ruby out, you see. But I know she'll be glad that I've found
someone to play with. And this is out-door exercise, isn't it? The
doctor says I need out-door exercise."

"Well, if you think it'll be all right. . . . Of course we're very
pleased to see you here." She smiled at him with that same expression of gentle sadness which he had seen on Cook's face when he
had at first refused to eat the birthday cake. Once again it made
him feel uneasy. It almost seemed as if they pitied him. Pitied him?
But why?

He worried over the question for a few moments only. There
were so many things to keep him and Ruby busy; and when they
had done all their jobs, there were still the calves to be played with.
These were three little Jersey heifers, faun-like creatures, with
black lustrous eyes and long legs. They sucked each other's ears
and the fingers held out to them.

They very nearly made him late for lunch. He and Ruby had

climbed into their pen, and were coaxing and petting them, when Mrs. Jones appeared in the doorway of the shed. "It's nearly ten to one," she called out. "Won't your aunt be expecting you home by now?"

"Gosh!" He heaved himself out of the pen, said a hasty good-bye, and set off at the double.

He ran in by the side door of the house, held his hands under the bathroom tap for a few seconds, and arrived in the dining-room just as the gong sounded. "Your hair!" Aunt Megs exclaimed. She stood with her hands balanced on the back of her chair, waiting for Uncle Kingsley to come in and say Grace. Then she pulled her handkerchief out of her belt and held it to her nose. "Oh!" she gasped. "Oh, oh!"

"What's the matter?"

"My dear Hugh, what have you brought in? Let me see your shoes." She made him turn up one sole and then the other. "Manure!" she exclaimed. "And look at your stockings—*and* your shorts! You're filthy. Where have you been?"

"I went up to Mrs. Jones's farm. I helped Ruby clean the pigs out."

"You what! Oh, really, Hugh. . . . It's too bad. You'll have to change all your clothes."

"Now?"

"Yes, now. I can't have you bring that muck into the dining-room."

At that moment Uncle Kingsley came in: before Aunt Megs could tell him, he had begun to murmur Grace in Latin. She waited with ill-disguised impatience for him to finish, and then as the last word was spoken, blurted out: "Hugh's been playing with that Jones girl. He's been in the pigsties and he just stinks to high heaven."

Uncle Kingsley stared at her, the silver cover which he had taken from the joint raised in one hand. "Do you mean our Mrs. Jones?" he asked.

"Yes, yes, our Mrs. Jones—who else?" she snapped. "It must stop, Kingsley. I can't have the child coming into the house with his clothes in that condition. In any case, it's—it's unsuitable for him to associate with that girl."

"Which child is it?"

"There's only one Jones girl—Ruby Jones. Don't you remember that whole business? I don't say it was the child's fault—probably it wasn't—but after a thing like that has happened to a girl, she's not fit company for someone as young as Hugh."

"I'd forgotten about all that," his uncle said gravely. "In that case we must certainly put our foot down."

"I knew you'd agree with me. In any case"—she gave a little titter—"it would make things rather embarrassing between us and the Joneses, if the two children became friends. They'd be sure to ask Hugh over to tea, and it would be difficult to refuse for him without hurting their feelings. You know how touchy these people are. . . . Now run along, Hugh, and change all your clothes. But don't go upstairs in those shoes, *please*! You'd better leave them in the hall, and I'll tell Mona to see to them. You heard what we said? There are to be no more of these jaunts up to Ash Farm. And we don't want you to play with Ruby. She's not really a nice girl."

"Of course you can say 'hello' to her if you meet her out," his uncle conceded. "But if she asks you to play with her, you must tell her that you're busy. Understand?"

"Yes, uncle."

As he changed in his bedroom, he wondered what could possibly be wrong with Ruby. Evidently she had done something wicked; and yet Aunt Megs had said that it wasn't really her fault. What could it be? And why did it make it impossible for him to play with her? He thought of many reasons—she was a murderess, or a thief, or perhaps she was just very, very naughty—but as Ruby's face came back into his mind, so kind and cheerful, he had to reject each of them in turn. He could not believe such things of her.

All at once he felt an extreme annoyance with his aunt and uncle. Whatever it was that Ruby had done, he was on her side, not on theirs. It made it rather exciting that there should be this secret about her; he felt he wanted to see her all the more; he wanted to find out what it was, perhaps he might even ask her. She had seemed just an ordinary girl before; but now she was touched with mystery; she became a figure in a legend. Certainly he would see her again—in secret, if that was necessary.

They met frequently after that. They played together in the water-meadows—French cricket, or hide-and-seek, or games of make-believe which Hugh invented. These last Ruby seemed to play half-heartedly, as if for his sake, and not from any real desire. She liked most of all to climb the trees which grew beside the estuary; she was amazingly strong and agile, and Hugh could seldom follow where she led. He became dizzy half-way up a tree, and had to cling to the trunk until she rescued him. She never complained when he failed her in this way; she would come back to the place where he had stopped and help him down to safety.

She never talked much. It was he who poured out his fancies to her, telling of his dreams, and his dislike of the relatives, and of his life in India. She listened to him without comment, her eyes fixed on his face.

He loved her in the innocently erotic way of children. The sun had already tanned her bare legs and arms; he liked it when she helped him down a tree, and he could feel her body against his own. He admired her strength, her dexterity with a cricket-ball, the way in which her hands were calloused. Her hair was thick and coarse, and the sun had bleached it to a yet more flaxen tint. He longed to caress it; and once, when they both sat together, high up in the forked branches of a tree, he attempted to do so. She was very close to him, her skirt rucked up to show a brown thigh. He put out a hand.

"Don't!" She pulled away in panic.

"What's the matter?" he asked. Her face was white and she was trembling all over. "Don't you like my doing that?"

She gave an unsteady laugh. "It's silly," she said, hoisting herself on to a branch which she knew to be beyond his reach.

"Why is it silly? You've got such beautiful hair. I want to stroke it."

"Well, you can't."

"Why can't I?"

Instead of answering, she swung herself yet further up the tree.

When he next met her, her hair had been bobbed. He was horrified. He stared at her speechless, and at last gasped: "You've had all your hair cut off!"

She shrugged her shoulders. "There was too much of it. It got in the way."

He felt utterly miserable. "Was it—was it because of me that you had it done?" he asked.

"Of course not, silly!" she retorted in a matter-of-fact voice. "And it's time *you* had *your* hair cut."

He could not understand her. She seemed to have become afraid of being touched by him. She no longer put an arm round his shoulders when she helped him up a tree. She even seemed reluctant to let him hold her hand. This withdrawal increased his love for her. Mysterious and unattainable, she appeared to him in his dreams. He dreamed much, not only of her, but of his uncle and Aunt Megs and Aunt Frances. When he dreamed of the relatives he awoke with only a confused memory of what had taken place; but all that day he would feel listless and tired, and uneasy in their presence. In his dreams of them, he had always done something wrong which he knew they would find out; and when they found out, he sobbed at their taunts and scoldings until weeping itself became a strange pleasure; it was as if the utter abasement of his soul brought him satisfaction.

In contrast, his dreams of Ruby were clear and definite and real. He had a sense of extreme brightness; nothing was ever said. He saw her face just above him, or he was touched by something which he knew to be her flesh or hair. Sometimes he awoke with her animal smell in his nostrils. They were all dreams of physical sensation, and he drew strength and refreshment from them.

Once when they were walking through the meadows they saw some soldiers milling about in a little creek where they had often sailed the boat which Mr. Andy had given to Hugh. The men were inexpert swimmers, but they seemed to be enjoying themselves. They shouted to each other, laughed, and splashed.

"Let's watch," Hugh said.

"Oh, come on!" She caught his arm and began to drag him forward. Her eyes were fixed on the horizon.

"But I want to stay."

"Well, you can't stay."

Sulkily he gave in. But before they moved out of sight, one

of the men had seen them. He let out a piercing whistle, and a moment later there were shouts and cat-calls. Hugh looked over his shoulder and saw that an immensely stout man was standing in the water up to his waist and making signs to them to go back.

"He's beckoning," Hugh said. "They probably want to talk to us."

"Run!" she hissed. "Run!" Still clutching his arm, she dragged him after her. He could not take his gaze off the fat man—his body was so large and white, and his breasts sagged—so that he kept on stumbling on rabbit-holes and the exposed roots of trees.

When they were at last out of sight and hearing, Ruby let go of him and threw herself panting on to the grass. "You were a fool," she said.

"What about you?" he retorted hotly. "They wouldn't have hurt us."

She pulled a face. "Cheek—calling out to us like that."

"I expect they only wanted to be nice."

"Nice! . . . Why didn't you run when I told you to?"

"I didn't see any point. I wanted to stay there."

"You don't understand! You're too young."

She spoke with a bitterness which brought a chill to his heart. He felt that now, if at any time, he would be able to solve the mystery about her. "What don't I understand?"

"You don't understand what those sort of men are like."

"Yes, I do. They're probably quite nice. They wanted to make friends with us." Wishing to flatter her, he said: "I bet they thought what a pretty girl you were, and that's why they wanted us to talk to them."

For a moment her whole body went rigid; he thought that she must be angry with him. Then, in a flat, peevish voice she said: "Don't talk nonsense. I'm not pretty. And you know it."

"You are pretty. I think you're—beautiful."

"Beautiful!" She said the word with the utmost derision. "I'm not beautiful. And I don't want to be."

"Why don't you want to be? I think it must be wonderful to be beautiful. Everyone wants to look at you and to do things for you."

"Oh, shut up!" she shouted at him. All at once she was crying.

She put her head between her knees, and attempted to choke back the tears by biting into her handkerchief.

"Ruby! What's the matter? What's happened? What have I done?" He put a clumsy arm round her shoulders, and tried to draw her towards him.

"Leave me alone!" she screamed. "Leave me alone! Don't touch me!"

He was frightened; from then on he was always a little frightened of her. He never again sought to discover her secret; he gave up trying to guess. He decided that it was something unique, even as she was unique. Whatever had happened could only have happened to her alone. He would never know everything about her; he realised that, and he acquiesced in it. Indeed, it was this sense of some part of her being perpetually withdrawn from him that bound him to her more than all other ties. It gave her that mystery which was essential before he could love anything or anyone. For, in herself, she was a very ordinary creature—beautiful, certainly, but without other subtlety.

Indeed, she only suffered his endless talk because she was tolerant and liked him; she knew it would hurt his feelings if she told him to shut up. But she really seldom listened to what he said to her. She let him run on, and his voice was pleasant enough, making an accompaniment to their various doings. In the same way she liked to hear the wireless while she did housework for her mother.

He only once spoke to her about the books he read. "Listen," he said on one of the earliest of their meetings. In a voice tremulous with excitement, he repeated for her the lines:

> "'The bailey beareth the bell away,
> The lily, the rose, the rose I lay.'"

When he had finished, he looked down at his hands and waited. Nothing happened for many seconds. Then he heard her giggle: "Silly! Where did you get hold of that one from? It's a nursery-rhyme, isn't it?"

"It is like a nursery-rhyme," he said seriously. "I'd never thought of that."

"'Ride a cock-horse to Banbury Cross . . .'" she shouted in an immature, boyish voice. She laughed once more. "'Here we go round the mulberry bush . . .'"

He knew then that she regarded it as no more than an eccentric joke of his.

So the days passed. While he was with her, he felt happy and carefree; she drew forth what was best in him, and restored his faith in his own powers. But as soon as he entered the house a dull weight of hopelessness descended on his spirit. He felt fretful and dissatisfied; he could not settle to anything; if he was asked to do a job, he did it clumsily and with only half his heart. He came to fear the house. Even on bright spring days it seemed both dark and clammy.

The fires had ceased to be lit in the evening; but the oil lamp still remained, giving out a steady and meagre flame. It burnt grudgingly, and made the air heavy with its fumes. So time burned away in the house.

He was often sent up to Aunt Frances's room to play cards with her. She never asked him if he wished to play, and they often continued long after he had wearied of the game. She liked bezique best. She pretended that they were playing for money, and entered all the scores into a note-book which she kept by her bedside. She became peevish if she lost to him; but when it was he who owed her money, her face brightened, her eyes shone, and she chaffed him about his ill-luck. "That's thirty-two shillings and eightpence. Do you think you can afford it? Shall I make you bankrupt?"

The flesh shown by the vee of her nightdress was red and coarse. All round the room there were medicine-bottles, and she had a magnifying mirror which she would sometimes make him hold in front of her. Squinting down at her reflection, he was horrified to see the rubbed texture of her skin, the many hairs and blemishes.

Miss Amberley, the American missionary, wrote to him to say that she was staying in Cambridge for a week. She suggested that he should visit her there; if the relatives would put him on the train, she would meet it, keep him for a night, and send him back the next morning. She enclosed the money for a first-class return ticket.

"Cheek!" He had shown the letter to Aunt Megs. "Fancy send-ing us the money like that!"

"I think she was only wanting to be kind."

"Oh, yes, I'm sure," Aunt Megs said acidly. "But we don't happen to be a charitable institution. I daresay that's the way they do things in America." She folded up the letter and the cheque and put them back into their envelope. A faint smile played about her lips.

"I may go, mayn't I?"

"I don't think so, Hugh. We'll ask your uncle and see what he says. But you're too young to go travelling about the coun-tryside alone—we don't know anything about this Miss . . . Miss Amberley."

"She's awfully nice."

The smile broadened indulgently. "You find so many people 'awfully nice'. You're rather uncritical, if I may say so."

"What are you going to do with the letter?"

"Keep it, for the time being. I want to show it to your uncle. Of course, he may let you go—he *may*. But in any case I'm sure he'll agree with me that the cheque must go back."

"But . . . you'll hurt her feelings."

"And what about our feelings?" she retorted irritably. "Does she think we have no pride? . . . Now run along, Hugh, I'm busy."

"I'd like my letter back, if you please, Aunt Megs."

For a moment she stared at him in incredulity. Then she snapped: "I've told you, I'm keeping the letter."

"It's my letter."

"That's enough, Hugh."

"It's my letter, and I want it back."

"Well, you can't have it."

All at once he pounced on it; there was a scuffle. The letter tore in half, and Aunt Megs fetched him a stinging slap across the face. He let go and began to cry.

"I've just about had enough," she said grimly. The contest had made her breathless, and there were red spots in either cheek. "You can go straight to bed. Go on! I don't want to see you again." He had learned his lesson. When, a few days later, another letter came for him, this time from Luchmann, he suffered her to look at it without question. Obviously written for him by some *babu*, it was full of quaint solecisms. "How too priceless!" Aunt Megs twittered. "Do look, Kingsley!" She showed it to the vicar's wife who called that same afternoon. The two women agreed that Indians were killing.

When at last the letter was restored to him, Hugh took it up to his bedroom and read it once more. The absurd, florid sentences told him nothing. He had thought that a letter would bring Luch-mann and India closer to him. Instead, they had never seemed so far away. What he read did not express any part of Luchmann; he had seen many such letters, they were all the same. In his heart, he hoped Luchmann would not write again.

Apart from Ruby, his only solace was the thought of going to school. Everyone told him how happy he would be. As the day drew near he experienced a wonderful sense of freedom. Since he would so soon be rid of the house, it no longer oppressed him as it had done in the past. He kept a chart on which he ticked off the days before his departure. He never tired of asking people about life at school—Uncle Kingsley, the vicar and Dr. Phipps all gave him thrilling accounts.

His last evening, he had arranged to meet Ruby to say good-bye. He slipped out of the house after tea on the pretext of going for a walk, and there she was, waiting for him, at the corner of the lane. They ran down the hill together, and then strolled on beside the estuary while Hugh poured out all his enthusiasm. "It's going to be wonderful," he said. "Oh, Ruby, I can't tell you! To be leaving the horrid old relatives! To be on my own!"

At last he fell silent, detecting in her a certain lack of warmth or sympathy. They walked without speaking. Beside them the estu-ary gave off a tender glow; the sun was sinking. Ruby picked up a stone and sent it skimming over the water; it jumped nine times.

"I say!" Hugh exclaimed in admiration.

"I'm going away, too."

"Are you?" he said politely. He was too intoxicated by his own future to think much of hers. "Will it be for long?"

"I don't know." She took aim, and another pebble lisped out-wards into the sunset.

"Where are you going to?"

"Don't let's talk about it."

"Tell me."

"To my Auntie Doris. Her husband's just died, and she's had another baby, and Mum says I must go and help her. . . . I don't want to go," she added miserably.

"Will it be far from here?"

"Birmingham."

"Birmingham! That's hundreds of miles away, isn't it?"

She nodded. "I don't want to leave the farm. I don't want to live in a town, and look after babies." Her mouth sagged, and he thought that she was going to cry.

"I don't expect it'll be for long," he said. But she shrugged her shoulders hopelessly.

"Will you ever come back here?" she asked.

"Oh, yes, of course! In the hols, you know. It'll be pretty beastly returning to a hole like this. But I shall look forward to seeing you."

"I wonder if we shall ever see each other again."

"Well, of course we shall."

She made him feel uneasy. He had been full of optimism when he had come out to meet her. But now everything had become rather flat. He felt angry with her because of this change: "What's up?" he asked. "What's the matter with you?"

She shrugged her shoulders, and for the rest of their last walk they said no more to each other. But at the gate, he asked: "I say, Ruby—would you mind—do you think—might I kiss you?"

She hesitated for a moment, and he saw her mouth phrase the word "no." Then she said "If you like" in a soft, expressionless voice.

He put his lips to her cheek, and as he did so he felt more afraid of her than he had ever done before. All at once she seemed much older than he was, and more powerful.

Her hands were pushing him away; that same look of panic had crossed her face. "Good-bye, good-bye," she called. Her voice was harsh and strange. She was running away from him, and soon he could see no more of her.

It wasn't until bed-time that he regained his former mood. "No one to tuck you up at school," Aunt Megs told him, as she opened the windows.

"I don't think I shall sleep a wink to-night. I'm so awfully excited."

"You may be homesick your first few days," she warned him. "But after that, I know you'll love every minute of it."

He almost laughed out loud at the notion of his ever feeling sad for the relatives. But in his new-found freedom he did not wish to hurt his aunt's feelings and restrained himself.

After she had left him he lay awake for a short time, imagining the life before him and making plans.

When at last he fell asleep he dreamed the old dream of the tunnel. He seemed to struggle in it for many minutes before he woke. In the light of dawn he saw that the walls were sweating; the moisture ran downwards in large drops.

CHAPTER XX

Fifteen shivering boys stood stripped to the waist in a passage-way. They chattered together in agitated whispers. "What does he do to you? What happens?" The question was repeated over and over again. No one knew the answer.

A sixteenth boy leant against a radiator which ran along the wall opposite to them. They eyed him with hostility, until one of them called out: "Get into line, you!"

"Yes, get into line," they all chorused.

The boy who had first spoken was easily distinguishable from the others. His arms and chest were sunburnt, and he had a flat, Chinese-looking face. Though small, with fine wrists and delicate bones, he possessed a physique superior to that of his fellows. "Get into line," he repeated.

"Why should I?"

"Because Matron said we were all to queue up."

"I can queue just as well here."

"No, you can't."

They wrangled, until the Chinese-looking boy, who was called Coppard, attempted to pull Hugh away from the radiator. "Come on; lend a hand," he commanded. A few boys shuffled to his assistance; one put out a foot and tripped Hugh, another pinched his arm. Between them, they loosened his grip on the radiator and threw him against the wall opposite.

He bruised his shoulder, and the jar made his head ache. Losing his temper, he set on the boy nearest to him, who had in fact remained aloof throughout the whole incident. He slapped his face, before Coppard had once more pinioned him from behind.

His arm was being twisted, and the pain was excruciating. But as he writhed between his half-naked tormentors, he was all the time conscious of the face of the boy whom he had just slapped. It was a small, peaked face, from which the dark hair was brushed straight back in a manner which seemed vaguely foreign. The blow had made tears run down his cheeks. Yet though Hugh had hurt him, he was gazing at him with pity.

"What are you boys doing?" The Matron had opened the door before which they had all been waiting, and now stood before them, pulling her starched cuffs well over her wrists. "I've never heard of such a thing. If you weren't new boys, I should report it to the headmaster. . . . The doctor's ready for the first boy. Come on, come on! Hurry up!" She clapped her hands together, and the boy at the head of the queue walked sheepishly in before her.

"What does he do to you? What happens?" The whispering began again.

All the new boys were in the same dormitory. It was a long room, with beds running down on either side of it; a table, with wash-basins, filled the centre. To Hugh, it seemed even more bare than his room at the relatives'. There were no curtains, the beds were made of iron, and the wooden floors were so slippery that one could slide up and down on them.

The first night, the boys seemed to be afraid of each other. Little was said; most of them were embarrassed at having to undress in public; only covert glances passed between them. When they had all climbed into bed and Matron had turned out the light, someone began to weep. It was a melancholy sound in the crowded hushed dormitory; it got on all their nerves. "Oh, shut up!" someone exclaimed. "Stow it!" Hugh recognised the voice for Coppard's.

But the sobbing continued until, suddenly, it ended in a hiccough. They all giggled, hysterically, as a release for their jangled spirits. A hush descended on the dormitory, and there was no more noise.

The second night was different; they had become rowdy and self-assertive. Coppard swung himself, like a monkey, from beam to beam of the dormitory. They took their treasures out of their suit-cases, and arranged them on their lockers. There were photographs in silver frames, ebony-backed hairbrushes, calendars, and torches.

The boy whose face Hugh had slapped the previous day—his name was Chorley—had a small case of crocodile, with silver fittings. He put it on his bed, looked round him apprehensively, and began to take out his belongings. He brought out a music-satchel, and then a photograph at which he stared for many seconds; Hugh saw the tears glisten in the corners of his eye; he was certain that it was he who had wept the night before.

"Whose is this?" Coppard came over to Chorley's locker in only his pyjama-trousers. He picked up the photograph.

"It's my mother." It showed the profile of a girl playing the piano; her hair was straight and dark, drawn into a bun, and she had a broad forehead and high cheek-bones.

"Your mother? What's your name?"

"Chorley."

"But this is signed 'Miriam Aaronson'."

"That was her maiden name. You see, she gave that photograph to my father before she married him."

"What's she playing the piano for?"

"She used to be a professional."

"I say, Badsy!" Coppard shouted to an obese boy who was cutting his toe-nails. "Chorley's mother used to be a professional." They both tittered.

"It's true," Chorley said angrily.

"We didn't say it wasn't. But . . . Miriam Aaronson. That's Jewish, isn't it?"

"Yes."

"Then your mother is a Jew?"

"I think so."

"What do you mean you think so?"

"I mean—yes."

"Then you're a Jew?" There was no answer. "Are you?"

"I suppose I am—partly."

"Did you hear that, boys? Chorley's a blooming Yid. . . . You are a Yid, aren't you, Chorley?"

"I've already told you—yes."

"And you know what the Yids did? They killed Jesus."

At this point Chorley broke down. As he wept, he bent over the crocodile suitcase, unscrewing and screwing up the fittings, so that the others should not see his tears.

"Chorley!" Coppard taunted him. "Chorl-ey!"

"Oh, shut up, Coppard!" Hugh intervened.

"Who are you telling to shut up?"

"I'm telling you."

"Oh, you are, are you?" He strode up to him, arrogantly, with his hands on his naked hips. "I suppose you're a bloody Yid, too."

"No, I'm not." He could hardly force the words past his lips. "But I'd rather be a Jew than a Chink."

Coppard flushed. "Who are you calling a Chink?"

"I didn't call anyone a Chink."

Temporarily at a loss for words, Coppard fiddled with the cord of his pyjamas. Then with a shrill: "I'll teach you!" he flung himself at Hugh. This time none of the others interfered; secretly they disliked Coppard, and welcomed any challenge to his authority. They gathered in a circle about the two combatants, who rolled over and over, panting and clawing at each other. In spite of his fear and the pain which was being inflicted on him, Hugh found a strange pleasure in the contest. They were now under the wash-table and Hugh had bumped his head; his mouth was full of dust.

Suddenly, Coppard yelled out: "Let go of me! You'll break my plate! Let go, you fool!" There was a second when they lay motionless, in tense hatred; they looked into each other's eyes and gasped for breath. Blood trickled out of Hugh's nose; it fell on to the floor in bright drops, and Coppard's chest was smeared with it.

"Let go!" he repeated. Hugh released him. Coppard got to his feet, and removed the gold brace which he wore over his front teeth. "If it's cracked you'll jolly well have to pay for it." He moved off towards his bed. "It cost twenty pounds, and if it's cracked, I'll go straight to Matron." He continued muttering to himself.

The others all grinned, including Hugh. They despised Coppard now, knowing him to have used the plate as an excuse for not continuing with the fight.

Hugh lay down with a handkerchief pressed to his nose. Chorley, who was already in bed, was looking at him in gratitude. "I say, are you all right?" he asked anxiously.

"Oh, yes, I think so." Gingerly he sat up.

"I'm sorry you had to do that. It was very decent of you."

"I wanted to pay him back for yesterday morning."

"They all seem so horrid. I don't know why it is. I'm sure they wouldn't behave like that if they were at home." He spoke in a melancholy, grown-up voice.

"I don't think they're too bad. It's only Coppard. He *is* a beast."

Chorley sighed. "Sixty-seven days!"

"Sixty-seven days?"

"Until end of term. Doesn't it seem a long time? Of course, there are parents'-days. My mother—or should I say 'mater' now——"

"You should. But don't."

They both laughed, with an uproariousness which was little more than a nervous overflow.

"Well, my mother's promised that she'd come the Sunday after next. But even that seems terribly far-off. . . . Do you think you're going to like it here?"

"I expect so."

"I suppose one has to come to school. Even if it does seem rather pointless at the time."

"Everyone says school's great fun—once one settles down to it."

"That's what they say."

At this point the Matron came in to turn out the lights. "No more talking, boys." She went to the windows, as Aunt Megs did at home, and pushed them open. It was not yet dark outside. The school-garden lay silent and deserted, the sun sank behind a row of poplars. It seemed very far off, and there was a touch of autumn in the air. Slowly the night came on, and with it the sobbing began again.

"Chorley!" Hugh whispered. "I say, Chorley!"

But there was no answer and he gave up. It was a long time before he could get to sleep; he was made uneasy not only by the sobbing, but by the presence of so many other people in the room with him. He wondered whether there were any of them awake; and if there were, what did they think of? Was Coppard awake? All at once he felt sorry for him. The memory came back to him of how, for a brief moment, they had lain motionless and close; Coppard had green eyes and, as Hugh had looked into them, they had been full of rage and misery.

It was too early to be dissatisfied with life at the school. In spite of what Chorley had said, he told himself that it was simply a matter of "settling down." Yet he could not prevent himself from feeling a twinge of disappointment. He had hoped for something —a warmth or an intimacy, he did not know what—and he had not found it. As at the relatives, he felt there was a lack; but he was unable to define it, and blamed himself for not being wholly grateful.

That night he had a vivid dream. He was walking through a garden, which he knew, by the scents, the colour and the atmosphere, to be in India. In the middle there was a pool, and he knelt by it, while from behind some trees there came to him the sound of invisible singing. When he had first come to the pool it had been half empty, but as he watched it, it began to fill, slowly, the water rising from beneath in great, gold bubbles which swam upwards, rested a moment and then exploded into a shower of spray. He wondered what would happen when the pool was filled to the brim; but though the water now lapped round the marble and the bubbles still came up, one after the other, the level seemed to remain constant. Perhaps the water flowed both in and out; but looking down into the clear depths he could see no place from which it might escape.

At last he wearied of looking down into the water, and he walked on in the direction of the singing. Behind the trees, there stood a temple; it was like the temple which his ayah had once taken him to, long ago, and before he entered, he remembered her commands and took off his shoes. It was almost dark inside; he moved up through a throng of worshippers, some standing, some kneeling with their foreheads to the ground, some cross-legged in rigid attitudes. He still could not see where the music came from; it was the same rhythmical monotone which the hillmen used as they trudged with their loads. Once again the sound of it filled his heart with strange longings. He moved on, to a corner of the temple from which it came loudest, until he was standing before a cross-legged idol, many times greater than he was. Behind the idol there was a screen of fretted ivory, delicate as lace; and the singing came from behind the screen.

He knelt down in terror and reverence; he began to pray. Strangely he did not pray as he had always been taught, asking for forgiveness for this and that, and making his own petitions. This was a silent communication, without words. He felt that his soul was being drawn out of him, upwards, into the idol; and a mysterious power flowed from the idol into him, flowed endlessly, as the water flowed into the pool. Each of the gold bubbles exploded like a star within him.

When he had finished, he slowly raised himself and looked for the first time up at the idol's face. It was very far away; but as he gazed it came nearer, the formal features broke up and changed, and it was Luchmann looking down at him. It was as it used to be, when they made their journeys by car, and his head was in Luchmann's lap. The dark face, though close to him now, was yet tinged with mystery: it looked down at him, and it seemed to smile.

He awoke, weeping, to the clang of a bell.

CHAPTER XXI

He and Chorley were in the same form; they were with boys two and three years older than themselves. Their form-master,

Mr. Burdock, was a young man who had just left a minor public-school; he wore grey flannels, a tweed coat and an old-school tie, his fingers were stained with nicotine, and he had red hair, cut close and then smoothed with hair-oil. He was an expert at the ironical comment—that most misused of all weapons, in life as in literature.

The first morning, he strode into the form-room, opened his desk, closed it, and then looked round until the class fell silent. "My God!" he exclaimed, scanning their faces. There was a nervous titter. He took a fountain-pen from his pocket, shook it so that a large drop splashed on to the floor, and drew his mark-book towards him. The class still watched him, as though bewitched.

He began to write laboriously in the mark-book, the tip of his tongue showing out of the corner of his mouth, "New boys? Any new boys?" he asked.

"Yes, sir." Hugh and Chorley put up their hands.

"Ah, yes." He scrutinised them both, tapping the end of his fountain-pen against teeth that were small and discoloured. The skin round his eyes was brown and wrinkled, and the eyes themselves seemed hostile and unnaturally close together. "Names?" he demanded.

They both spoke at once, and he said coldly: "I beg your pardon? I didn't quite catch." There was another feeble titter. "Would you mind—do you think you could oblige once again? Not in chorus, this time." He pointed the pen at Hugh. "You first, sonny."

"Hugh Craddock."

"*Hugh* Craddock." He brought a derisive emphasis to the Christian name. "And a very nice name, too. But if it won't bother you, I think we'll just put you down as 'H. Craddock.'" The laborious writing began once more.

"Now you." The pen was pointed at Chorley.

"Chorley, sir."

"Oh, so you're Chorley! Pleased to meet you, Chorley. The Honourable Brian Chorley, isn't it?"

"No, sir."

"Your father's a baronet, isn't he? Sir Denvers Chorley, Bart.?"

"Yes, sir. But the sons of baronets aren't called Honourable."

"Aren't they? My mistake! You must forgive my ignorance. I'm afraid I'm just one of the *hoi polloi*. I don't know much about these things."

So the lesson continued. Everyone, except the victim, tittered and grinned at these sallies. It was nervous laughter, for each boy feared that he would be the next to be subjected to Mr. Burdock's satire. But both Hugh and Chorley found it impossible to join in the merriment. Mr. Burdock noticed this, and it did not endear them to him.

Nor did an incident of a few days later. In their history books there was a quotation from Horace Walpole, and one of the boys, wishing to seem keen, put up his hand: "Please, sir?"

"Yes. What do you want?"

"Please, sir, who is Horace Walpole?"

"Horace Walpole?" Mr. Burdock considered, sucking the top of his pen. "You know who Horace Walpole is," he said at last, "Wrote the Jeremy books, *Jeremy at Crale*, and *Jeremy and Hamlet*. You know them, don't you? Damned good they are, too. . . . Well, Chorley? What's the matter? Haven't you read any of the Jeremy books?"

"Oh, but surely, sir. . . . You're thinking of Hugh Walpole."

"I'm thinking of Horace Walpole." Mr. Burdock flushed.

"But wasn't it Horace Walpole . . . ? I'm sure I've heard my father speak about him. He wrote letters—oh, a long time ago." He was genuinely bewildered.

"Well, of course, Chorley, I should hesitate to contradict you. Since you're such an authority on the matter, perhaps you'd like to change places with me. Would you?" There was no answer; Chorley stared down at his exercise-book. "Come on, Chorley, don't be modest! We're all just hanging on your lips. Come and sit up here, instead of me. . . . Chorley!" His voice became harsh and commanding. "Did you hear what I said? Come and sit up here." Chorley shook his head faintly. "I warn you, Chorley. There are certain punishments for disobedience—rather painful ones, so they tell me. Now do as I say . . . at once."

Chorley stumbled up to the dais on which the desk was set. He was made to sit down in Mr. Burdock's place, and was told to start the lesson. "I can't," he said in a voice which rasped with tears.

"Can't you? Oh, I'm sure you can. You're so clever, Chorley. You must be able to do better than that."

The other boys howled with laughter; they rolled about in their desks, and clutched their sides. "Oh, sir! Don't, sir! I shall die of laughing!" But anyone who had looked into their eyes would have seen that they were empty of all mirth.

Mr. Burdock was the only master who ill-treated Chorley and Hugh; but since the greater part of their day was spent in his charge, they acquired an exaggerated sense of persecution. He seemed to wish to humiliate them more than any other of his pupils: his malice sprang from an inherent knowledge that they were in every way superior to him—in birth and breeding, morally and intellectually.

The other masters—and in particular the headmaster, Mr. Baldstone—tended, on the contrary, to show favouritism towards Chorley. They recognised how great an asset his father's name must be to the school. "Well, Chorley," Mr. Baldstone would say, with an indulgent smile. "I see that your father has made another first-rate speech in the House. . . . Knocked the Socialists for six!" When Lady Chorley came down to see her son, she was asked to take tea at High Table, with the masters; they all fussed round her, except Mr. Burdock, who sat chewing bread in moody silence.

It became the custom for Chorley to be pointed out to anyone who was being shown round the school. "That's Brian Chorley— son of Sir Denvers Chorley. Nice kid. Got all his father's brains." Parents seldom failed to be impressed.

But in spite of his privileged position, Chorley was unhappy; and Hugh knew, in his heart, that he was unhappy also. He knew it, but would never admit it openly. The thought of school had been his one anodyne for all that he suffered with the relatives. Without school, there would be nothing else. If he once admitted that life at Frimley Towers was no better than life with the relatives, he would truly be in the tunnel, with no escape.

So he still clung to his belief that all that was necessary was to settle down. "It can't always be as bad as this," he protested to Chorley. "If we work hard we can get out of old Burdock's form before next year."

But Chorley was inconsolable. Hugh realised that it was worse for him; he missed his home, his mother and father, his pony and his dogs; he talked about them ceaselessly, until Hugh caught the infection of his nostalgia, and memories crowded back—memories of his mother in her blue evening-dress, of Luchmann and Hetty, and the house that had been burnt. Sometimes it seemed to him that he had ceased to live since those days; the past was definite, the events following were no more than a blur in his mind. After the fire everything had somehow lost clarity; the machine had only run at half-strength.

Chorley spoke often of leaving the school. He was going to ask his mother to take him away and get a tutor for him. He was going to slip out one night, and take a train home. He was going to save his pocket-money and live in an hotel. But though they often discussed such schemes they both knew, secretly, that nothing would ever come of them. They accepted the necessity of being at school, because all the grown-ups said that it was necessary; they were too young to challenge that authority; and since rebellion was out of the question, they endured, as children endure, because their elders say they must.

"Don't you ever feel you want to run away?" Chorley asked Hugh.

Hugh shook his head. "There's nowhere where I could run away to."

"But you could go home."

"I'd just as soon be here as at—where I live."

"Where *do* you live?" Though Chorley had often discussed his own family with Hugh, there had been no return of confidences.

"With relatives."

"Then . . . have you no parents?"

By degrees, Chorley learnt the truth. He stood aghast. "But that's terrible," he said. "I'd no idea. Oh, Hugh, I am sorry."

"There's nothing to feel sorry about," Hugh mumbled.

"I've done nothing but tell you how unhappy I am. And compared with you . . . I don't know how I should bear it if Mum and Dad were to die suddenly like that. I think I should kill myself. You must be very brave."

To talk of his father and mother after so long a time had wrenched the scab off the half-healed wound. All the time that he had been telling Chorley, he had been like a silk-worm from which the inexorable engine strips off its shining thread. As each inch was unravelled, his nerves became more exposed.

"One gets used to it," he said. "It's funny. One thinks one will never be able to bear a thing like that, but when it happens . . . You know, one can bear pretty well anything."

"I can't."

"If there's no escape, I mean. If you can't run away, you stay put. What else can you do?" Suddenly embarrassed at thus speaking his inmost thoughts he broke off: "But don't let's talk any more about it. I'd rather not."

Chorley insisted that at the next parents' day Hugh should join him and his mother. "That is—I don't suppose your aunt and uncle will be coming down, will they?"

Hugh shook his head. "They say it's too expensive. Aunt Megs said that seeing them so soon after the beginning of term would only make me more homesick." He gave a bitter laugh. "That was only an excuse," he added.

Lady Chorley came down by car. There was a cricket-match on that day against a neighbouring school, and all boys were expected to watch it. "Well, what do we do now?" she asked, when Chorley had introduced Hugh to her. "I suppose you boys ought to be watching the match."

"We ought to," Chorley agreed doubtfully.

"But you'd much rather not," she put in with a smile. "Well, to tell you the truth cricket bores me to tears. Let's do something else until tea."

"Don't you think Mr. Baldstone might be angry?" Chorley asked.

"Oh, I don't see why he should. After all, what are parents' days for, except to enjoy oneself? You both choose what you want to do, and we'll do it."

"We could play clock-golf," Chorley said. "At least, only the prefects are really allowed to play it. But if we played it with you, I don't think it would matter. In any case, everyone is up at the match, so we're not likely to be seen."

"Clock-golf it is then! You'd better get the clubs, and balls, will you? I'll wait for you out here."

They went to the chest in the hall, and having first looked all round them, took out the things. Hugh felt a certain anxiety. "Do you think it's all right for us to take them?" he whispered.

"Oh, yes. If Mummy says it's all right. Old Baldstone wouldn't dare to row with her."

"But we might get into trouble after she had gone."

Chorley had already run out into the garden, carrying two clubs. Hugh followed after him. He still felt uneasy; but once he was in the confident presence of the other two his qualms vanished. Lady Chorley had offered a prize to whichever of them won. She herself played shockingly; either she gave the ball so light a tap that it rolled only a few inches, or it flew across the lawn and buried itself among Mrs. Baldstone's irises. She always laughed at these mishaps, and at first Hugh was rather scandalised at her nonchalance; games were meant to be played with complete seriousness—he had learnt that from Mr. Burdock's withering cry of "Duffer!" when one missed an easy catch at cricket. But bit by bit he was won over to this new attitude; he realised that it was possible to enjoy a game, regardless of one's skill at it.

At the end of their match he was proclaimed the winner. "I haven't forgotten the prize," Lady Chorley said. She took a slab of motoring chocolate out of her bag and held it out to him.

"No, really . . ."

"Go on. It's for you. You won it." She took one of his hands and put the slab into it. Her fingers were cool and slight, and for the first time he realised how kind a face she had. It was like the face of the girl in the photograph which Chorley had, but there were small wrinkles round the eyes and the hair was tinged with grey.

"Let's have some to eat now," Chorley said.

"But, darling . . ." She laughed. "It's for Hugh. I want him to keep it."

"Come on." Hugh had already fallen in with Chorley's suggestion and was breaking the slab into large squares.

"Not for me," Lady Chorley said. "We'll be having tea soon. . . .

I really think I must go in and powder my nose. Brian—will you show me the way?" She turned to Hugh: "We'll be back in a moment."

After they had gone he experienced an extraordinary exhilaration. His mouth still full of chocolate, he began to drive the ball from one end of the lawn to the other. Each time that he hit it, he raced to the place where it had landed, and took aim once more. He became breathless and hot.

Suddenly he heard a voice: "Craddock! What on earth are you doing?" The drawing-room window had been thrown open and Mrs. Baldstone was looking out. Of middle age, she dressed smartly and wore her hair in tight yellow bubbles: her face was hard but still handsome. "Come here!" she called, as he dithered with the golf-club. "And put that club down. Hurry up!"

"Yes, Mrs. Baldstone?"

"You know you ought to be at the match. And you know you've no right to be playing clock-golf anyway. And look at my irises. . . . I shall have to speak to Mr. Baldstone about this."

"Well, you see——" he began.

"Don't speak to me with your mouth full! What are you eating?"

"Some chocolate."

"Chocolate! You're not allowed to eat chocolate. Where did you get it from?"

"Someone gave it to me."

"Someone? . . . Who gave it to you?" Suddenly her face was suffused with a smile which Hugh imagined to be intended for himself. She put her head on one side, and called out: "How are you, Lady Chorley? It is nice to see you."

Chorley and his mother had come out of the house and were crossing the lawn, arm-in-arm.

"I'm afraid I've been rather naughty, Mrs. Baldstone. I made these two boys play clock-golf with me instead of watching the match. Is that a very serious crime?"

Mrs. Baldstone laughed lightly. "As a matter of fact I got so bored myself that I came away."

Hugh was at a loss to account for this sudden change of mood. He looked from one woman to the other. Mrs. Baldstone was admiring Lady Chorley's ear-rings; then she made a flattering reference to Sir Denvers' last speech.

"But I mustn't keep you," she broke off at last, as she glimpsed the first of the parents returning from the match for tea. "You must come and have a chat with me later on. Perhaps you could stay to dinner?"

While Lady Chorley was excusing herself from the invitation, she heard her son say to Hugh: "Give us some more chocolate." She turned round: "Brian—offer Mrs. Baldstone some chocolate. I'm sure she'd like some."

Mrs. Baldstone shook her head. "No, really, thank you, Lady Chorley. It's very good of you. I won't rob the boys."

At that moment Hugh's bewilderment turned into scorn. There came to him an exultant sense of power and a contempt for all those who spend their lives cringing and fawning on their betters. Mrs. Baldstone no longer frightened him; he pitied her.

When they went up to bed that night they found the other new boys huddled together in a circle, so absorbed that they did not turn round at the noise of their entry. The air was pungent with the smell of struck matches. They both felt listless and rather melancholy, and at first did not go to see what was happening.

"Put it under him! Closer!" they heard one boy say. A few moments later there was a gust of excited laughter.

"Where's he got to?"

"He's by that jug."

"Blast! That's another match wasted."

Many of them were now crouching under the wash-basins; there was the scrape of a match being struck. Reluctantly, Hugh and Chorley moved up to the group.

Coppard held a lighted match in one hand; he was stooping over a large spider; his hand descended until the naked flame touched the creature's body. Immediately it scurried away from him, one leg already shrivelled; there were titters from the onlookers. Again he lowered the match. He had caught the spider in a corner, and as he passed the flame slowly across its back it wriggled, capered, and then slowly reared itself as if it were trying to stand up.

"Did you see that?"

"Trying to do a bloody dance."

"Phew! What a stink!"

"Ouch!" The match had burnt up to Coppard's fingers; he hurriedly dropped it and lit another.

Hugh and Chorley looked on in horror. It did not occur to them that they might protest; they had grown to accept such happenings as part of the life they now led. What was being done was no more outrageous than other acts of callousness and cruelty which they witnessed daily. At least the boys were not hurting each other, but a creature of a supposedly lesser order. In any case, it was hard to feel sympathy for a spider—and this one was exceptionally ugly. There was nothing left of it now but a corpse, which looked like a charred knot of string; that, and a bitter smell. They went back to their beds and began undressing.

But the memory of the spider would not leave them. It had seemed almost human when it had reared up; the smell still filled their nostrils. There had been a strange atmosphere of excitement in the dormitory; it had not yet quite gone. Everyone seemed flushed, and spoke quicker than usual.

"Perhaps we should have tried to stop Coppard," Chorley said, when they were both undressed.

"What would have been the good? That's what they're like, and we can't really do anything about it."

"It seemed so beastly," Chorley said. "I can't explain. . . . Perhaps it's just that I'm feeling homesick."

"Are you? It's funny . . . so am I. I like your mother most awfully, Chorley."

"She likes you."

Hugh had drawn the bed-clothes well up over his cheeks. "I don't mean that I'm homesick for the relatives. But that awful stink . . . that burning smell. . . . In India we had hundreds of spiders in our house. Particularly during the rains. I remember . . ."

He remembered how he had gone out on to the verandah to give Luchmann the silver pencil, and a spider had run out across his path. He had been about to squash it, but then he had picked it up, and it had stung him. It, too, had had hairy legs. He could feel them pushing against his cupped hands, as he stood looking down at it. The mist wafted over the verandah, and there was a musty smell of dead geraniums. A smell not unlike the smell of used matches. . . . As Coppard had leant over the insect, his face had appeared strangely lurid in the flame; it had seemed to be transformed, into the weak yet somewhat sinister face of a grown man.

But before he could say anything of this to Chorley, Matron had come in: "Lights out, boys! Lights out!" She used the word as a figure of speech; there were, in fact, no lights to be extinguished; the late sunlight filtered through the windows, and once more he thought how far away the sun seemed in England. There was no warmth to it; it was like a deity, half withdrawn. As it sank, his heart went out in a prayer: "O Sun, come nearer, come nearer."

He turned over, smiling. It was absurd to be praying to the sun. What would Aunt Frances think? But the sun had burnt low and steadfast in India; since he had left that country he had never been truly warm; since he had moved out of that influence he had never been truly happy.

CHAPTER XXII

Chorley was as voracious a reader as Hugh himself. He had been brought up on certain books which he knew by heart—*The Lays of Ancient Rome, Alice in Wonderland*, the Arthur Ransome stories, Kingsley's *Heroes*. Hugh, in turn, introduced him to his own favourites; he told him the lines, "The bailey beareth the bell away," and together they recited verses of Swinburne on Sunday walks. They understood little of the Swinburne, but the rhythm intoxicated them.

To this list Mrs. Baldstone's mother, Mrs. Corabel, provided a further addition—Malory's *Morte d'Arthur*. Each Sunday evening she invited the new boys into her sitting-room to read to them. It was her husband who had first started the school, and she could remember a time when there had been only fifteen pupils; they had all eaten together at one table, and she had often supervised prep. The school had been like a private house then, without a gymnasium, changing-rooms or the new red-brick extension. When her husband had died, the school had passed out of her control; Mr. Baldstone had put in the new plumbing, and the numbers had risen. But she felt that something had been lost; it was no longer the same. Fretful and discontented, she stayed on, to do small jobs, because she had nowhere else to go to. Her hands were ugly and swollen with rheumatism, she wore a knitted coat and skirt which had long ago lost shape, and a number of long grey hairs grew above her mouth and on her chin. She often quarrelled with the other members of the staff.

Her sitting-room was small, and crowded with knick-knacks; on either side of the fire rested brass tongs and shovels, gleaming boldly; the mantelpiece was covered with silver cups, won by her husband; there were innumerable photographs on the walls, and the arms of the chairs had over them shields hand-embroidered with eidelweiss. Hugh liked to come into this room; it was a change. The rooms in which they usually spent their time were big and bare; the floors were of parquet, and there were no curtains to the windows. She would let them squat on the floor at her feet, or if they wished, they could sit on the sofa; many of the boys fooled about, pressing the knob which let down the arm, so that the end-occupant tumbled sideways. They giggled among themselves, and administered surreptitious kicks and nudges. At one end of the room there was a great china vase, covered with blue dragons; it was about six feet high, and they played a game with it, all the time that she was reading to them; they made small pellets of paper and tried to flick them into its mouth, scoring one mark for each pellet home. Perhaps she never noticed that they did this; perhaps she thought it best to feign ignorance. Only occasionally she would look up and, lowering the book to her lap, would murmur: "Do try to be a little more attentive, boys."

Hugh and Chorley loved the story of King Arthur. They always arrived early, so that they could squat on the floor just below her, leaning their heads against her chair. She had a sing-song, yet expressive voice; she could read tirelessly for an hour on end. The June sunlight filled the room with eddying notes; the atmosphere became heady and blurred, so that they did not notice the behaviour of the others but went into a kind of trance under the gentle hypnosis of her voice. The sun showed up cruelly the frayed patches of the carpet, the worn cushions and the blotched wall-paper. But strangely it concealed more than it revealed. It bathed them in a timeless fluid, washing away all dross and refuse.

The death of King Arthur was most moving of all the episodes that she read. Hugh cried silently all through it. But just before the end there was a crash and a tinkle, and her voice stopped. He turned to look at her, his cheeks still bathed in tears. Her face had blanched, her lips were quivering.

"Who did that?" she asked. The china vase lay in pieces on the floor. There was no answer and she repeated in a strange, harsh voice: "Who did that? Who was responsible?" With hot cheeks and lowered eyes, the boys remained silent.

"Is no one going to own up?" she asked. There was still no answer. "Very well," she said quietly. "I think you'd all better go." No one made a move, until she repeated: "Please go, will you? I don't think I want to read any more." Then they rose to their feet and filed out, one behind the other. In the corridor someone tittered.

Hugh and Chorley were about to follow, when she called them back: "You didn't have anything to do with it. Would you like me to go on?"

"Oh, please."

"I'd better clear this up first, though." She went on her hands and knees, and they joined her. "Do you think it can be mended?" Hugh asked.

She shook her head. "I don't think it would be worth while." She took from them the broken fragments which they had col-lected and tipped them all into the wastepaper-basket. Something still remained in her hand—a pebble. She looked down at it for a while; it lay hard and smooth in her rough, crooked fingers. "A catapult, I suppose," she said. She got to her feet, her joints crack-ing, and put the stone with the other fragments. "It was rather unnecessary of them."

"Was the china very valuable?" Chorley asked.

She did not answer the question. She went to the open window and stood there, a breeze ruffling her thin, white locks. The back of her neck was covered with a criss-cross of deep wrinkles. "They're all so destructive now," she said, as if to herself. "Why is it? What's gone wrong? They weren't always like that." She turned round and faced them. "Why is it?" she asked them both.

"They're not really so bad," Chorley said. "I don't expect they do those sort of things at home."

"Exactly. But here . . . Oh, why, why?"

"It just seems to happen—of its own accord. I don't know why it should be so. We're all so much together, and we're . . . we're all so young."

"But there are the masters."

"They don't really count," Hugh put in. "They tell us what to do, of course. But that's not the same thing."

"Some things can only be transmitted through example and affection and intimacy—is that what you mean? One can't give lessons in being civilised. . . . You're all herded together, to rub on as best you may. It usen't to be like that. We used to see much more of the boys—my husband and I. . . . It was more a family, then."

She stopped, for they were both looking at her blankly; she realised that they understood little of what she was saying to them. They both tried to grasp at her meaning; they were fond of her, and they felt that they owed her this much. But there were too many words, and only one stuck in their minds. It was the word "rub", and to both of them it suggested graphically the constant friction of their raw and exposed spirits, one against the other. It was as if the pain so produced did something to alleviate that greater pain—the pain of growth and change and approaching manhood.

"Come," she said. "We'll go on." She patted the arms of her chair, and they both went and perched on them, one on either side. "Let's go back a bit, shall we? But first . . . here's something to fortify you." She opened a drawer and brought out a bottle of bull's-eyes. "I'd better not take one, or I won't be able to read properly. But you help yourselves." The sweets were deliciously hot and soothing.

When she had finished the tale, she lowered the book and took off her glasses. For a while, none of them said anything; they looked out of the window on to the sunlit garden. Hugh and Chorley had both been crying.

"That was sad," she said, "I've read that so many times, and it always makes me feel sad. But it's a nice sadness, isn't it?"

She was right; they both nodded.

"It's funny," she said. "It's only a story, and yet, do you know, I mind far more about poor King Arthur than about that vase of mine. I've grown into a hard old woman where other people are concerned. But books and music—they can still move me. I suppose that's what it means to have an imagination." She touched Hugh's hair. "I can see that you two boys are imaginative, also. You should be glad of that. If you have a world of your own, it's easier to bear with the world of other people. . . . And now, one more sweet and you must get along to bed, or Matron will be angry with me."

After that, none of the other new boys were asked up to her room; but Hugh and Chorley often went there. She read to them and talked to them, and showed them her treasures. She had photograph-albums full of women in long skirts and men with whiskers; she had pictures of herself as a girl, and of Mrs. Baldstone, lying naked on a cushion, at the age of two.

Hugh and Chorley had already begun to make up a saga, modelled on *Morte d'Arthur*. They elaborated it to each other whenever they had a spare moment, using the archaic diction which they had picked up from Mrs. Corabel's reading. The saga was about themselves; they were knights, who fought against the mythical "enemy"—Mrs. Timpson, Captain Curtiz, Aunt Megs, Uncle Kingsley, the Baldstones, Mr. Burdock, Coppard and anyone else whom they disliked. Although Chorley had not met half of these characters, he was quick to seize on their weaknesses.

The saga extended itself into Hugh's dreams. Many of the incidents which he wove into it had first come to him during the hours of sleep. His dreams were wonderfully vivid now, and there were few nights without them. In the end he came so much to live in this world of dreams and books and imagining, which only Chorley shared with him, that the "real" world became even more hazy and disconnected than it had been before. He was not troubled by this. It was easy enough to live through hours of malice, cruelty and boredom, knowing that he held inside himself the key to a place where he would be free of these things. Mr. Burdock's sarcasms and the behaviour of his fellows had become unreal; they troubled him only momentarily, as a nightmare troubles one, to be forgotten soon after waking.

He dreamed many dreams over and over again. There was the old dream of the idol to whom he bowed in prayer; that he dreamed most frequently of all. But there were others. They were dreams full of sounds and smells and colours; they were dreams in which an indefinable atmosphere would transmit itself. They were full of tenderness, pity and reunion.

There were two dreams which were particularly vivid, apart from the dream of the temple. In one he stood on the edge of a boundless plain; it was brown and sere, and the grass was withered, either from drought or from the intense cold; for a gritty wind blew at him from all four corners of the plain at once, making his eyes water, his face sting. Far away, at the other end of the plain, there rose a hillock with a flat top; it was strangely green in all that brownness, and as he looked at it the wind seemed to raise him up and bear him with a great rushing noise along the plain. He could see now that there was a fire lit on top of the hill, and a circle of naked figures moved round and round it, their hands joined. The wind had carried him far, far above them, so that he could not see their faces or their sex. They chanted as they moved round the fire, their brown bodies disappearing and appearing through the smoke. The fire burned fiercer, and began to give off white exhalation, through which their movements appeared slightly distorted to the eye. The flames leapt high, and cast dwarfing shadows on them. They began to circle faster and faster; their chant grew shrill and there were strange shouts of ecstasy. Suddenly, one of the figures detached itself and whirled into the fire; there was a small puff of smoke, no bigger than a man's hand, and that was all. The dance continued. Another figure detached itself. Faster and faster they danced; one by one the flames consumed them. In the end there was a solitary figure left; he leapt into the air, there was a loud scream of pain or triumph, and he too was gone.

The other dream was, in part, a recollection of an incident which had taken place in India. The car had broken down on a lonely stretch of road, and while his father and Luchmann had attempted to mend it, he had wandered off by himself down a cart-track. After a few yards he had come to a field across which there moved a bullock dragging what seemed to be some sort of agricultural implement; a man followed behind. His father later told him that the labourer was distributing fertiliser over the field; the Commissioner of the district had done much to spread modern methods of agriculture.

It was a vast field, stretching on and on, at a gentle incline, until it met the white gauze of the horizon. The bullock and the man moved unwearyingly across it, back and forth, back and forth, stopping only to load more fertiliser on to the contraption. Wherever they went, the brown of the earth became grey, as if with spent ashes. The man's naked arms and chest, his hair, and the bullock were all of the same colour. Gusts of wind fountained clouds of the fertiliser up into the air, and then let it waft back, like motes of dust.

In the dream, he was standing at the opening of the field and watching the slow progress of the bullock and the man. Both were bigger than in reality, and the bullock had great curving horns, like a stag. They moved for a long time before him, and the earth where they had passed bloomed like snow and gave off a tingling brilliance which dazzled the eye. In the bushes round the field, the birds sang very loud—a ceaseless descant of love and longing. All at once, the man halted the bullock with a guttural word of command; he stooped and picked up another sack of fertiliser, untied the string at its neck, and began to pour it into the distributor. At that same instant the wind blew very strong, and the powder, instead of falling downwards, shot up into the air in a thick cloud, which spread outwards, split into other smaller clouds, and then began to drift downwards, all over the field. It fell like snow, obliterating the man, the bullock, the distributor, and even the bushes round the field. It fell out of a grey sky, flake on flake; it was covering Hugh's own clothes, his face and hands; it was stopping his eyes, and filling his ears, and he was floundering deeper and deeper in it. At first he struggled against this new and yielding element; but just because there was no body to it, and because, like water, it was brushed away only to return once more, he had, in the end, to give in to it. Then a delicious sensation stole all over his body. Completely relaxed, he suffered himself to be covered by the flakes; he nestled deeper into them, and found them warm and soothing. He lay blissful and without conflict, each flake alighting like a feather on his body. There was no sensation now but his utter abandon to the element.

He told Chorley of this and the other dreams, and a few days later, when he awoke from sleep, it was to find that Chorley was pulling at his bed-clothes: "I say!" he whispered. "It's happened to me also, I've just dreamed that same dream."

"What dream?"

"That dream of the temple. It was all exactly as you said." He was still flushed from sleep, and his eyes shone.

"What happened exactly?"

"Oh, just what happened to you." He went over the incidents of the dream.

"But the pool. Tell me about the pool. When it began to fill, what were the bubbles like?"

Chorley's brows creased. "Oh, not ordinary bubbles. They were gold and large—like oranges. They came up one by one, and exploded."

Hugh felt his scalp prick with goose-flesh. As far as he could remember, this was a detail of his dream which he had never told to Chorley. It had seemed an irrelevant decoration.

He thought a moment; then he said: "Chorley—can you remember? Did I tell you that about the bubbles?"

Chorley shook his head. "No. There were hundreds of things in the dream which you hadn't told me. And it was all so unlike anything that I had ever seen before. That singing . . . it was awfully queer, Hugh. And round the temple, there were bushes of flowers—like rhododendrons, only a greenish-white colour, with mauve centres—much bigger, too."

They stared at each other, invisible tides of wonder, fear and sympathy moving between them. "I've never heard of a thing like that happening before," Hugh said at last.

Chorley shook his head.

"And yet I suppose it isn't really so funny," Hugh continued. "After all, it's just as real *there* as it is *here*: and if we both meet here, then why shouldn't we . . . ?" He broke off, and once again he felt his scalp tingle.

"But other people don't have the same dreams, do they?" Chorley voiced the doubts which nagged beneath their exhilaration. "It may be just a coincidence. And yet . . . it was all so clear, you know."

"I've told you all about it."

"Not all."

"It's so difficult to be absolutely certain."

They were never absolutely certain; sometimes Hugh believed that he and Chorley shared a dream-world together; sometimes he doubted and it seemed merely a matter of coincidence and suggestion. They both hesitated to put it to any real proof. Chorley once suggested that they should cease to tell each other their dreams for a whole week; they should write them down in a note-book, and then compare them. They discussed the scheme, but went no further with it. They were afraid; they did not dare to put it to the test. For while they both doubted and believed, a mysterious force, stronger than friendship or any human intimacy, seemed to bind them irrevocably together.

CHAPTER XXIII

A week later Chorley fell ill. He had a cough, and the Matron excused him games. While Hugh and the others went up to the cricket-field he read for a while, strummed on the piano in one of the music-rooms, and at last mooned disconsolately about the garden. Mrs. Corabel discovered him there, and asked him up to her room. She gave him tea, and showed him the glove-puppets which she had been making for a nephew of hers. "He's very clever with his hands," she told Chorley. "He's made himself a puppet-show. But he doesn't like doing the dolls, so I take over all that side." She explained how the dolls' faces were made out of papier

mâché; then she put one of them on her hand and, crooning in a
strange falsetto voice, made it dance for him.

When Chorley left her room to join the others for tea, he was
full of ideas for a puppet-show of his own. Mrs. Corabel had lent
him a book on the actual construction of the theatre, and she herself had volunteered to make the dolls. He told Hugh, and infected
him with his own enthusiasm. Hugh was to write the plays, and
Chorley was to compose the music. At their next carpentry lesson
they would speak to Beddows, the school carpenter, and get him
to assist them.

The theatre progressed rapidly. Beddows helped them over
all difficulties; he produced some special wood, cut the dove-tail
joints for them, and showed them how to do the painting. Chorley worked at the job all the time that the others were up at the
cricket-field.

"It's almost ready," he told Hugh at lunch one day. "There's just
the proscenium to be painted. I daren't do it myself—you know
what a bad artist I am." There were Corinthian pillars on either
side, which had to be painted gold. "I wish you could help me this
afternoon."

"I wish I could, but I've got nets with old Gallstones." Mr.
Golston, the English master, occasionally took the boys in cricket;
he wore flannels, yellow with age, and bowled under-arm.

"You could cut it. He wouldn't notice."

"Cut it?"

"Yes. Easy as pie. Just don't turn up. You can slip out of the
changing-rooms into the carpentry-shop."

Hugh hesitated. "I don't mind about old Gallstones. But what
about Burdock?" Mr. Burdock made out the games lists. "He might
notice."

"Why should he?"

"Oh, he's like that. You know."

Chorley knew.

"Then there's Beddows," Hugh continued. "If he sees me in the
carpentry-shop, he's sure to wonder what I'm doing there."

"No need to worry about him. He told me that he was taking
his girl to the pictures to-day. Anyway, he's all right. He's pretty

decent, and wouldn't make trouble. . . . Oh, I wish you would come. We could finish it in one more afternoon. Mrs. Corabel has all the puppets ready for us."

It was tempting, and Hugh hesitated. He was naturally obedient; it required a certain effort for him to break a rule. "I'll see," he said.

"There *can't* be any risk," Chorley put in. "Coppard often does it—even when it's Burdock taking nets. He told me so. He goes down to the village, and has an absolutely super time. Well, that *is* running it rather close. But if we just stay in the carpentry-shop, no one can possibly see us."

It was the mention of Coppard which won Hugh over. Ever since their tussle on his second night at the school, a sense of rivalry had existed between them both. Their very hatred had become a subtle kind of longing; they were at once overwhelmingly attractive and overwhelmingly repellent to each other.

All went well. Hugh slipped out of the changing-rooms while Mr. Golston was arguing with one of the prefects, and found Chorley waiting for him. They set to work at once. They went about their jobs in silence, both receiving a wonderful sense of achievement from the sight of the theatre, completed now except for its last coat of paint. "I'd much rather be doing this than hitting a ball about," Hugh said.

"So would I." They paused in their work and looked at the theatre. It was not perhaps a professional job of work; it was somewhat unsteady, and Chorley had split one side with a too large nail—he should have used screws. But there it was, and they had made it. They knew that it was their one real achievement during their four weeks at the school.

Suddenly, they heard footsteps on the gravel outside the shed. They both looked at each other, in horror. "Hide!" Chorley whispered. But already a face had appeared at one of the cobwebbed windows. It was Mr. Burdock's.

They waited for him to walk round and come in through the door. They waited in tense silence, neither of them daring to speak. Some glue was boiling on the hearth, and all at once its smell became oppressive and nauseating. Chorley shifted a foot, and from the shavings which covered the floor a dust rose to prick their nostrils.

"Well, well, well!" Mr. Burdock eyed them both from the doorway. Then, without saying anything, he strolled up to them, his hands deep in the pockets of his soiled flannels, and looked them up and down. They blanched beneath his gaze, and shame and terror flowed over them like a hot liquid. "H'mph!" Plunging his hands deeper into his pockets, he leant forward on his toes, and then kicked out at the shavings. The dust rose thickly, and Chorley began to cough. He coughed for a long time, until the exertion brought the tears streaming down his cheeks. Mr. Burdock eyed him with irritation.

"When you've finished that—that pandemonium, Chorley, perhaps you'd be good enough to explain what you two are doing in the carpentry-shed."

Regaining his breath, Chorley told him that he had been excused games by Matron.

"Oh, yes." Mr. Burdock was palpably annoyed at hearing this. "You seem to have been off games for a very long time. What's the matter with you?"

"I've a cough, sir."

"A cough! Tck-tck!" He made a sound of ironic commiseration. "That's too bad. You must take care of yourself. You never know what might happen—pneumonia, pleurisy, T.B."

"Yes, I have had pleurisy," Chorley said with quiet dignity. He fixed an unflinching gaze on Mr. Burdock's face.

"And you?" Mr. Burdock turned away from this scrutiny, as if from a light too dazzling for his eyes. "What's the matter with you?" he asked Hugh.

"Nothing, sir."

"Nothing?"

"No, sir."

"Then perhaps you'll be good enough to tell me why you didn't go up to the cricket-field. You saw my notice, I suppose? . . . Well—did you?"

Hugh hung his head. "Yes, sir."

"And you deliberately disobeyed it?"

"Yes, sir."

There was a silence until Chorley put in: "It was really my fault, sir. I persuaded him." Mr. Burdock's face was white and strained; he was trembling with rage, and his small eyes had a red tinge in them.

"I was not asking for your opinion," he snapped vindictively. His hands moved restlessly in his trouser-pockets. "You're both slackers," he said. "You're nasty, idle little shirkers! I've had my eye on you both. I'm up to your snivelling little tricks. I know that supercilious attitude of yours. You're snobs—you're both bloody snobs." A yellow scum appeared at either side of his mouth; he was screaming at them in shrill hatred. All courage seemed to drain out of them as they listened to him. "And what did you come here for? Eh? Eh?" He thrust his face towards Chorley. "What have you been doing here?"

"Some carpentry, sir."

"Carpentry!" He gave a high-pitched, hysterical cackle. "Carpentry!"

"Yes, sir." Chorley backed against the wall.

"Carpentry! I see, I see. So you cut nets, not to go to the cinema or to the sweet-shop, but to do some carpentry? That's it, is it?" His voice was rough with sarcasm.

Chorley nodded. "It's true, sir."

"You're a scruffy little liar!"

Chorley pointed at the theatre. "We were working at that, sir. It's a theatre."

"You weren't working at that."

"Yes, sir." In a despairing effort to be believed, he added: "You can ask Mrs. Corabel, sir. She knows all about it."

The suggestion was a fatal one. All the masters were agreed that Mrs. Corabel interfered too much in the affairs of the school. Moreover, she and Mr. Burdock had had a feud of long standing. She had seen him strike a boy, and the matter had been reported to her son-in-law.

"I don't care a damn about Mrs. Corabel!" Mr. Burdock screamed. "What I do care about is that you two have been fiddling about when you ought to be on the cricket-field. You've no public spirit.

It's people like you who let down the school." Speechless with rage, he looked about him until his eyes fell once more upon the theatre. "A theatre!" he shouted. "You cut games for a theatre! And what kind of theatre is it, anyway?" He went up to it, and suddenly put out a foot. The theatre toppled over backwards; there was a dry splintering of wood. He gave another kick and the whole thing buckled inwards.

Both boys stared in horror at the ruins of their project. Then Chorley gave a sob: "You've spoiled it, you've spoiled it all!"

"It wouldn't have lasted a minute anyway. That'll teach you not to take French leave."

"You've spoiled it. I hate you, I hate you!"

Hugh gripped his arm, afraid that his words might drive Mr. Burdock to some fresh act of destruction. But he need not have troubled. Mr. Burdock's anger had spent itself, leaving behind a residue of shame and remorse. He was too graceless a character to do more than bluster his way out of the situation; he would never admit that he had lost control of himself.

"Don't be a fool," he said to Chorley; there was no longer rage in his voice, but only a peevish obstinacy. "It was your own fault. It would never have worked. You can mend it in a jiffy." He retreated from one defence to another. Still speaking, he hurried out of the shed.

Chorley went to the theatre and attempted to raise it; but as he did so the proscenium-arch came away in his hands. He flung aside the splintered piece of ply-wood: "It's ruined," he said.

"We can mend it."

"We can't. It's ruined, ruined!" Kneeling among the shavings, he pressed his knuckles to his eyes and began to weep and cough at the same time. Hugh tried to put an arm round his shoulders, but he wrenched free. "I hate him, I hate him!" he sobbed. "I'll kill him!" The tears flowed from under his hands, and dry excruciating sobs shook his whole body. "I'll kill him," he repeated in an abandon of grief. As he opened his mouth to say the words, saliva ran out and fell on to the dust at his feet. It was threaded with scarlet.

CHAPTER XXIV

The next day, Chorley was in the sick-room; Hugh was disconsolate. It was raining outside, the big drops hissing on the shiny leaves of the laurels which flanked the paths outside the school-room. He stood at one of the windows after prep and watched the evening close in, premature and grey. Three boys behind him were making paper aeroplanes. They spoke in shrill, falsetto voices, and one of them threw his aeroplane so that it hit Hugh in the back. "Zoom! Bang! Crash!" he yelled. They all clapped their hands and laughed.

"Oh, shut up!" Hugh said angrily.

Mr. Burdock passed through the school-room, a ping-pong bat in one hand, a ball in the other. He put the ball on the bat and patted it four or five times into the air as he walked. "Oh, sir!" one of the boys exclaimed in admiration. Mr. Burdock turned and scowled.

"Burdock is a swank," someone remarked at Hugh's shoulder. It was Clarry, a podgy boy with dimples, who was devoted to both Hugh and Chorley, and possessed no other qualities than an extreme good nature. Hugh did not answer, and he queried: "What's bitten you?"

"Oh, nothing."

"Like one?" He held out a bag of sweets in a grubby palm.

Hugh shook his head. "Go away, can't you?"

Clarry put one of the sweets into his mouth, and all at once Hugh felt sorry for having spoken so roughly to him.

"Burdock'll catch you with those sweets," he said.

Clarry giggled. "I bought them last parents' day. Try one. Go on. They're darned good."

Again Hugh shook his head, and a silence fell between them. The rain was lisping into the water-butt outside the window; one of the maids, with a green oilskin umbrella, darted down the drive with a pile of letters clutched against her breast.

"She'll miss it," Clarry said. "It's gone six. I suppose they'll have to wait till morning."

Hugh turned from the dimming light of the evening to the rosy face behind him. "Can one write to people in the sick-room?" he asked.

Clarry shrugged his shoulders. "I don't know. Never tried. I don't see why not. . . . I say, you're not going to write to Chorley, are you?"

Hugh nodded. "I think so."

"I'll write too!" Then seeing Hugh's look of exasperation, he said hurriedly: "No, I won't. It's silly for too many people to write. But you can give a message for me. You will, won't you?"

He followed Hugh as he went to his locker and fetched a pen and paper. Hugh sat down at a double desk, and Clarry perched beside him. The pen moved over the paper.

"What are you saying?" Clarry asked.

"Oh, nothing."

"I say, you do write quickly. I can never think of anything. That's nearly a page already."

"Don't talk so much."

Clarry fell silent. He watched Hugh as he covered half a dozen sheets of paper. Mr. Burdock came back through the class-room, still carrying the ping-pong bat. As he passed Clarry, he gave him a playful smack on the head with it. "Oh, sir!" Clarry looked up at him, grinning, and yet with tears welling from his eyes. After Mr. Burdock had passed into the other room, he murmured: "Swine!"

Hugh was looking pensively out of the window, his pen raised above the sixth sheet of note-paper. "How should I end?" he asked.

"Oh, I don't know. 'Yours sincerely,' I suppose."

"That sounds unfriendly."

"When I write to my brother, I say 'Lots of love.' I expect you like Chorley much more than I like my brother. He's awfully stuck-up—my brother, I mean."

Hugh wrote "Lots of love" above his signature. He paused.

"No kisses?" Clarry asked jocosely. Seeing Hugh hesitate, a smile about his lips, he urged: "Go on—just for fun. Why not?"

Hugh made a neat row of four crosses. As he looked down at them they seemed childish and he felt irritated and ashamed. If it hadn't been for Clarry he would never have put them in. "Must you breathe down my neck?" he asked. He raised his pen to scratch out the crosses and then stopped himself, realising what a mess it would make. He gave Clarry a push, so that he toppled off the edge of the desk on to the floor. "Oh, go away," he said.

Clarry hoisted himself to his feet; he was trying to grin, but there was hurt in his eyes. His grey suit was thick with dust from the floor. "See you later," he said. He sauntered off, whistling, his hands in his pockets.

Hugh felt miserable. He had not wished to be rough with Clarry; he was the only person with whom he could now talk freely; he was good-natured, and since he would never seek revenge for any slight, it made his own conduct all the more shameful. It was almost dusk outside. He could not see the rain any longer, but he could hear it, falling past the windows with a melancholy, swishing noise. Only one of the three boys with the paper aeroplanes was now left; he was playing with a yo-yo in silent absorption, the reel spinning outwards and then whirring back for many minutes at a time. It was getting cold, and without the light he had difficulty in re-reading his letter. He suppressed a shiver as he turned back to the first page.

Going over the sentences that he had written, he was all at once filled with hopelessness. He had said none of the things that he had wished to say. He folded the sheets and stared down at them. He thought of the days ahead, of waking each morning with the bed empty beside him, and of doing without Chorley's company through meals and games and lessons.

"When's your bath-night?" a voice cracked out from the door-way.

"Who, sir? Me, sir?" It was Mr. Burdock.

"Yes, you, sir. When's your bath-night?"

"Wednesday, sir."

"Wednesday! And what day of the week is it?"

"Sorry, sir!" He hurried to his feet, scooping up his writing materials.

"You're ten minutes late. Get a move on." Mr. Burdock went out.

Rage jagged inside him. He stared through the open door at Mr.

Burdock's retreating figure; his hand closed round the ink-pot as if to hurl it after him. Then his brief mood of defiance left him. He felt defeated and alone, and he wished that Clarry were with him. Why had he sent him away?

He unfolded his letter and wrote at the bottom of the last sheet: "Come back soon. I miss you terribly." The words seemed to detach themselves from the rest of the letter with a pensive urgency.

He wrote daily after that. The first night he was afraid to ask the Matron to deliver the letter for him; but she slipped it into the pocket of her starched apron without question, and even smiled at him. She was a severe but not unkindly woman. "Is he better?" Hugh asked, taking courage from this first success.

"He's comfy."

"Will he be up soon?"

"I expect so."

"How soon?"

"What questions you do ask! I don't know how soon. It all depends. . . . Now, run along and don't worry me any more. I won't forget your letter."

As he wrote each evening, he poured out all his emotions— his loneliness, his dislike of Mr. Burdock, his desire for Chorley's return. There was no single event of the day which he omitted to mention. He wrote as if he were talking to Chorley; his pen raced over sheet after sheet of paper, making a thick wad of manuscript which could barely be slipped into one envelope.

At first there was no answer to his letters. He was disappointed, and ventured to Matron: "He didn't give you anything for me, did he?"

"Heavens, no. He's not allowed to write yet. I write his letters home for him."

"But he reads my letters?"

"Oh, yes. He seems to like getting them."

The next day, as he was going up to the cricket-field, he heard a window being opened above him and there was a low whistle. He was late, and there was no one else about. He looked upwards, and at the same moment a note fluttered towards him and landed on one of the rose-bushes. For a moment he saw a face and an arm which he recognised as Chorley's, and then the window slammed shut again.

It was a brief note, scribbled in pencil on the back of one of the sheets of his own letter. He held it in trembling hands, and read it over and over again; the relief and pleasure were exquisite. Chorley said little—the food was wizard, he was not supposed to write, he hoped to be back soon. The signature was merely "B. Chorley." But it was enough to have heard from him. He tucked the note into the pocket of his flannels and raced up to the cricket-field.

That evening his own letter was even longer than usual; he wrote from a full heart, urging Chorley to be certain to write again —he would stand under the window at the same time every day. He wrote the old postscript: "Come back soon. I miss you terribly." The words looked even more urgent than before; they made him feel uneasy without knowing why.

When he gave the letter to Matron it seemed to him that her smile was somehow different from what it had been on previous occasions; it was a slow, lingering smile, which made him feel that for some reason she felt pity for him. Usually, she smiled in brisk and friendly fashion; now there was a tinge of sadness; and she smiled only with her mouth, not with her eyes. Her eyes were grave, even stern.

That night he thought of that smile of hers. He wondered what it meant. It gave him a vague pang, and his uneasiness when he had read those words "Come back soon. I miss you terribly" was now strangely intensified. He had difficulty in falling asleep, and when he did he dreamed his old dream of the tunnel.

CHAPTER XXV

The boys were all falling into line before going into lunch. They made a crocodile round the four walls of the school-room, chattering, giggling and pushing each other. Mr. Burdock, who was standing in the centre of the room, brought his hand down sharply on a bell. "Silence!" he called. Hands in pockets, he began to read out the roll-call.

Before he had gone through more than a dozen names, Mr. Baldstone entered the school-room. A retired army officer, he had a neatly-clipped moustache and wore tweeds. The two men talked together in undertones, while the boys lolled against the walls, whispered and shuffled their feet.

Hugh felt faint with hunger; there had been kidneys for breakfast, and since he did not like them he had put them surreptitiously on to Clarry's plate. He wished that Mr. Baldstone would hurry up. Giddy and sick, he leant against the boy in front of him.

"Craddock!"

The sound of his name, spoken in a rough, official voice, made him jerk to attention. Then, in his confusion, he wondered if he had imagined it.

"Craddock!"

"Yes, sir." It was Mr. Burdock.

"Why can't you answer the first time? We all want our lunch."

"Yes, sir." He knew that the answer was a foolish one, but could think of no other. One or two boys tittered.

"The Headmaster wants a word with you." Mr. Baldstone was waiting in the doorway. The shadow of the lintel fell across his face, making it seem dark and strange and somehow intimidating. He raised a hand and beckoned to Hugh; then, without saying anything further, he turned on his heel and walked towards his study.

In the hall, Mrs. Baldstone stopped him. She was wearing a hat and coat, and Hugh heard her say: "I'm getting the car out. Do hurry or we'll be late." She glanced at Hugh with what seemed to be both curiosity and repulsion.

He followed Mr. Baldstone into the study. "Shut the door." He shut it. "Sit down." He was facing Mr. Baldstone across the high desk, which was littered with papers. There was a smell of tobacco and furniture polish in the air; it aggravated his nausea, and he gripped the leather arms of the chair in which he sat. There was a cumbrous green satin shade on the lamp beside him; flies crawled over it, and buzzed on the ceiling.

Mr. Baldstone was gazing at him. It was a grave, steadfast look which Hugh associated with doctors. And as he gazed his hands raised a pile of letters which had been lying out of sight on the desk before him. Hugh watched the hands, fascinated as if by a conjurer.

"I wanted to speak to you about—these. . . . You know what they are?"

"No, sir."

Mr. Baldstone brushed a fly away from his face with a gesture of irritation. The room seemed uncomfortably hot and crowded with furniture. "They're the letters you've been writing to Chorley. Remember?"

"But what . . . what . . . ?" His eyes had begun to prick and ache with staring at them.

"But what are they doing in my study?" Mr. Baldstone put in for him. "That's the whole point. I—I happened to see one of these letters. It—interested me." His lips twitched in what might have been a smile, and he flushed slightly. "You mustn't imagine that I normally go round reading the letters of you boys. As you know, there's no censorship of letters at Frimley Towers. We don't believe in it. It was just by chance that I saw your letter. I was visiting Chorley in the sickroom, and while I talked to him I happened to see it lying open on the window-sill. I saw your signature, and some crosses . . . some kisses." He paused, and his hands unfolded the topmost of the pile of letters.

"There," he said. He held it out to Hugh. The blood mounted to the boy's cheeks as he once more read the postscript: "Come back soon. I miss you terribly." The thought that Mr. Baldstone had read that message which voiced his inmost wish, horrified him; he felt utterly exposed.

"I told Chorley that I wanted to read the whole of the letter. I must say that it rather sickened me." He looked critically at Hugh. "I suppose you know what was wrong with it. You do, don't you?"

"Wrong with it? No, sir."

"Good heavens, man! The whole tone . . . it was nauseating. Boys don't write to each other like that. It was the sort of letter that might have been written by—by a schoolgirl. Those kisses at the end—that postscript. . . . You do see what I mean, don't you?"

"I don't think I do, sir."

Mr. Baldstone rose to his feet. "Look here, I don't want to have any argument from you." He went to the lamp and shook it, to frighten away the flies. "You can take my word for it that that letter was not the sort of thing that one expects to read in a boys' school. It was namby-pamby—sentimental . . ."

The door opened at that moment, and Mrs. Baldstone put her head round. "Aren't you ready yet?"

"Just a moment."

"Oh, do hurry."

"All right, dear. All right!"

She went out, and he continued: "After that, I gave Matron instructions that all your letters were to be brought direct to me. They only confirmed my first impression. They were thoroughly morbid and unhealthy. In particular, this last letter of yours. . . ." He pulled it out. "Your whole attitude seems to be wrong. There was one passage which decided me that I must speak to you at once—*at once*. That's why I had to have you in now. Mrs. Baldstone and I are going away for four days. . . . You know what I'm referring to?"

"No, sir."

"I'm not surprised," he retorted acidly; "There are so many things in it which might call for comment. But I was thinking of this." He cleared his throat, and began to read: " 'That beast Burdock hit Clarry with a ruler this morning . . .' "

"I remember, sir," Hugh put in.

"I simply can't have that sort of remark bandied about the school. You've no right to comment on the behaviour of the masters. It's insolent. It's impertinent. It destroys all discipline."

He continued in this strain, concluding: "I'm not going to punish you. But I warn you. I shall be watching your conduct in the next few weeks. You must realise that you occupy rather a special position in the school. I'm making allowances for your education to the tune of sixty pounds a year. I expect something in return for my money. When I took you on, I explained to your uncle that you would only stay here just so long as I was satisfied with your work and your conduct. Do you understand that? Do you?"

At that moment Hugh burst into tears. He clutched the polished edge of the desk and bowed his head onto his hands. He heard Mr. Baldstone draw his breath in sharply, as if in exasperation; then he spoke with an attempted gentleness: "There's no need to 'blub' about it." He used the schoolboy 'blub' because he imagined that it sounded friendly. "If you're willing to turn over a new leaf, I'm willing to forget all about this." He picked up the pile of letters and threw them into a drawer. "You can go now," he said. "I've told Simpson to put some lunch aside for you."

Still weeping, Hugh rose unsteadily to his feet. Mr. Baldstone patted him on the shoulder. "Now let's have no more of this morbid nonsense. Eh?" A kind but unimaginative man, he was shocked at having so easily reduced Hugh to tears. He put a hand under his chin, and raised his face to the light: "You must learn to be a man," he said. "You're growing up. Men don't cry . . . or write silly letters like that. Be a man!" He pushed Hugh out into the corridor with a hearty slap on the back.

Instead of going into the dining-hall, Hugh shambled down the corridor which led on to the garden. The tears flowed ceaselessly. He felt frightened yet rebellious; he did not understand in what way he had really offended Mr. Baldstone, and the mystery oppressed him like some great weight thrust between his shoulderblades. There had, of course, been the remarks about Mr. Burdock and the other members of the staff—he could understand Mr. Baldstone being angry at them—but he knew that there was some misdemeanour which he had committed far worse than this. He remembered the adjectives Mr. Baldstone had used when alluding to it: unhealthy, morbid, nauseating, namby-pamby. But what had occasioned this plethora of epithets? He could not imagine. It seemed that, in some curious grown-up way, the fact that he and Chorley were friends had angered Mr. Baldstone. Why shouldn't they be friends? Was that unmanly? It was at this point that he felt rebellious. He could not believe that it was wicked for them to like each other.

The noon sun came off the gravel in a white glare; there was a loud thunder of bees in the holly-hocks on either side of him. The heat and the noise of the bees made him feel giddy and sick once more. He had been misunderstood, utterly misunderstood. Dragging his feet over the scorched gravel, self-pity swept through him, an annihilating wave: it brought with it a strange feeling of tranquillity and pleasure. His tears flowed effortlessly now, and he was utterly abased.

"Hugh! Hugh!" Someone was calling his name. "What's the matter?" Mrs. Corabel was seated at the open window of her room, a lunch-tray before her. Hugh had passed, so abandoned to his grief that he had not noticed her.

"It's nothing," he sobbed.

A kinder but less understanding woman would have pursued him with questions. Mrs. Corabel merely called out: "Why not come up and talk to me?" He shook his head. "I'm feeling rather depressed, too. It's a long time since you came to see me. It's lonely up here, by myself."

Put like that, the invitation became attractive. "All right," he said, blowing his nose and attempting to smile at her.

She made him eat most of the lunch that was on her tray. At first he refused, but she urged him: "Go on. I don't want it. If I send back a full tray Cook gets in a huff. She thinks I'm choosey." She gave a sigh. "I have enough rows here without that. . . . Oh, I'm so sick of them all," she said, as if to herself. "I wonder how much longer I can stick it."

"You wouldn't leave here?"

"I don't want to. I've nowhere else to go to. But it may come to that, in the end." She looked round the room at all her small possessions.

His mouth half full of food, he cried out in distress: "Oh, don't leave here, Mrs. Corabel. Don't leave here. You're my only friend now."

She looked at him tenderly, and one of her ugly, crooked hands closed on his. For a moment their eyes met. "It's nice of you to say that. We are friends, aren't we? . . . You know, I come more and more to believe that that's all that matters in life—'the marriage of true minds.' The atoms are, in themselves, dull, senseless things, but when they touch each other, they strike off eternal sparks." She was muttering to herself now, and he did not know what she

was talking about. Yet in some fashion, she had confirmed him
in his rebellion against Mr. Baldstone. The enemy were still the
enemy. "Manliness" was not all.

CHAPTER XXVI

He had had confirmation from Mrs. Corabel; yet when he next
saw Chorley, nearly two weeks later, he felt ashamed and uneasy
in his presence.

It was the mid-morning break. He shuffled along the paths
in the garden, his hands in his pockets. In the ha-ha there were
great, straggling bushes of lavender, and he snatched a branch and
pressed it between his fingers. It was a cool smell on that hot morning. "Look out!" A cricket-ball shot over the wall, and the stem of
one of the bushes was snapped in half. The two boys responsible
climbed down into the ha-ha and agitated whispers passed between
them.

"We've broken it."

"It's all right."

"It won't grow again."

"Yes, it will." Clumsy hands attempted to straighten it.

"I told you it was broken."

"Oh, shut up! No one will know it was us."

Hugh moved out of ear-shot; the sun was making his head ache.
He stood awhile watching Coppard and another boy play French
cricket together. Coppard looked up at him and scowled, and he
scowled back. His hair had been bleached white by the sun, and his
bare throat and fore-arms were brown against his flannel shirt. He
bowled over-arm and got the other boy out. "We said no bowling
over-arm," the boy exclaimed sulkily. "Rot!" "I'm not playing if
you cheat." "I didn't cheat."

All at once they were fighting. Hugh watched them as they
rolled over and over each other; then he turned away. Small bubbles of heat seemed to be exploding inside his head.

As he walked the path which flanked the masters' garden,
someone called his name. Chorley was looking over the hedge. He

was grinning, but his face seemed wan and meagre. "I say! I was hoping I should see you. Matron told me not to leave this seat. Are you all right? You look fine. I didn't really have too bad a time in the sickroom. . . ."

He, at least, felt no restraint. But Hugh was tongue-tied and embarrassed. It was as if he were confronted with a stranger. His face hot, the blood thumping in his ears, he stared down at the gravel of the path.

"Why don't you come over?" Chorley suggested.

"I'd better not." Boys were not allowed in the masters' garden.

"Oh, no one will see you. They're all guzzling in the common-room. Anyway, there are bushes right round this seat. Come on!"

Hugh hesitated. "It's risky."

"It'll be all right."

In the end he went round and joined Chorley. The seat was placed in an arbour of syringa-bushes; they gave off a sweet, heady smell, overpowering to the senses.

Chorley grasped both his hands. "I was standing on the seat when I was talking to you," he explained. "But I'm not really supposed to be on my feet at all. Let's sit down."

The touch of Chorley's fingers had jolted him like a blow in the stomach. He sat down beside him and, wishing for something to do, picked a branch off the syringa. He held it to his nostrils, and while he listened to Chorley's excited chatter, he breathed in the scent. It nauseated him, and yet he felt he could not stop. It was a hot, dry smell, unlike the lavender; it was more a taste than a smell.

At last Chorley fell silent. He had become conscious of the restraint which now existed between them; it frightened him, and he wondered why he had been so long in noticing it. Faced with such situations, adults are quick to improvise; children lack the technique. Miserable and baffled, they both sat staring before them at the frothing mass of the syringas.

What had happened? Why could they find no words to say to each other? Whose fault was it? Hugh knew that it was his. But he could see no way out of the impasse; his will seemed to have been stunned, even as his senses were stunned by the perfume from his fingers.

"What's wrong? Is anything up?" In desperation Chorley forced the issue.

"No. Nothing." Panic seized him; he felt hot with shame. His whole spirit seemed to put up a last resistance, while he blinked dizzily at the white blooms before him. He thought he was going to faint or be sick. . . .

Instead, he told Chorley of his interview with Mr. Baldstone. As he told him, he tore off the petals from the branch which he had plucked; like confetti, the wind blew the fragments all about them.

"I wondered why you'd stopped writing. . . . Oh, but it's ridiculous." Chorley became indignant. "Anyway, he's no business to read other people's letters. Nosey-parker! . . . I suppose it was all pretty beastly, having him tick you off and everything."

Hugh nodded. There was no longer any need to say anything. When words came, he would speak them: that was as it should be. It is only when there is an insecurity in personal relationships that words for their own sake become needful. There was no insecurity now. A crisis had been overcome; and their success in overcoming it had been due to Chorley's courage, not his own. He acknowledged that debt with gratitude, and with love.

Part III

SWITZERLAND

CHAPTER XXVII

It was half-term. Matron came round the dormitories with a school-list. First, she read out the names of those boys who would be going home for the week-end: there were various instructions for them—they must change into clean underclothes and remember to take their tooth-brushes. Next, she read out the names of the pathetic remnants who always stayed behind on such occasions. There were boys with parents too far away to come for them; there were boys without parents; there were boys whose parents could not be bothered. At the end of this list, she read out Hugh's name.

He and Chorley looked at each other in consternation.

"There must be a mistake," Chorley said. "Go and ask her."

"Shall I?"

"Of course. Go on."

Hugh pulled on a pair of trousers and followed her out into the passage.

"I say, Matron!" he called after her.

"Yes?" There was much to be done, and she did not wish to stop.

"Matron, you did read me out on the second list, didn't you?"

"I really don't know," she said irritably. She looked at her list: "Yes, that's right. Why?"

"I think there must have been some mistake. I'm going out to-day. Chorley asked me."

"There can't be any mistake. I had this list from Mr. Baldstone." She glanced down at it again, and then held it out to him. "No, you're down for the picnic. You can see for yourself."

"But Chorley asked me to go home with him——"

"I can't help that. You must speak to Mr. Baldstone about it. It's nothing to do with me." She saw the look of distress on his face, and softened: "I suppose you've had your permit?"

"Permit?"

"You know you have to get a permit from your parents or guardian before you can go out with another boy."

"Yes, I know that." He had written twice to Uncle Kingsley; but though the letters had been answered, there had been no mention of half-term.

"And it hasn't come?"

"I'm sure it'll come this morning," he said desperately.

"Well, if it does come, you can go. But if it doesn't. . . . It's a rule, you know."

"It *must* come. I've written twice for it. I can't think what has happened." He was on the verge of tears.

"It's not really so bad, staying behind," she said in a brisk, yet kind voice. "You'll have lots of fun. A picnic in the woods. . . . Mr. Burdock has arranged it all. I happen to know that there's cold chicken for lunch, and you're going to play rounders."

"But I want to go home with Chorley," he pleaded.

She lost patience with him. "I must get on," she said. "You must speak to Mr. Baldstone about it. It's really none of my business."

Mr. Baldstone repeated what had already been said. If there was no permit, he could not go out. "It's a matter of responsibility," he explained. "I can't make any exceptions." He, too, was fussed by his many duties, and he added maliciously: "In any case, are you certain that Lady Chorley really wants you to go home with her son?"

Hugh had not considered the question. He hung his head and made no reply; Mr. Baldstone had implanted a doubt in his heart.

"Who invited you?" Mr. Baldstone pursued.

"Well . . . Chorley."

"Exactly! . . . I bet he never even consulted his mother. She probably doesn't know about it. Is she expecting you?"

"I suppose so. That is . . . I'm certain Chorley must have told her."

"You don't know boys as well as I do!" Mr. Baldstone laughed. But it was half-term, and everyone must be happy. He patted Hugh on the shoulder: "It's going to be a grand picnic. Bathing, rounders, birds'-nesting . . . I envy you. What a day to go up to Town! Mrs. Baldstone insists on dragging me up to a concert."

Hugh went and told Chorley. "Of course Mum knows about your coming. Silly old fool: I wrote and told her, and I've got her letter here saying how pleased she'd be."

"I can't think why Uncle Kingsley didn't send the permit."

"Forgot, most likely."

Hugh was not sure. "It'll be a beastly picnic," he said.

"Oh, don't worry. Mum will put it all all right."

Hugh shook his head gloomily. "It's a rule, you see. You've got to have a permit."

Nothing Chorley said could cheer him. They stood together at one of the school-room windows watching the cars crunch over the gravel and halt at the front door. Most of them were large, expensive vehicles; the arrival of anything cheap or shabby aroused the derisive comments of the onlookers. The parents also came in for their share of criticism. Hugh wondered wryly what would be said of the relatives if they ever came to visit him.

It was melancholy seeing the cars draw up, the parents embracing the reluctant boys, the chauffeurs punctiliously opening and shutting the doors, Mr. Baldstone chatting to the more influential of the visitors, and the final departure through the school gates. Jealousy, contempt and self-pity filled his heart. He even felt angry with Chorley, because in a few moments he, too, would run out and be whisked away. He was alone, and there was a certain pride in being alone.

Chorley was looking at him. "Don't worry," he said. "It'll be all right."

Hugh shrugged his shoulders, and at the same moment he heard his name: "Craddock! Anybody seen Craddock?"

It was Mr. Burdock, in a white Aertex shirt and khaki shorts; his legs thus revealed seemed strangely thin and hairy. "Come on, come on!" he said to Hugh. "What are you doing? I've been looking high and low for you. You know you were supposed to be in the changing-rooms at half-past ten. Drawn your lunch rations yet?" In spite of his irritation, he too was speaking in a tone to match the festivity of the occasion. He brandished his walking-stick: "You haven't woken up yet. You can't come out for a picnic in those clothes. You're holding us all up. Buck up, man! Buck up, buck up!"

"Craddock's coming home with me, sir."

"What's that?"

"He's coming home with me, sir. My mother'll be here any moment now."

"That's the first I've heard of it." He, too, had a list which he produced from his trouser-pocket. "No, no," he said. "It's down here. Craddock's to come on the picnic. Look!" The list was thrust at them. "Anyway, it's too late to back out now. We've picked up teams, and Craddock's with the Blues."

Chorley continued to argue with him. During this discussion, which was to decide his fate, Hugh stared listlessly out of the window. He said nothing, and hardly heard what passed between the two others. A strange apathy had enveloped him; sooner or later they would reach some conclusion, and then he would accept it. He saw Coppard stroll out to an empty Daimler, give a few brusque directions to the chauffeur, and then disappear into the back. He saw Clarry scramble into the dickey of a Morris Cowley, where two girls were already seated; he raised a hand and waved to Hugh, and everyone in the car began giggling.

"Come along, Craddock!" The voice was sharp and authoritative and Hugh knew that Chorley had lost. With a shrug of the shoulders, he followed Mr. Burdock down the stairs into the cloak-room hearing Chorley say at the same time: "But she'll be here any minute, sir—any minute." He sounded tearful.

"Shorts, cricket-shirt, gym-shoes!" Mr. Burdock seated himself on one of the lockers opposite him while he undressed. "Quick! Quick!" Hugh put his shirt on back-to-front and one of his gym-shoe laces broke. Mr. Burdock heaved a sigh: "You're all thumbs. I've never seen anyone so clumsy. . . . Have you got your lunch?"

"No, sir."

He rose wearily. "I'll get it."

He returned with a package wrapped in grease-proof paper. "What on earth have you been doing all the time that I've been away?"

"Doing up my shirt, sir." Although it was a warm June day, his teeth were chattering.

"Got any bathing-drawers?"

"No, sir."

"Never mind. You'll have to bathe in your birthday clothes." Hugh flushed with shame. Mr. Burdock gave him a playful tap on the bottom with his walking-stick: "Quick march! Hurry! Hurry!" Hugh stood hesitating: "Well—? What's the matter now?"

"I want to go to the lavatory."

"You'll have to wait."

"I don't think I can, sir."

"Oh, God! . . . All right, all right. Get on with it. Go on!" Hugh could hear him walking up and down on the concrete outside the lavatory; his footsteps rang out, and the sound of them had the effect of making him even slower than he would normally have been.

When they went out into the yard behind the changing-rooms where the other boys were waiting for them, a groan went up. "Craddock! Craddock!" they jeered at him. "Trust Craddock to keep us waiting." One of the boys had a length of rubber tubing in his hand, with which he hit Hugh on the back of his neck. "That's enough, Melton," Mr. Burdock reprimanded him. "Leave him alone." The masters were not meant to countenance bullying. But he was at pains to look the other way when another boy surreptitiously pushed Hugh into a rose-bush.

"Come on, chaps!" Two by two, they wound their way round the back of the school-buildings and cut across the garden. Hugh, who had no one to walk with, found himself beside a boy called Müseler; he was a German and he was supposed to smell. Neither of them said anything to each other. Hugh walked with downcast eyes from which he knew that the tears would soon trickle.

"Hi, there! Stop!" Mr. Burdock had halted the crocodile. Hugh shuffled to a standstill with the others; he did not speculate on the cause of their halt.

The boy in front turned round. "Phew!" He held his nose. "Shall I tell you something, Müseler?" The German boy flushed but made no answer. "There's an amazing whiff of cheese round here. I wonder what it can be. Don't you?"

Hugh listened dully to this conversation. At each sally, there were derisive peals of laughter. The boy in front had begun pinching Müseler, who was short and fleshy: "I believe you're turning into a woman, Müseler. Look at your bosoms. Does that hurt?"

"Craddock!" Someone was again calling his name. Wearily he looked backwards in the direction from which it came.

"Yes, sir?" It was Mr. Baldstone.

"Fall out, Craddock. Lady Chorley's here, and she's just putting a call through to your uncle. . . . All right, Guy." He nodded in Mr. Burdock's direction, and the crocodile moved on. "Of course, I don't know whether your uncle will be in; I don't know whether he'll give his permission. Anyway, we must wait and see. If the answer's no, I'll have to take you to the picnic in my car. . . . Come along in."

Hugh followed Mr. Baldstone across the garden. Although he did not really believe that his uncle would allow him to go out with Lady Chorley, he could not help feeling a certain excitement. "You must remember to thank Lady Chorley," Mr. Baldstone told him over his shoulder. "Trunk calls in the morning are very expensive. . . . Not that Lady Chorley has to worry about money," he added with a touch of pride. "Still—it's very good of her to go to so much trouble on your account."

The first thing Lady Chorley did when she appeared from the telephone was to greet Hugh: "Hello!" she called. "How are you?" She shook his hand vigorously.

"Is it all right?" he asked.

"Is what all right? . . . Oh, yes, right as rain. Your uncle was a bit sticky at first. I don't think he quite trusted me—probably thought I wanted to kidnap you. But I got round him." She gave a clear, ringing laugh.

"Splendid!" Mr. Baldstone put a hand on Hugh's shoulder; he made a point of being affectionate to the boys in front of parents. "You're a very lucky young man. Very, very lucky. . . . Aren't you?" he prompted.

"Thank you very much, Lady Chorley," Hugh got out.

"It was nothing."

"Oh, but it was," Mr. Baldstone corrected her. "I think it was wonderful of you to go to all that trouble."

"Hugh and I are friends," she put in quietly.

"You must change back into your clothes," Mr. Baldstone told Hugh. "That is, if Lady Chorley can wait. Matron has packed your suitcase for you."

Hugh raced into the changing-room and flung off all his clothes. It was a strict rule that nothing should be left lying about, but for once he did not bother. He kicked off his gym-shoes so that they hurtled across the floor. At that moment Mr. Baldstone came after him: "All well?" he queried.

"Yes, thank you, sir."

"Er . . . I can't remember . . . Did you draw a picnic lunch?"

"Yes, sir." The grease-proof packet was in the trousers of the shorts which he had just removed.

"Well, I don't suppose you'll want it now, will you? Shall I take it?"

Hugh gave it to him, and he smoothed the grease-proof paper with both hands. "Better not to waste it," he explained.

Chorley and a borzoi were seated in the back of the car. "Lovely fellow," Mr. Baldstone gushed. He drew one of the silken ears through his fingers. "How old is he?"

Either Lady Chorley did not hear the question or she could not be bothered to answer. "Hop in!" she called to Hugh.

As the car swept out of the gates both Hugh and Chorley looked back. Mr. Baldstone stood waving at them, a grin on his face, and for some reason the spectacle sent them both into peals of laughter. It was many minutes before they could control themselves.

Their first halt was at the village sweet-shop. Chorley and Hugh both chose gob-stoppers—sweets the size of billiard balls, which changed colour while one sucked them. "Revolting," Lady Chorley said. "You'll get one stuck, or you'll choke, or something." But she bought them as many as they wanted. At home, Aunt Megs had forbidden him to eat them; she said that they were "vulgar."

They had their lunch in London. At the restaurant, each of

them was handed a menu, and the joints were trundled round on trollies by men in tail-suits. They were allowed to choose whatever they wanted, and the meal concluded with vast glasses piled with pink ice-cream, cream, fruit, and strawberry-jam.

They drove on, through the country now, until they came to two great gates of wrought iron with a cottage set beside them. "Home at last!" Chorley exclaimed. He leant over in the car and kissed his mother's cheek. A man had come out of the cottage and the gates clanged back. He touched his cap as they drove past him, and Chorley called out: "Hello, Parsons."

It was a Queen Anne house, but certainly not the best that that period achieved; a wing had been added on, and also a great deal of unnecessary decoration. Sir Denvers preferred it so. A boy of fourteen or fifteen sat out on one of the lawns reading a book. He looked up as they passed him and waved languidly. "That's Alan— he's my cousin," Chorley explained. "He lives with us during the holidays. His father and mother are in South America. It's his half-term also." A number of dogs ran out from the porch, barking at them; but when they saw who it was they leapt on to Chorley, licking his face and almost throwing him off his balance.

"Show Hugh his room," Lady Chorley said. "He's in the Blue."

"Oh, Mummy!" Chorley protested. "Couldn't we sleep together?"

"Well, if you'd rather . . ." she smiled.

Chorley looked at Hugh. "It would be much nicer, wouldn't it?"

"Oh, yes."

At tea, which they ate out in the garden, Lady Chorley asked them what they wanted to do with themselves. "Let's go riding," Chorley suggested. "Hugh can ride Kitty."

"Can he?" Alan, who had said nothing so far, put down his plate of cake. He was a slight, missish boy, with glasses and a stoop; he wore immaculate flannels, and drank his tea with a slice of lemon in it.

"You don't mind, do you?" Chorley asked.

"Yes, I do. You're always borrowing Kitty. When Noel Griffiths rode her, she was lame for a whole week. I don't like having strangers ride her. It makes her mouth so hard."

"Hugh's every bit as good a rider as you are."

"I don't care whether he's a good rider or not. I don't want Kitty ridden."

"Dog-in-the-manger!"

"I'm not a dog-in-the-manger!" the other protested, his mouth full of cake. "How would you like it if someone you'd never met before came along and borrowed your pony——?"

"Boys, boys!" Lady Chorley pacified them. "Hugh can ride Teddsie."

"Oh, can he really, Mum?" Chorley exclaimed excitedly.

"If he thinks he can manage him. . . . But I do think it's rather selfish of you, Alan." Alan turned away from them, pouting.

"Teddsie's a super horse," Chorley explained to Hugh. "He's Mum's own. He's an Arab, and he's a wonderful jumper."

"You'll have to take Godden with you," Lady Chorley said. "I can't have you boys out with Teddsie alone."

"Oh, please, Mum!"

She shook her head. "No, really, darling. I'm responsible for Hugh."

"Responsible!" Chorley exclaimed. They had so often heard that word; it had a forbidding sound, and was always used by grown-ups to excuse their fussiness.

It was a memorable ride. Alan joined them, in black riding-boots and a canary sweater; Hugh had borrowed some riding-breeches off Chorley. At first Godden, the groom, would not allow them out of his sight; but when he saw how easily Hugh managed Teddsie, he gave in to them. Hugh led the way, and neither of the others, on their Welsh ponies, could keep up with him. Strength and courage seemed to come to him out of the horse. They careered over a rough meadow, the clods flying behind them, and then down through a spinney, their hooves pounding the blue-bells into dust. He felt a wonderful exhilaration; he was at last alive.

At the end of the spinney there was a low hedge, and a ditch beyond it. Without hesitating, he gave the horse the office; there was a second of mingled panic and excitement as he crouched low and felt it rise beneath him. Oh good, good! He had cleared the hedge, and he could hear Chorley behind him.

A cry rang out. The horse swerved as he tried to stop it; looking over his shoulder, he saw Alan kneeling on the ground, with Kitty a few yards away from him. He hurried back: "Are you all right?" Chorley was dismounting.

"I'm quite all right, damn you!" He was groping in the ditch for his spectacles. His breeches were plastered with mud, and his eyes, exposed now, were brimming with tears. "Get on!" he shouted. "I'll follow in a moment. What have you stopped for?"

"We thought you might have hurt yourself." Hugh said.

"Oh, don't be such a bloody swank!"

"Come on, Hugh!" Chorley called. Alan had got to his feet and was putting on his glasses. He climbed into his saddle and whipped the pony savagely, making her rear and prance.

Hugh and Chorley rode abreast now; Alan had left them, cutting off down a lane. "He's like that," Chorley said. "He hates not being able to do things well. He's awfully stuck up—he's at Eton, you know. I'm supposed to be going there, too. Where are you going when you leave Frimley Towers?"

"I don't know. It depends if I can win a scholarship."

"I hope we don't have to separate."

"So do I."

"Oh, well—don't let's talk about it. It's such a long time yet."

They dismounted by a stream and rested, their horses cropping the grass. The water flowed leisurely between banks that were covered with sallows and willow-herb; the willow-herb was strung with a cotton-wool substance which stuck to their hair and clothes. Far away they could hear a hay-cutter at work; at that distance its din blended with all the other sounds of the late afternoon—the birds, the plock-plock of the water against the bank, their own voices, and the champing of their mounts.

Lying deep in grass, Chorley murmured: "Oh, it's wizard being home."

"It is nice here, isn't it?"

"I suppose I'm terribly lucky. I've been born here, and all this belongs to the family. I'd never really thought about it before. And one day it will all be mine . . . and yours," he added on an impulse.

"Mine?"

"Of course. We're friends, aren't we? We must always share things."

Hugh did not argue with him. He knew that there would come a time when this offer would be disregarded; he had lost all confidence in the future, knowing it to be a treacherous ally, rich in promises which it never fulfilled. But it was a pleasant make-believe; he almost accepted it. Acceptance was easy, lying beside Chorley on such an afternoon.

When they had got back to change for dinner, Hugh saw that a dinner-jacket had been put out for Chorley. "Are you going to wear that?" he asked.

There was a moment's hesitation. Then Chorley answered lightly: "Oh, no. It's too hot. I shall just wear my school suit."

"Don't mind about me."

"It's not that."

Hugh was not deceived; momentarily the incident saddened him. Chorley was not a snob and he was not a snob, but however much one regarded it, money had a power of its own. There would be many such difficulties, and no doubt they would be able to surmount them as tactfully as they had surmounted this one. But that most jealous of gods would always attempt to separate them.

Alan met them in the passage; he was, of course, wearing his dinner-jacket. "Haven't you changed yet?"

"I'm not changing," Chorley said.

"Why the hell not?"

"Because I don't want to."

Alan looked at them both, his lips twitching in a derisive smile; then he went on ahead of them.

Sir Denvers had returned from the House. He was a tall, powerful man, many years older than his wife. He spoke in a soft, beautifully modulated voice about things which were incomprehensible to the two boys. He seemed a little heavy and lacking in humour, and there was a trace of weariness in everything that he did or said. It was a weariness admirably controlled, until Alan attempted to argue with him on some point of politics. Then he snapped irritably: "You don't know what you're talking about."

"I do. We learnt it in form last term."

"Do you think something picked up from a fourth-form master can be accepted as an argument?" he asked his wife with ponderous irony. "Don't be such an ass, Alan. You young people think you know everything."

Alan's face went crimson with rage and shame; as soon as dinner was over he excused himself and retired to his own room. "You must try and be more tolerant to him, darling," Lady Chorley whispered.

"Tolerant, be damned! Insufferable little prig!"

"He's at that age. Most boys pass through it."

"Well, let him pass through it. At the present he seems to have got stuck."

He gave a dry, humourless laugh and went into his study.

There was a fire lit in the drawing-room and the butler brought in coffee. Chorley sat on the arm of his mother's chair. "Play for us," he said.

"Oh, darling. I'm so out of practice."

"Never mind. Play for us."

She went to the grand-piano and they stood on either side of her. Hugh watched her fingers moving deep in the satin of the wood; it was like a reflection seen in water, shimmering slightly. The curtains had not yet been drawn, and outside the great windows the park lay empty in the last rays of sunset. She was playing an odd little piece; it seemed to consist of one simple phrase, repeated over and over again. But somehow it united them, and drew them closer to each other. Even the garden, as it dimmed and faded, seemed to be leaving them to themselves. Under the tranquil arch of evening they were utterly reconciled.

The door opened. "Miriam, I simply can't get on with that report. You must stop playing."

"Must I?" she asked simply, like a child.

"You can play any other time when I'm not here."

"Oh, very well. It was for the boys, that's all."

"I'm sorry. But there's so much to be done. I can't concentrate."

"Never mind." She shut the lid. When he had gone, she turned to Hugh: "My husband doesn't like music. I think he considers it rather childish of me to bother with it." There was an edge of bitterness in her voice which shocked him profoundly. It struck him for a moment that she was unhappy; then he dismissed the thought.

The next morning he and she were alone together. "My husband's going to drive Brian over to the dower-house to see his grandmother," she said at breakfast. "I'd suggest your going with them, but she's a very old lady now and bedridden—you know how it is. You'll have to put up with my company for a short while."

Sir Denvers looked up at her over the *Observer.* "Aren't you going to church?" He had just returned from early-morning service.

She coloured slightly. "Not to-day, dear."

"As you wish." He shrugged his shoulders.

As if in extenuation, she turned to Hugh: "We've a new vicar. He used to be an actor, and he's very popular with the whole parish. But his sermons are so theatrical." Sir Denvers made a noise from behind his paper which was either a cough or a short laugh. She broke off: "What's the matter?"

"Nothing." He crackled the pages as he turned over. They all fell silent, oppressed by the atmosphere of unspoken enmity.

When the others had gone, Hugh sat with her in the drawing-room. She was making a bead-bag and Hugh offered his assistance. She gave him the tray on which the various coloured beads were placed in small compartments, and he picked out the colours she wanted and threaded them for her. It was a finicky job, but he soon got used to it. Already half her pattern was completed; it showed a unicorn in a wood, and it delighted him. She had made it up out of her own head. The unicorn's horn was gold, and the trees glittered all about it, with leaves which were like bells of green glass. One hoof pawed the ground, its head was lowered.

At first they worked in silence, but as he got used to the task they began talking. Without seeming inquisitive, she got him to speak about his life in India. He described the house to her, and Hetty, Luchmann, and his pony. As his mind returned to the past, he remembered many little things which he thought he had forgotten; he told her how, when they had mangoes, he used to make a pig out of the stone, by sticking in used matches for the four legs and then drawing an eye and a snout in ink.

"There's white hair on a mango-stone. It's just like a pig's hair."

She was astonished by the clarity of all this visual detail. "How well you remember it all!"

"Yes, and do you know, it's funny, but I feel that I shall always remember it. I shall remember it after I have forgotten everything that has happened since—except coming here, of course, and one or two other nice things."

She was touched by the compliment. "You must come here often. I'm glad Brian has you as a friend. Before he went to school he had so few friends. I thought it might be my fault—we did so much together."

"He's very fond of you."

"Perhaps too fond. That's the trouble with only children. Brian's everything to me, and I can't bear the thought of losing him. He'll grow up, and he'll want to break away—that's only natural. It's all right for him: everything lies before him, and of course no woman should stand in her son's way. But it is rather sad for us mothers. We grow old, and it's seldom that we can find any substitute; so even though we know it's wrong, we cling—we can't help ourselves. I've made up my mind that I shall let Brian go without any fuss, but it's easier said than done. A mother's love can do so much harm." She saw that his cheeks were flushed, his eyes lowered. "I expect you miss your parents terribly. But though it's an awful blow to find yourself all alone like that—so awful that I can't bear to think of it—perhaps one day you'll see that you've got some good out of it. Independence is the most difficult thing in the world to achieve, and you've achieved it very early. . . . Do you mind our talking like this?"

"Of course not." He had felt panic when she had first begun to speak of his affairs; but her subdued and kindly voice gave him reassurance, and now he took courage from her words. He saw that there is no disaster in the world which cannot be minted into a fresh coinage, if only one has the fortitude.

"I expect you miss India very much?"

"Yes, very much. It's awful to say this, but do you know, sometimes I think I miss India itself more than the people—more than Hetty or Luchmann or even my father and my mother. I hate England," he added simply.

"Isn't that only because you've been unhappy here?"

"Perhaps," he pondered. "I don't know. It seems so cold here— even in summer it seems cold. I can't explain what I mean, but the sun always seems so far away. And the cold seems to have got into the people. It seems to be inside them."

She nodded her head. "I know what you mean. I feel that also. My home isn't really in England. My people came from Baghdad, and though I was born here and I've spent all my life here, I don't really belong. The English have so many qualities—and so many *important* qualities—that perhaps one shouldn't complain. But they do lack something which one can't help missing. Perhaps, as you say, the climate has got inside them. . . . Being a foreigner, I get impatient with their qualities—honesty, integrity, truthfulness. It's stupid, of course, because those things are more important than mere warmth. Or are they?"

At that moment Sir Denvers came in, and she busied herself with her work, the blood slowly mounting to her cheeks and forehead, as if they had been discussing him. He looked over her shoulder at the bead-bag; he made no comment.

"What do you think of it?" she asked in the end.

"Very pleasing. But what a waste of time! You've been working at it nearly six months."

"One has to do something," she said in a strange, controlled voice.

He stared at her for a moment, and then moved away. As he did so, his hand brushed the tray of beads at which Hugh was working, and it tipped over on to the carpet. "Damn!" The beads lay inextricably jumbled; some had trickled under the settee and, as he took a pace forward, he trod on others with a brittle, crunching sound.

Lady Chorley had gone on her knees with Hugh, and together they began to scoop them up and empty them back on to the tray. Sir Denvers stood watching them for a few seconds. Then, he exclaimed: "Oh, leave it, Miriam. I'll get one of the servants."

It was a command, and they both rose to their feet once more as his hand pressed the bell.

CHAPTER XXVIII

Somehow they had failed to set off at the hour that they had intended. Chorley had wanted to show Hugh the organ in the small, private chapel, and the chauffeur had been slow in bringing the car round. "Haven't you gone yet?" Sir Denvers exclaimed, coming out of his study to find them in the hall.

"Well, of course not, dear. Brian hasn't said good-bye to you yet."

He looked at his watch. "You really mustn't break school rules like this. You'll only get them into trouble. Rules must be obeyed—I wish I could convince you of that."

"Say good-bye to your father, Brian."

Both the boys were worried. In the car, Chorley kept urging his mother: "Oh, do go faster, Mummy. Can't you go faster?"

"I expect old Baldstone will be in a fearful bait with us," Hugh said gloomily.

"I'm taking all the blame," Lady Chorley put in. "There's nothing for you two boys to worry about."

When they arrived, at eight o'clock, the school was deserted. There was thunder in the air. From upstairs they could hear distant shouts and laughter; there was a dry crackle, and a few drops of rain hissed on to the laurels. The drive smelled of stale petrol-fumes. Under the black sky, desolate but with the lights burning, the school seemed a strange and forbidding place. A pang of fear came to the hearts of both of them.

Lady Chorley went to Mr. Baldstone's study and they followed after. "I'm afraid we got rather delayed," she explained to him. "It was all my fault and I'm truly sorry."

"Oh, that's all right." He brushed away all excuses with a sweep of the right hand. "Did you have a good week-end?" he asked the two boys.

"Oh, yes, sir," they chorused.

"I bet you did. . . . Well, I think you'd better get along upstairs as soon as possible. Tell Matron that you've seen me." Obedient to his command, they turned to file out of the study, when they heard him laugh: "And aren't you two young men going to say good-night to your hostess?"

Hugh saw Chorley hesitate, ashamed to kiss his mother before Mr. Baldstone. But she went forward and kissed him on the cheek, as if they had been alone together. "Good-night, darling." Next she turned to Hugh; he put out a hand for her to shake. But she bent down, and he, too, felt her lips on his cheek. "Good-night, Hugh."

They both made their way through the deserted school-rooms, their footsteps ringing out with unnatural loudness. In the library, one of the servants had swept up a small heap of rubbish which he had then forgotten to collect; they walked round it, glancing down at the cigarette-ends, sweet-papers, and grey rolls of dust. It brought a renewed sadness, intensifying the mood which had fallen on them when she had kissed them both.

Someone was walking towards them; although they could not see who it was they could hear the slow shuffle of his feet, and then the crash of something being knocked over. As they came into the main school-room they saw Mr. Burdock clumsily pick up and straighten a chair. He looked up at them as if he did not know who they were; he was swaying slightly on his feet.

They both felt afraid, expecting that they would have to explain their lateness to him. "Well?" he said, scrutinising them as they halted before him. They noticed that his face was covered with small bubbles of sweat and his eyes were blood-shot. "Did you have a good half-term?"

"Yes, thank you, sir," Hugh replied, tremulously polite. "Did you, sir?"

"No—bloody!" The unexpectedness of the words and the emphasis with which he said them made them both jump. "You've heard about the picnic?"

"No, sir. We've only just come in."

"Wilson broke his arm. It was my fault. We were climbing trees and the bloody little funk wouldn't go any further. I told him he'd have to, and he fell. I've been well and truly hauled over the coals."

Neither Hugh nor Chorley realised what was the matter with him, until he added: "And now I'm drunk. I'm sozzled." They both stared at him in horror and repulsion; they were still at an age when drunkenness and cigarette-smoking seemed to them the depths of vice. He put a limp hand to his forehead: "Christ, I feel awful! I think I'm going to be sick."

They shifted uneasily towards the staircase, but at their first movement he swayed after them: "You're not going, are you?"

"Mr. Baldstone told us to go straight to bed," Hugh replied, edging his way on to the first step.

"Don't go. I want someone to talk to. I want to talk to you both."

"But Matron will wonder what has happened to us——"

"Oh, damn. Matron! . . . God!" He belched quietly and sat down at one of the desks. "I forbid you to go upstairs. Orders is orders. I want you to talk to me and you must stay and talk to me." But even as he said the words, his voice trailed away and he buried his head in his arms.

They stared at him for a moment, fascinated. His whole body was shuddering, as if with ague; then they heard a sob. "Everyone hates me," he whimpered. "I'm so alone . . . alone."

Of one accord they ran up the stairs. But on the landing they turned back and looked at him. He still sat huddled up at the desk, but he was silent now; the shuddering continued. The naked bulb above him seemed to gleam unnaturally on the white flesh of his neck, and they could see, even from this distance, the scurf which powdered the shoulders of his blue suit. He sat in the empty school-room, which seemed much bigger now than when there were boys in it; hunched like that, in the first of a long row of desks, he appeared as no older than they themselves were. His grey socks were rolled down to his ankles, and between them and his trousers there was a rim of flesh.

As they left him and continued on their way up to the dormitories, Hugh exclaimed: "He was drunk! Did you hear? He said that he was drunk." He could not help being excited by so extraordinary a happening.

"I felt sorry for him," Chorley said in a subdued voice. "He looked wretched like that. He—he looked like one of us."

"Yes, didn't he?" All at once Hugh felt ashamed of his own shrill excitement. "It was beastly seeing him. I think he was crying, you know."

"It's funny. We've always hated him so much, and now we feel sorry for him."

"Shall we tell the others?"

"No," Chorley said. "We must tell no one." He looked to Hugh for confirmation, and Hugh nodded.

At the door of the dormitory they both stopped: "It's been a wonderful week-end," Hugh said.

"I think so, too."

From inside they could hear a din of voices.

CHAPTER XXIX

Two weeks before the end of the term, Chorley fell ill once more. They were rehearsing a play for their puppet theatre; it was a dramatisation of the Epic which they had been composing all that term, and the characters included the relatives, Mr. Baldstone, Mr. Burdock, and the rest of the "Enemy." Chorley was an admirable mimic, and on that afternoon he was elaborating his impersonation of Mrs. Baldstone. It was so funny that Hugh began giggling and before long Chorley joined in also. He tried to suppress his laughter so that he could continue with his impersonation, but this only made him giggle more.

Suddenly he began coughing as he laughed. He took a handkerchief from his pocket and pressed it to his mouth. Then he took it away, and held it out to Hugh in both hands. They stared down in horror, still flushed and breathless from their laughing.

"What is it? What's happened?" Hugh broke the silence.

"I don't know. It happened once before. The night of half-term. I didn't tell anyone. . . . Do you think I ought to?"

"Of course you must."

He folded up the handkerchief and put it in his pocket. "I feel afraid," he said.

"But why? It isn't anything serious. It isn't, is it?"

"I don't know. I don't expect so."

He went up to tell Matron, and Hugh did not see him again. All the next afternoon, Hugh had to play cricket, but when he came back for tea, Clarry, who had been excused games for some trifling ailment, told him that Lady Chorley had come down and gone off again. The news seemed more ominous than the visit of the doctor the night before, or anything else that had so far happened. Hugh wanted to question Matron, and yet feared to do so in case that, too, like his letters, might anger Mr. Baldstone in some inexplicable way. Anxiety made it impossible for him to do his work properly, and Mr. Burdock kept him behind after he had let the others out of a Latin lesson. He used his tongue on Hugh, but for once this weapon failed in its effect.

Hugh slept little that night, and the next morning went to Matron's room; she was reading a novel before the open window. "Yes?" she asked.

"Matron, I . . . I wonder if you could tell me what is wrong with Chorley?"

She closed the book, put it on her table, and then reached for her starched cuffs. "I can't keep on answering your questions about my patients," she said, not unkindly, but in a brisk matter-of-fact voice.

"I'm sorry, Matron. I just wondered . . . is it serious?"

"Now, don't you worry. He'll be all right. He's gone into hospital and in six months he'll be as right as rain."

"Six months!"

"Thereabouts." She had got some temperature charts out of a cupboard, and then produced a small glass tumbler which contained thermometers. She looked up, and seeing that he had not yet gone, she said: "Six months is not much. It'll be gone in no time. Now run along. I can't have you in here—that's the rule, you know."

It was the rule, and he obeyed it. But dismay filled his heart. Six months! As he thought of it, it seemed endless. He had only been ten weeks at school, and now he must live through a period three times as long as that before he again saw Chorley. But the days passed, the six months grew shorter in his mind; he became reconciled to the separation, and in the end he accepted it, as he had accepted so many other disappointments.

So the term drew to its close; they had exams and he came out top in them; he also won the Junior Essay Prize. There was an atmosphere of excitement in the school, and tuck-boxes had been brought out of the cellars to lie about the big school-room where the boys had their lockers. Hugh was going through the papers in his desk on the afternoon before the school broke up when Mr. Baldstone came into the school-room. Everyone fell silent, and two boys who had been milling together in one corner looked sheepish and tried to pretend that they were doing nothing. Mr. Baldstone looked about him.

"Oh, there you are, Craddock!" he exclaimed, catching sight of Hugh. "Lady Chorley's here, and she wondered if you could give her a hand with collecting all Chorley's belongings. You must know where his things are. Can you spare a moment?"

Hugh followed him on to the private side where Lady Chorley was waiting. "Hello, Hugh." Although her manner was subdued, she seemed pleased to see him. "I'm sorry to worry you like this. But I wanted some assistance. Can you possibly give me a hand——?"

"He's only too willing," Mr. Baldstone put in for him. "It's the least he can do after all the kindness that he's had from you."

"I shouldn't like his help for that reason," she snubbed him gently.

Hugh showed her where Chorley kept his books, and together they went through them and put them into his tuck-box. Behind them, a boy was chanting:

> "No more Latin, no more French,
> No more sitting on a hard board bench.
> No more spiders in my tea
> Making googly eyes at me. . . ."

As she stacked the books on top of each other, Lady Chorley seemed to be listening to the jingle. An exercise-book spun across the room and landed a few inches short of the wastepaper-basket. "Rotten shot!" Another book followed, and this time it reached its destination. The wastepaper-basket, which had once been a tea-chest, was piled high with crumpled sheets of exercise-paper, used books and blotting-paper black with age. Clarry stood beside it, and there was a tearing sound, as he ripped one exercise-book after another into tatters. He looked up at Hugh, and a grin spread over his stupid, kind face.

"You won't want to pack these school-books, will you?" Hugh asked.

"Oh, yes. They'd better go in as well."

"Will he be having lessons then?"

"Later . . . we hope."

Hugh looked at her in bewilderment. "Before coming back here, you mean?"

"I don't know if he will ever be able to come back here."

She saw Hugh blench, and at the same moment heard the old jingle:

> "No more beetles in my bath
> Trying hard to make me laugh."

She slammed together the two books which she was holding, so that a cloud of dust rose upwards to prick their nostrils. "Let's go out into the garden for a breath of air. This dust is choking me."

They walked over the smooth, shaven lawns and then down the ha-ha. A fresh breeze was blowing; there was a chill in the air which seemed autumnal on that midsummer day. The longest day was over, and for a moment they were conscious that already the sun was moving away from them.

They sat on a seat in the ha-ha, and Hugh began shivering; Lady Chorley drew her light coat closer about her. "No," she said, as if no time had elapsed since the last sentence she had spoken to him. "I don't think he'll ever come back."

"Is he . . . is he seriously ill, then?"

"I'm afraid so. Of course we have hope, we have faith—we must have, we must never lose them. Everything possible is being done for him, and there's no reason why he shouldn't get better and become as strong as any other boy." She had picked a twig off the lavender and was tearing it to pieces. All at once he was reminded of how, on another occasion, he and Chorley had sat together in the masters' garden and he had done the same thing—only, it had been syringa then. There were innumerable echoes if one had an ear for them. "Sometimes I feel frightened," she said. "Oh, Hugh, I feel so frightened. If only I could bear some of his suffering for him. He's no good at bearing pain—it's not his fault, he never has been. Some people are like that. Not that I'm much better . . ." she added wryly.

"Do you mean—he's in pain, then?"

"Off and on. Sometimes it's not pain, it's just discomfort. That can be worse. They have to do all sorts of horrible things to him—many of them don't hurt, but of course he hates them. My poor Brian!"

In a rush of self-pity, he said: "I'll miss him terribly." He spoke almost resentfully, because he thought that his own sorrow was being overlooked. He despised himself for this attitude, yet could not bring it under control.

"I know," she said, turning to him and placing one of her hands over his, "you will miss him." He looked into her eyes; they were full of compassion and tenderness. "I'm awfully sorry. And he'll miss you, I know he will. He's asked for you so often. When he's better, you must go and visit him. Perhaps you could spend part of the holiday with us. We mustn't lose touch—whatever happens, we mustn't lose touch."

They went back to the school-room and continued with the packing of the books. They worked in silence; all about them they heard shrill, immature voices; someone was whistling. There was an endless bustle and excitement. Suddenly Hugh saw that she was crying. Behind her veil the large tears trickled downwards. She did nothing about them, and he was too embarrassed to say anything to comfort her. One by one they went through the books and placed them in the tuck-box.

After she had driven off, Hugh went down to the changing-rooms and locked himself into one of the lavatories. He had discovered that this was the only place in the school where one could be certain of being left alone. He sat down on the seat and cupped his chin in his hands. Through the frosted window behind him the light came meagre and diminished.

It was strange; he could not cry, and there was a certain triumph in not being able to do so. Men did not cry, he had often heard it said at the school; and it struck him that perhaps he had now entered manhood. Yet tears would have helped. There was an abject pleasure in tears, which soothed all aches and fevers; tears were the soul's utter surrender and abasement, and after them there could be nothing more.

He wished to cry; he thought of Lady Chorley's tears and of Chorley himself; he thought of separation and death, and the indifference which is worse than either. Then he repeated to himself two words, "Never again, never again." They would make him weep if anything could. He said the irrevocable syllables many times. But no tears came.

In his loneliness, he decided to go and see Mrs. Corabel. It was several days since he had last seen her; he had been up to her room but she had always been out. He thought of her now with love and gratitude; it is the fault of the young that they must always either idolise or despise the old. He, too, had made this mistake.

She was kneeling on the floor, and all about her were littered books, letters, papers, knick-knacks, and photographs. She looked up at him and smiled; he smiled back, but as he did so he felt all at once afraid of her. She seemed remote from him, a stranger, and he wondered what he was doing in her room. There was an odd, unfocused expression in her eyes, and by a transference of the same image, her smile, too, seemed to be somehow out of focus. "Did you want something?"

"Yes. . . . May I come in and talk to you for a moment?"

"Come in."

She went on with her sorting of her papers, scrabbling with her fingers at snapshots that were yellow and blotched with age. She tore one or two of them across, and chucked them into the wastepaper-basket. But there seemed to be no method in the way she went through them; she churned them about, and picked from them whatever caught her eye.

Hugh waited; but when there was no sign of her asking him what he had come about, he began to mumble: "I'm feeling rather miserable, so I came to see you. You know about Chorley, do you?"

"Yes, I did hear something. I'm sorry." Without looking up at him, she continued to busy herself with the debris about her.

"His mother's just been down here. I spoke to her. She says he's very ill."

"Is he? Yes, I suppose he must be." Each sentence that she spoke, in a flat voice edged with what was almost irritation, seemed to take her further from him. He had the impression that he was pursuing her down a tunnel—the tunnel in his dream; her words did not come direct to him, but echoed along the walls and were subtly changed by them.

"He's not coming back," he said desperately. "Never. He's leaving the school."

Then, for the first time she looked at him. A wisp of white hair lay across the raddled cheek, and she held one of the faded snapshots in both hands. "Everyone seems to be going away. I'm going, too."

"You! Are you going?"

She nodded and went on with her work. "But why?" he asked. "Why?"

"They've told me to go."

She said it without sorrow or rage or any other emotion. The thought came to him: *She does not care!* This was the final wisdom or inanity of age—to move into a light so blinding that the atoms and their sparks seemed to be as one. It was an attitude which horrified him.

He said a few more words, and then left her, her eyes unfocused among the accretions and rubbish of her days.

CHAPTER XXX

He returned home, and found that Aunt Frances had now left the sick-room. Just as he had formerly been made to play bezique with her, so now she made him move her deck-chair when the sun came round into her eyes. They went for short walks together, during which she leant on his shoulder. The edge seemed to have been blunted off her personality. She lacked all incisiveness; she no longer appeared to be able to make up her mind, and if she thought that she had been slighted or overlooked, she became sulky rather than angry. Her voice had in it a perpetual note of whining; she could be easily flustered, and as easily pleased.

She no longer disgusted Hugh. He found that he pitied her. Even her greediness could do no more than arouse compassion in him. One morning, he had entered the dining-room before the gong had gone for lunch, and discovered her with the bowl of Devonshire cream held under her chin; she was helping herself from it, so absorbed that she did not see him. "Oh! You did give me a fright!" she exclaimed when she at last realised that someone was watching her. "I was just tasting this cream to see if it had gone off. It smelled rather queer."

"And has it?" he queried.

"Has it what?"

"Has it gone off?"

The question seemed all at once to fluster her. Her face became hot and red, and she stammered: "No—no . . . I don't think so. . . . This weather, you know. . . ."

He had wanted to laugh, not unkindly, but as grown-ups laugh at a child, indulgently and with no intention to wound.

She seemed to be fond of him. Each morning they read the Bible together. "You have a nice reading voice," she told him. "Perhaps one day you'll read the Lesson in church." He liked the stories, and she mistook this enthusiasm for religious fervour. She often went to church, taking him with her, and on one occasion she whispered during the hymn: "I'm going to faint, Hugh." He did not know what to do about it. She sat down and took some smelling-salts out of her handbag.

"Are you all right?" he asked.

Inhaling deeply, she murmured: "I think so. I'll feel better in a moment."

"Shall we go out?" he suggested.

"No, no." She sat through the rest of the service, and when at last they made their way out into the sunlit churchyard, she had to wait and tell all her friends of the occurrence.

As soon as Hugh returned from the school, he thought about

Ruby. That evening he walked over to the farm; he did not dare to go in and ask for her, but loitered at the gate, until her small brother appeared with a bucket full of chaff. Hugh called out to him.

"Hello," the boy said. He did not stop, but continued on his way to the stables.

"I say," Hugh shouted. "I want to talk to you."

"Haven't much time to spare," came the brisk retort.

"Oh, come on!"

The boy toddled towards him; he was even fatter than when Hugh had last seen him, and his hair was now greased down above his white forehead. "Well?" he asked.

"Is Ruby about?"

"No."

"Where is she?"

"Away."

"Is she coming back soon?"

"I don't think so."

He asked a number of such questions; but the boy was either unwilling or incapable of giving him any real information. He became sulky with Hugh, and at last began to walk off: "Can't wait any longer," he called out. "I'm very busy."

Hugh walked home perplexed and disconsolate. Truth to tell, he had not given a thought to Ruby all the weeks that he had been away; but now the desire to see her was very strong in him. He thought of her coarse hair, her strength, and the strange way in which she had kissed him at their last meeting. He felt ashamed that he had never written to her. What had become of her? Where was she?

At breakfast next morning, Aunt Megs let fall some information. Aunt Frances was still in bed, his uncle was reading his letters. "Kingsley?" she said. He did not answer and she repeated: "Kingsley?"

"Yes. What is it?" He did not like others to talk at breakfast. He, himself, sometimes read the news out of *The Times* between mouthfuls.

"I was speaking to Mrs. Jones yesterday. For once, she was at the W.I. meeting."

"That's a wonder."

"She really is rather slack. . . . She was telling me about Ruby. I'm afraid it's quite true what we heard."

"I can well believe it."

"She's in some sort of home. You know what I mean. Mrs. Jones can't understand it. It seemed to happen as soon as the child got to Birmingham. She just went from bad to worse."

"I never had a very high opinion of that child," Uncle Kingsley said. "I always said that she was a bad lot. That court-case—I never for one moment imagined that she was as innocent as she was made out to be. There's always some provocation in cases like that. But what can one expect? Look at the upbringing she had. It's a wonder she kept so long off the streets——"

"Sh, Kingsley!" Aunt Megs had realised that Hugh was listening to their conversation. She made a gesture in his direction, which she imagined that he could not see.

"You began the discussion," her brother reminded her.

"Yes, I know, I know. But there *are* certain things. . . . Do get on with your porridge, Hugh! You've hardly touched a mouthful. We can't keep the servants waiting all morning."

His uncle had cut open another envelope with his knife, and was now unfolding a stiff sheet of paper: "Your report, Hugh," he said. "H'mph, h'mph." As his eyes travelled down it, he made an odd snorting noise at the back of his nose. "Not too bad, not too bad," he murmured. Then he stopped: "What's this? 'Games: Could show more enthusiasm.'" He looked across the table at Hugh, as if in inquiry. "You know what that really means," he said at last.

"Really means?" Hugh echoed.

"It means that Mr.—" he looked down at the report for the name—"Mr. Burdock considers you to be a funk."

"I don't think so, Uncle."

"Yes, it does. Don't contradict, Hugh. It's a polite way of saying that you're a funk at games."

"I don't think I'm a funk," Hugh defended himself. "I'm just not very keen."

"Not very keen, eh?" his uncle said sarcastically. "Oh, that's different. I beg your pardon. . . . I'm afraid you may be becoming an intellectual snob, Hugh."

"Oh, no, Uncle." He was not certain what the phrase meant, but knew it to be something detestable.

"Oh, yes, Hugh. I'm afraid so, I'm very afraid so. You happen to be possessed with a fair share of brains. But that's no reason for looking down your nose at those fellows who are not as clever as you yourself are."

"I don't do that, Uncle."

His uncle gave him a smile of mingled patience and exasperation. "Listen to what Mr. Baldstone has to say. 'Tends to keep too much to himself. His form work is excellent, but there is a danger of his "losing the common touch." He must become more public-spirited and take a greater interest in the school.' . . . Well, there you are." He folded up the report as if he had proved his point conclusively. "Brains are not enough, Hugh. You'll find that out later for yourself. What one wants is Character. Character and—and—and Character," he concluded rather lamely.

When Hugh was next able to slip into the kitchen he asked Mona if she knew what had really happened to Ruby.

"Now don't you worry about that," Mona said briskly. "She's been a bad girl, and she's got what she deserved. Her only fifteen and all!" she exclaimed.

"But what did she do, Mona?"

"What did she do? Why, didn't she——?" She caught a warning glance from Cook. "You're too young to hear about that sort of thing, Master Hugh. Now no more questions. You take my advice, and don't you mention 'er no more."

Hugh did not mention her again; but often he thought about her, and a perplexed uneasiness made his heart heavy. Once or twice he dreamed about her. They lay close together, their fingers locked, and he could smell that warm, animal smell of hers.

CHAPTER XXXI

In the middle of the holidays they all went up to London for ten days. Aunt Frances had to have some treatment at one of the big hospitals; moreover, they had been fortunate enough to find a tenant for the house. It was for this reason that they usually stayed in town during the summer months; it was impossible to find a tenant during the winter.

They had rooms in a boarding-house in Earl's Court. Hugh had imagined that London would be exciting, but most of his days were spent in accompanying Aunt Megs round the shops or Aunt Frances round the Gardens. He preferred the Gardens to the shops; the shops were detestable, but in the Gardens there was always the chance that Aunt Frances would allow him to go off and play by himself for a while. She liked to sit on a bench in one of the walks laid out with shrubs and flower-beds; no dogs were allowed there and she disliked dogs.

On one such morning, she had told Hugh that he could go and sail his boat on the Round Pond while she read a book. "For only ten minutes, mind. We don't want to be late for lunch. . . . Shoo! Shoo!" She flapped the *Daily Sketch* in the face of a terrier which was straining forward to sniff at her ankles.

While Hugh sat on his hunkers beside the Round Pond, watching his boat veer round in an unambitious circle, he heard a voice beside him: "Good God! It isn't . . . ? It is! Hello, Hugh! How are you, old chap?"

It was Mr. Andy.

"I'm home on leave," he told Hugh, exuberantly. "And I'm married. You look well. You've grown. Tell me all about yourself."

Hugh felt shy and diffident. Mr. Andy seemed to have changed so much. His face had begun to sag, and though it was impossible, he seemed to have shrunk since their last meeting. He no longer emitted that irresistible vitality; it had simply become an affectation, like any other. But had he really changed? Or was it that he was seeing him with different eyes? Hugh felt angry. Time seemed to have played a shabby trick on him; his old friend had vanished, and a shoddy counterfeit had been offered in his place.

He picked his boat out of the water, and holding it so that it dripped on his shoes, he looked down at it. It was his last link with the old Mr. Andy. "Do you remember?" he said. "You gave this to me."

"Did I? By Jove, so I did!"

He had failed; the last link had snapped. Mr. Andy was dead also. This other person, in the grey suit baggy at the knees, and the battered trilby, gave a laugh which seemed to be forced out of him like a cough: "What a coincidence! I often wondered what became of you. . . . You heard about Mrs. Timpson?"

"No."

"Oh, she's divorcing Timpson. She doesn't mean to go back to him."

Hugh was not interested in the stranger, nor in the other strangers of whom he talked. "What time is it?" he asked.

"Ten to one."

"Oh, I must get back to my aunt. She said only ten minutes, and it's nearly quarter of an hour."

"I'll walk back with you."

"All right." He acquiesced without enthusiasm. He felt discouraged and bored in the presence of his old friend, and wished it were not so. For a moment, he wondered if it would be the same if he were to meet Luchmann or Hetty. It would not, he hastened to assure himself; but doubt nagged at him.

Aunt Frances liked Mr. Andy. It is easy enough to ingratiate oneself with invalids; one has only to show an interest in their health. He assisted her to her feet, and soon she was telling him those details of her malady which always revolted Hugh, however often he heard them. They turned slowly to the 'bus-stop, and there waited. It turned out that Mr. Andy was living in a private hotel only a few minutes' walk from their own.

"Do you like this part of the world?" Aunt Frances asked.

"Oh yes, I think so. It's cheap, and it's near the West End."

"I must admit that I'm very fond of Earl's Court—though it has gone down rather."

Their 'bus came, and Mr. Andy was quick to help Aunt Frances on to it. When they got off again, she smiled at him: "It's very good of you to be so attentive to an old woman like me. Nowadays, young men have no manners. Oh, but you've been in India—that makes all the difference."

Mr. Andy looked down at his feet. Then he turned to Hugh: "Well, young fellow-me-lad! When am I going to see you again?"

He put out a hand and tweaked Hugh's ear. "We must go out one afternoon. If that's all right for you?" he added to Aunt Frances.

"Oh, quite all right. I'm afraid Hugh finds life in town just a little boring. It's not like the country, is it? Not for children, I mean."

Two days later Hugh was shown into a sitting-room very much like the sitting-room of the hotel in which they themselves were staying, except that it was smaller and dingier and less full of people. Mr. Andy rose to shake his hand vigorously. "Welcome!" he exclaimed. "So you found your way all right." He indicated a woman who sat opposite him, knitting. "Meet the wife! I told you I was married, didn't I? Well, there she is!"

Mrs. Andy did not for a moment stop her work; she smiled at Hugh, and said "Hello" in a soft, slightly nasal voice. Her face was sallow, and the hair, which she wore in a small roll, was wispy and lacking in any real tint. Even in summer, her lips were chapped, and her broad nose was covered in unbecoming freckles.

"Sit down!" Mr. Andy said.

They talked for a while, and Mr. Andy laughed so heartily that his wife often had to tell him not to make so much noise.

"Sh, darling!"

"What's the matter?"

"Everyone can hear you."

"Let them hear me."

When she next said "Sh" he turned on her irritably: "Oh, do stop saying 'Sh' all the time. Can't a man have a decent laugh? One would think we were in a hospital ward."

Her face reddened, but she made no answer; for the rest of the time that they sat there her eyes were fixed on her knitting, and no word passed her lips.

It had seemed to Hugh that she was unnaturally fat, and on the 'bus Mr. Andy explained this to him: "We're expecting a baby next month. That's why my wife was a bit on edge. I don't blame her."

"You'll like that, I expect," Hugh said politely.

"Oh, rather!" But the exclamation lacked any real conviction. "Of course it means rather a scrape for us. And then there's the responsibility—it's no joke bringing a child into this sort of a world. But Vi's a grand pal; she'll stick by a bloke, through thick and thin."

They went to the Science Museum, and it became apparent that Mr. Andy knew every foot of it. "I often come here. It's a cheap way of passing an afternoon. Better than the cinemas by a long chalk." He had to show Hugh how all the demonstration models worked; and in his excitement with one of them—a steam-engine which ran round a circular track—he was unfortunate enough to jam the handle. He wrenched at it, pushed it and then began banging on the glass with the palm of one hand. Everything failed; he looked rueful. "We'll have to tell one of the johnnies, that's all. I've never had a thing like that happen to me before."

When the commissionaire had heard of the accident, he turned to Hugh: "You lads mustn't be so rough with the models," he told him, reprovingly. "They must be treated gentle like."

"It wasn't my fault——" Hugh began.

"I'm afraid it was me," Mr. Andy stammered. "The boy had nothing to do with it." There was a twinkle in the commissionaire's eye.

After they had finished their tour of the museum, they went to the A.B.C. for tea. Mr. Andy ordered sausages and mash, which Hugh ate dutifully, though he did not feel hungry. "Tuck in, tuck in!" Mr. Andy urged him, pushing across the cakes as soon as the sausages were eaten. "Oh, don't worry about that fork thing. Use your fingers." He bit into an éclair, and the cream ran down his chin.

As they walked home, they passed an ice-cream man. "Come on," Mr. Andy insisted. "Let's have one. . . . Hi, there!" he called.

"I don't really think I can manage an ice-cream."

"Of course you can. I know all about boys' tummies. . . . Two fourpenny-tubs, please."

"No, really, Mr. Andy——"

"Bob," he corrected.

"No, really, Bob——"

"Go on! Put that in your mouth."

Half-way through, Hugh had to say: "I'm afraid I can't eat any more of this. I shall be sick if I do."

"Oh, nonsense."

"What shall I do with it?"

Mr. Andy was momentarily angered. "Oh, throw it away," he said. ". . . No, don't throw it away. I'll have it."

But the ice-cream had already fallen into the gutter and splattered outwards. It mingled with the grime and dust; it was an ephemeral thing, and already it was melting.

For a while they walked on in silence; Hugh knew that he had annoyed Mr. Andy. The sight of the ice-cream lying in the gutter had made him even more ashamed than the irritation in Mr. Andy's voice. It was not the waste, but something more subtle that worried him, he did not know what.

"How do you like school?" Mr. Andy asked. "Enjoying it?"

"Oh—ye-es."

Honesty made him hesitate; but Mr. Andy had no ear for such niceties. "I bet you are!" he exclaimed. "You know, I do envy you. I'd give anything to be back at my first term at school."

"Would you?"

Once more an inflexion was lost on Mr. Andy. "Of course I would," he said. "No worries, no need to work if one doesn't want to. Money doesn't matter. The worst that can happen to one is getting six of the best. And think of the friends one has! One never makes such friends after leaving school—I don't know why. They were a grand crowd, my old friends, and I've lost touch with all of them."

They said good-bye outside Mr. Andy's hotel. "I won't ask you in," he said. "A lot of old fogies. . . . It's been grand meeting you, old chap." He wrung Hugh's hand.

"I hope the baby will be all right."

"Oh yes, I'm sure it will. I want a boy, that's all. If it's a boy, I don't care about anything else—it can be black, green, or khaki. I don't think I'd like to have a daughter. I'd never know what to say to her when she grew up," he added with embarrassed candour.

They said good-bye, and there was some talk of seeing each other again. But Hugh was resolved that that would never happen. "Best of luck!" He walked off with the words ringing in his ears.

As he walked up the Earl's Court Road, he had a sensation of relief and freedom; it made him stride along, whistling and swinging his arms. Mrs. Corabel had once read to them a Greek myth in which a boat is followed on its voyage by a host of ghostly presences. Wherever the boat goes, the ghosts follow after it, weeping and supplicating and stretching out their hands.

He thought of the story now, and of how the ghosts had at last been exorcised by the speaking of certain words.

CHAPTER XXXII

The next term had begun and was over. It had seemed interminable enough at the time, but looking back on it, on his first night at home, he was astonished to find that it had telescoped itself out of all recognition. He remembered its incidents as one remembers the confused incidents of a dream. Chorley, Mrs. Corabel and Mr. Burdock were all gone. Mr. Burdock had met with some obscure disgrace—drunkenness, was it? no one seemed to know—and he had heard that Mrs. Corabel was living with a sister in North Wales. Chorley was now in Switzerland with his mother, and he and Hugh wrote to each other—letters which Mr. Baldstone did not intercept.

Half-way through the term, Hugh had had a few days in bed; and from then on he had become one of Matron's "favourites." He knew the ignominy of this position, but there were too many advantages that went with it for him to wish it otherwise. He was delicate, she told him, and he was often excused games.

He won his form prize, he showed an aptitude for P.T., and he was now seldom bullied. Perhaps they had been right after all; it was just a matter of settling down. But what had he settled down into? He preferred not to ask the question.

On the third day of the holidays, he received a letter from Lady Chorley suggesting that he should go out to Switzerland to spend a week with them. She made it clear that they would pay all expenses.

"... Brian had a tutor but that's stopped now, so I've asked Cherrie—Miss Cheriton, his old governess—to come out here for a few months so that he doesn't get altogether rusty. You could travel out with her, and we have friends who would see you back.

"Do try and come if you possibly can. Brian is up now, and he feels the need for someone to play with. We so look forward to seeing you. . . ."

As he read the letter, during breakfast, his hands began trembling with excitement. Aunt Megs was watching him: "Who have you heard from, Hugh?" she asked. She pulled the empty envelope towards her. "It's a Swiss stamp, isn't it?"

"Yes. It's Lady Chorley." He felt himself shrinking as he made the effort to speak about the invitation. "Actually"—he cleared his throat—"actually, she—she wants me to go out there."

"Go out where?" Aunt Megs demanded.

"To—to Switzerland."

"To Switzerland! . . . Did you hear that, Kingsley?"

The pages of *The Times* rustled, and Uncle Kingsley looked round them. "What's that?" he asked. "I don't know why you chatter so much at breakfast."

Aunt Megs told him. They both began asking questions. How could he travel alone? Who would pay for the journey? How long was he going for? Hugh answered as best he could; but as he met each new objection, hopelessness descended on him. He knew that they would never let him go.

". . . We don't even know anything about this—this Miss Cherrie," his uncle was saying. "Who is she? Is she competent to look after you? You know what Continental travel is—anything might happen. . . . But that's not really the point. I object to this scheme on principle. Yes, principle." Hugh's heart became leaden as he heard the word; it meant that Uncle Kingsley wished to say something disagreeable. "For one thing, you'd be putting yourself so very much in their debt. You'd be accepting hospitality which you could never hope to repay."

"But they don't want repayment," Hugh put in.

His uncle raised a hand: "Don't interrupt me, please. They don't want repayment—of course they don't. But that's not the point. It would be bad for you to accept so much from them, and what's more, it would be bad for them." Hugh did not understand this argument, and his brows creased in perplexity. "Of course, you're too young to realise that. But you can take it from me—that sort of dependence is the one way to destroy all friendship that exists between people. It's deadly, utterly deadly. . . . Another thing," he added. "You may think it fine to have these grand friends of yours. But in the end they'll give you all sorts of expensive tastes which you can't possibly afford. You'll want to make the sort of splash that they make, and then you'll find yourself in difficulties. They belong to one sort of world, and you belong to another. It's better not to keep up with that sort of people. Choose your friends from those who live in the same style as you do—it's the only way. Otherwise you'll find yourself made to feel miserable and uncomfortable." This last argument voiced a fear which had often nagged at Hugh since the incident of the dinner-jacket.

"Don't you remember how you told Aunt Frances that you wished you could ride again?" Aunt Megs put in. "I'm sure that was only because you'd ridden when you went out with them at half-term."

"I was always against that outing," his uncle reminded him. "But you'd somehow got round Lady Chorley, and she rang up, and I was stupid enough to give in against my better judgment."

It was decided; he could not go. He could not tell them: "Yes. All that you say is true. But you've overlooked something. They're my friends, and our friendship is strong enough to surmount all such obstacles." Instead, he hung his head and sulked.

After breakfast, he went as usual up to the sick-room to read the Bible with Aunt Frances, who was bedridden once more. She, herself, read a few verses, but her voice became hoarse and she told him: "Now you read, Hugh." He had lost the place. He had been thinking of the journey which he would never make, and of the friends whom he would never see again. She told him irritably: "Third chapter, ninth verse," and he began in a dull voice, faltering at every long word in his effort to gulp back his tears.

"What is the matter with you?" Aunt Frances asked. "You usually read so well. You're making absolute nonsense of all this." He looked up at her, and she saw the tears glisten on his eyelashes. They had been reading the story of Absalom's death and she at

once imagined that he had been upset by it: "I know this is all
very sad, dear. But you must remember that it happened years and
years ago—hundreds of years ago."

He had leant forward in his chair, and buried his face in the
eiderdown. She heard him sob incoherently: "It's not that. It's not
that."

Scenes frightened her. All her life she had avoided them. She
disliked emphasis; life was full of it—noise, bustle, people wanting this, that and the other. If only the atoms would remain still,
instead of colliding together. "Hugh, Hugh! Stop, oh do stop!" In
panic, she looked around her, put a hand on his shoulder only to
withdraw it, and at last made up her mind to ring the bell.

But before she could do so, she heard him say: "I'm so unhappy,
Aunt Frances—so unhappy!"

"Unhappy!" What reason had he to be unhappy? Two weeks ago
she had been told that the cells were multiplying themselves with
such energy that no more could be done for her. "What are you
unhappy about?" she asked, with a faint awakening of curiosity.

He told her about the invitation. As the words choked out of
him, between sobs, she kept saying: "Yes, dear, yes. But do stop
crying. Do control yourself." The sight of his red face, streaming
with tears, filled her with agitation. She felt touched, obscurely,
within herself; and she did not wish to be touched. She had grown
used to having her disordered body subjected to every exposure
and indignity; but she shrank, in spiritual modesty, from having
hands laid on her soul.

When he had finished, she said in a flustered voice: "Well, of
course, it must be a disappointment for you, dear. But I'm sure
your uncle knows what's best. You must trust to his judgment . . .
yes, to his judgment. It's not as if there weren't a hundred and one
things for you to do here. You can have a grand holiday, without
going to Switzerland for it. Can't you?"

"But I'm so miserable here," he said simply.

"Miserable! . . . Miserable here! What are you talking about?"
He nodded his head, and she repeated: "What are you talking
about? What do you mean, Hugh? You're happy aren't you? Aren't
you?"

"No, Aunt Frances. I—I wish I was dead."

The words startled her, making her blench and tremble. "You mustn't wish such things. It's very wicked of you. God gave us life—God gave us . . ." She found she could not go on. She was horrified; all at once the phrase seemed meaningless and empty— had it always been so? In panic she hurried on: "But what's all this nonsense about not being happy?"

"It's true, Aunt Frances." The sobbing had ceased; he spoke in a perfectly flat, even voice, but the tears still rolled down his cheeks.

"You've no right not to be happy. It's most ungrateful of you. You don't seem to realise all that we've done for you. You don't seem to realise——"

"I do realise!"

Breathlessly, she went on: "It's been a sacrifice for us. We know nothing about children, we've never wanted any. We're not even well-off, and this illness of mine. . . . We've spent money on you. Of course we were glad to spend it," she added hastily. "We did it for your poor dear mother's sake. But you must see that it hasn't been easy for us. We've made our sacrifices, and it's cruel of you to turn on us like that and say that we've not made you happy. We have tried, Hugh, we have tried! I've been ill—you know that—and when one's ill one wants rest and quiet. But I've tried to do my little bit. I've had you up here to play cards with me—we've read the Bible together. Don't you see how ungrateful you're being? Don't you?"

He made no answer; she was appalled. As she had listened to her own words, they, too, had seemed meaningless and empty. She must not stop to think: "Have we ever denied you anything? Have we underfed you? Have we ever beaten you or maltreated you in any way?"

"No, no!" He was sobbing once more. "You don't understand. I shouldn't have minded that. One gets over beatings and hunger and all those sort of things. It's just feeling that one's not wanted. Oh, don't you see? It's feeling that no one wants one or cares for one."

"But we want you. We care for you," she protested feebly. One hand was pressed to her side; she was feeling ill.

Once again he shook his head, in a way which carried more conviction than any words. "I know that it was only because of Mummy that you took me. You felt it was your duty. You thought me a nuisance, and you wondered if you could get out of having me; but there was no way of getting out of it, so you took me."

"Hugh!" she exclaimed, scandalised. Then she stopped. It was true, all that he said. Suddenly she saw that they had done none of the things which they ought to have done. Shame and pity burst painfully from the recesses of her heart; her whole spirit felt exposed and raw.

His head was on the counterpane once more; he was beating on it with one fist. "I must see Chorley again. It may be my last chance. He's been ill, and—and perhaps he may die." He had been hysterical when he had said the words; but once said, they brought a chill of terror to his heart. Perhaps he may die. . . . "Oh, help me, Aunt Frances. Please help me. I must see him. He wants to see me—he's been terribly ill. . . . Look—you can see the letter. Look, it says here . . . Oh, Aunt Frances, make it all right. Please make it all right. He's the only real friend I've had since I left India. Oh, Aunt Frances . . ."

She put one arm round him and then the other. Without disgust, he felt her trembling wasted body; his nostrils filled with the smell of her dressings, and he heard her crooning to him: "Don't cry, dear. Don't cry. We'll fix it. I'll speak to them. We'll fix it somehow. We'll fix it. Don't cry, dear."

In the abasement of her soul, there was also triumph; she had at last seen the atoms move together; they had touched and their sparks lit up the night before her. "It'll be all right. Hugh darling, it'll be all right."

CHAPTER XXXIII

"Miss Cheriton!" Hugh called from the window of the railway-carriage.

Miss Cheriton stirred sleepily, took a comb from the breast-pocket of her suit, and ran it through her hair. "Yes? What is it?"

she asked with a touch of petulance; as she spoke, she yawned. There was a knot in her closely-cropped grey hair, and she had to tug in order to release the comb. "Well, what is it?" she repeated. The comb came out threaded with several strands of grey. She stared down at them angrily.

"Oh, look, Miss Cheriton! The snow . . . the sun!"

"Can't you be quiet, Hugh?" She glanced at the watch which dangled from her jumper. "It's barely eight o'clock. . . . Oh, what a night, what a journey!" Groaning, she pressed her head back into the leather upholstery, and closed her eyes.

At the border, a customs official had snapped the clasp of one of her valises; she had mislaid a book; there had been a wrangle with the porter because she had undertipped him, and she had over-tipped the car-attendant. Travel on the Continent was a disastrous business.

Alone at the window, Hugh stared at the countryside which revealed itself in the first light of dawn. He was entranced. It was a white, rounded world through which they moved; beside them the telegraph wires hung downwards in great ropes; bushes scurried sheep-like across his vision. Far away stood the mountains, and as he watched them the sun rose and they began to flush coral; they deepened, they became red, and heat seemed to come off them, as if they were smouldering. The whole countryside began to turn pink; it bloomed strangely, and it seemed to give off a radiation so that he threw off the rug which had lain over his knees. They passed beside a lake, frozen and desolate, and in it was mirrored the whole scene; it was as if a fire burnt beneath the ice.

Breakfast was brought, but still he stared out of the window. The pink glow faded, the sun rose. It rose, and it grew nearer; it moved above them now, it followed them, and the valleys opened to its presence. "Come nearer, oh come nearer!" The god had heard him, and he had come.

At the station, Brian—he was no longer Chorley—ran forward and grasped both his hands. "I'm so glad you've come. I was afraid that they'd say no."

"They jolly nearly did."

"Was it difficult, persuading them?"

"Awful. I'll tell you all about it later."

"There's so much you must tell me about."

They were all glad that he had come. When they were alone for a moment, in the hotel, Lady Chorley said: "It's wonderful having you here. Brian's made himself almost ill with excitement."

"He looks wonderfully well."

"Yes, doesn't he?" She snatched at the words eagerly, and then her face became grave once more. "But that means nothing. He is better, of course he's better—and yet . . . one never knows with this illness. That's what's so awful—one never knows." She moved restlessly in her chair, as if to shake off the thoughts which weighed upon her. "But I wanted to tell you, Hugh—you must enjoy yourself all you can, and not worry about leaving Brian to himself. He's not allowed to be very active, and obviously you'll want to ski and skate and go for long walks. There are three German children here—they're very charming—so for all those things you must join them, and I know Brian will understand."

"Oh, no, Lady Chorley. I want to do exactly what Brian does."

She tried to persuade him, but could not. His loyalty touched her. He joined Brian in his lessons every morning, and in the afternoon he rested with him. "This is called 'doing a horizontal,'" Brian explained. They went out on to the terrace which led from their room, carrying rugs, books, and hot-water bottles.

"Won't it be cold?" Hugh asked.

But his fears were groundless. As they lay full length in the wicker chairs, the sun hung above them, burning their face and hands and forcing them to put on dark-glasses. The three German children were ski-ing on a slope before them; they wore only shorts, and their bodies were brown against the tingling whiteness of the snow. "Like Indians," Hugh said. As yet they were inexpert with their skis, and they often toppled over, making the snow rise in dense clouds. From the terrace the two boys could hear their laughter and their friendly, guttural shouts.

The days passed. One morning they went for a walk to the English cemetery. It stood on the brow of a hill, beside the ugly little church, and all the time that they wandered over it, the wind blew up a snow which cut their faces and made their eyes sting. It blew with crude malevolence, the spot being exposed on all sides, and for a while the sharp powder hid everything from them—the road, the valley, even the sun. To escape from it for a moment, they sought protection in the church.

A woman was playing the harmonium in one of the bare aisles, and as they tip-toed past her, she smiled and coughed and nodded at them, all at the same time. "That's Miss Minnie," Brian whispered. "She's awfully plucky. Everyone says that she ought to have died years ago."

They went through another door, and for a moment the wind stopped. In the lull, they stood and looked at the crosses, some blown crooked, all weighted under snow. Brian went to one and stood before it. "Mr. Acton's buried there. He was my tutor, you know." He put out a hand and scooped away the snow.

"I didn't realise . . . I didn't know that he was dead."

"He was awfully nice. He was only twenty-two, and it was all so sudden. They said that he was getting better."

Hugh shivered slightly; the wind had begun once more, and the sand-like powder cut into him.

"It seems funny I . . ." he began. His lips were sore and numb; he could not continue.

"What? . . . People dying, you mean?"

"Yes."

"It used to make me terribly afraid—I mean before I fell ill or anything. I used to wake up sometimes in the middle of the night, and it was awful, thinking about it and knowing that there was no escape. Every second that passed seemed to bring it nearer. Even now . . ." Brian drew his scarf further over his face. "I was an awful baby, I suppose. After all, everyone has to die sometime. It doesn't worry me now—at least, not much."

They walked back into the valley, passing the pond where people came to skate. "Look!" Brian pointed across the blue sheen. "Do you remember I told you I'd met Coppard here? He's staying at the Majestic. . . . Well, there he is."

Skaters circled round and round the pond, and in the midst of them there moved a solitary figure. Terror and admiration filled Hugh's heart. From far up in the sky a handful of snow-flakes drifted downwards; they fell about Coppard, one by one, like petals, and through them Hugh saw his face, shut, remote and indifferent.

All at once Coppard caught sight of them. He ceased to circle with so much grace, and cut out briskly to where they had been standing. His face changed, and became normal, flushed and a little embarrassed. "Hello."

"Hello," they echoed.

They looked at each other. He wore a white fur cap and white fur gloves. There was colour in his cheeks, and his eyelashes glistened with tears from the wind. They talked for a while, and when they separated it was decided that they should see more of each other.

"He seemed quite different," Hugh said.

"Quite different. Everyone is different—away from school. Do you remember our discussing that with Mrs. Corabel? . . . I think he's lonely. I never see him with any other children, and I heard Miss Minnie tell another of the people in the hotel that his mother spent all her time with someone else's husband. It must be beastly for him."

"I'm glad we shall be seeing him again."

Coppard came to tea. As they ate it out on the terrace, they noticed that the boy who did odd jobs in the hotel was dragging dead laurel branches out of the wood-shed, and stacking them up in a heap in front of them. "What are you doing?" Coppard called over the railings.

In his abominable English, the boy told them that he was making a bonfire of the branches which were too small for use in the hotel as firewood.

"Let's help him," Hugh said.

"Yes, let's, let's."

They ran down and began pulling out the branches, dragging them or lifting them on to their shoulders, shouting to each other, laughing and churning deep furrows in the snow. Sometimes the leaves were dead and made a dry, scraping sound; sometimes they were still green and glossy, and buds had formed on them. The hotel-boy was pouring paraffin over the heap; he splashed it out generously so that it dripped downwards and stained the snow beneath. Then he set a light to it. "It's lit! It's lit!" they cried.

A tongue of flame shot skywards; there was a crackle and a sizzle; smoke rolled out towards the setting sun. "Quick! Quick!" Breathlessly they rushed to the shed, snatched at the branches and hurled them on to the flames. "Here, take this." Hugh's hand met Coppard's; he felt a thrill of pleasure and then he was joyfully flinging an old stump into the heart of the blaze. The three German children had appeared from somewhere; they took off their skis, and they, too, began to run back and forth, from shed to bonfire. The sweat ran down their chests and faces, and they shouted to the others, incomprehensibly, in their own tongue.

Now it seemed as if they were all circling round the bonfire. One of them broke away to fetch a load; he returned, and someone else left the ring. Exultantly Hugh carried the dark branches close to his face, and he could not help shouting as he hurled them downwards. "There!" It was a meaningless cry, but it expressed his mood of exaltation.

The flames cast shadows on the naked arms of the German children, on Coppard's face, and on the façade of the hotel. Round the fire the snow was melting in a circle; it melted, and they splashed about in the slush, making their legs muddy and stinging them with the cold.

At length all the rubbish of the last year had been burnt, and they stood silent in the gathering dusk, silent and motionless, and gazed into the heart of the fire. On one branch something small and red moved. An insect was it? A spider? Hugh put out a hand to snatch it from the flames. But already it had shrivelled, and was nothing.

The fire seemed to bloom and open like a flower; its petals unfolded, unfolded slowly, until at last they looked into its heart. There was a bluish tinge—like the sheen on blue silk—and then that, too, had vanished. The sight of it, for that brief moment, brought a pang to Hugh's heart; it troubled him, he knew not why, like the incident of a dream.

He gazed deep into the fire; perhaps it would appear again. His face was scorched, and his nostrils filled with the bitter reek of smoke. He shook off this new mood. "We must rake it together," he shouted. "We must rake it into a heap again. We must burn it all." His voice was loud and confident, and they obeyed him.

In the end, Miss Cheriton came out and called: "Bed, children! Bed!" They grumbled and pleaded with her. But in the end they said good-bye to Coppard and went in. They felt tired, yet still exhilarated. "You know you shouldn't have done so much," Miss Cheriton chided Brian. But he took no notice of her.

"That was fun," Hugh said, as they undressed together in their bedroom.

"Yes, wasn't it? . . . Oh, Hugh, it's only two more days now. It is awful. Will you hate going back very much? Will it be very beastly? I wish we could do something for you. I wish you didn't have to go to school, but could stay here with me. I wish there were no relatives."

"It won't be so bad now. I've got used to it, and I know it can never be so bad again. My other aunt—Aunt Cecil—will be coming home next spring. I like her, and perhaps I can stay with her. Even school seems less awful. I'll never like it, but I think I'll get on all right there. The great thing is not to care too much. Nothing matters if one doesn't let it matter. . . ." A few flakes of snow fell past the window; more followed, and he put out a hand to catch them. They fell slowly, out of a clear sky, and drifted on to the terrace. Once again he was troubled by something—an echo, a memory? What was it?

He turned: "I've nothing to worry about. But you . . . I hope you get well, soon. You remember what you said at the cemetery? Well—you don't feel that now, do you? I mean, you don't feel frightened any more."

"Oh, no." He said it lightly, but with utter conviction. "It's funny. They've done all sorts of nasty things to me, and I find that I can bear them. One can bear anything, if there's no escape." It was an unconscious echo of something which Hugh had once said himself.

Brian had joined him at the window, and together they looked out. Under the arch of night the fire still smouldered; it looked like a volcano, and at each gust of wind brilliant granules shot up into the air and whirled outwards, into the snow and dark. "Oh, I wish you weren't going," Brian exclaimed again.

"So do I. It seems only yesterday. Time flies so."

"Time, time!" He spoke the word resentfully.

Hugh shook his head. He looked into the bonfire, consuming the last year's dross and rubbish, in acceptance and surrender. He found himself saying those words "Never again, never again." There was no melancholy in them now, but freedom and reconciliation and a strange sort of triumph.

"Do you know," he said. "It's exactly a year—a year almost to a day—since I was told about my parents?"

They drew closer to each other, still watching the fire. All about it the snow was pink; even the sky seemed to be tinged with that colour.

"It'll burn all through the night," Brian said. "I expect it'll burn till the morning."

THE END

ALSO AVAILABLE FROM VALANCOURT BOOKS